It Won't Happen Again

Susan Hoffman

Hardcover ISBN 978-0-9799168-2-3

Paperback ISBN 978-0-9799168-3-0

Collegare Press

It Wont Happen Again

Susan Hoffman

CHAPTER 1

THE WALLOP

The first time it happened I was seven years old. I got spanked for not eating my mashed potatoes. Mother and Joe had just returned from their honeymoon in Mexico and the three of us were eating dinner together now as a family. Joe had just shoved the last piece of bread in his mouth when his eyes became fixed on my plate. Breadcrumbs flew from his mouth as he spoke. "Stefanie how come your mother and I are done eating and you've barely made a dent in your food?"

I gave him a blank look and shrugged my shoulders.

He sat back in his chair and folded his arms across his chest, watching and waiting for me to take a bite. "You still got a pile of potatahs you haven't even touched."

I picked up my fork and let it hover before pushing the potatoes to the other side of the plate.

"Quit yur lollygaggin' and get busy and finish yur dinner!"

I shook my head. "But, I don't like these potatoes." That's when I felt a big hand clamp down on my arm. It was Joe. In one single action, he yanked me from my chair and out of the cramped kitchen so he could get a better swing at me.

I was so scared that I wet my pants, which made Joe even angrier. To avoid getting peed on, he dragged me into the bathroom and dangled me over the bathtub, with one hand holding me in the air, while the other pelted my backside. With my free arm I tried to cover my bottom, but it was no match for the power behind the wallops that were coming hard and fast. Crying out for my mother was all I could do, "Mommy, Mommy, help, oww... ouch... puleez help me!"

I got a glimpse of Mommy standing at the bathroom door, raking her hands through her hair when she saw me. She was pleading, "Joe, stop, that's..." but Joe kicked the door closed in her face and yelled at her to go away. She did.

Joe was shouting, "When I tell you to eat what's put in front of you, do it!" Swat.

"Don't pretend that you don't hear me or shrug your shoulders... you think I talk to hear my head rattle?" Swat.

"Who the hell do you think you are, pushin' your food around on the plate like it's a game!" Swat.

"You. Do. Not get to choose what's put on your plate. This isn't a restaurant, God dammit!" Swat.

"And the next time you start pickin' at your food and refuse to eat, you're gonna get more where this came from, got it?" Swat.

Sobbing, "Yeeessss."

"Now take off those wet clothes and get back in the kitchen! Shit, peein' yur pants like some two year old."

I hobbled to the bedroom that I had shared with my mother before Joe came along and pulled out some dry underpants and trousers from my chest of drawers. As I was changing, I wondered if Mommy was as scared as I was? Did she know before they got married that Joe was so mean? The shock of what had just happened felt like a lightening bolt had struck our house. Was this how things were going to be? Was this my life now?

When I returned to the kitchen, Mommy was sitting at

the table, her cup of coffee untouched, her burning cigarette resting in the notch of the stamped metal ashtray and Joe was in her face. He was out of his seat lunging across the table with both his hands splayed across the table holding his weight and leaning so close to her that if she pressed herself any closer to the back of the chair it would surely split.

"I know she should try to eat all of her dinner, but she doesn't usually like potatoes," Mommy explained.

"It's my fault. I shouldn't have served them to her, I should have made her something else."

Joe, short on patience, pounded his fist on the table, coffee splashing from her cup. "See Marge, that's exactly what the problem is!" he shouted, as he berated me to her.

"She's never heard the word 'no'. That kid ain't the one runnin' the show; what she needs is discipline!"

My mother nodded and said nothing.

"So quit defendin' her and makin' excuses, the little spoiled brat. She eats what we eat and that's that! And what the hell is that pissin' all about? She's too old to be wettin' her pants."

When I sat back down at the now cleared table he continued his condemnation as if I wasn't there. He was on a rant. As a way of soothing myself, I tuned him out by tracing with my finger the yellow and red flowers on the oilcloth table covering.

"Look at me when I'm talkin' to you!" That jolted me from the tablecloth fixation. I hated what I saw, the egg-shaped head with the receding hairline, bloodshot colorless gray eyes and wall to wall freckles covering every inch of real estate on his face.

"In case yur wonderin' I don't feel the need to justify my actions," Joe announced. "I'm here to tell ya I am now man of the house and I'm gonna show everyone who's boss."

Yeah, he showed us all right. From his soapbox on the
linoleum tiled floor, he recited the first rule which was: "you
clean your plate." To further drive the point home, he began
his monologue. "Do you know how many people are starvin'
all over the world?" Pause.

"When I was stationed in Korea, I saw it everyday, kids
gettin' a bowl of rice once a day, that's it," he continued.
"Over here we take food for granted and waste more than we
eat. You don't know how lucky you are to have enough to eat,
so next time you have food put in front of you, I don't want
to see anything left on your plate when you're done. Whatcha
do with her plate, Marge?"

"I already washed the dishes."

He swept his hands in an upward motion across his
forehead. "Jesus–fuckin'–Christ! See that's what I'm talkin'
about. You shoulda made her eat the cold potatahs, that'd
teach her a lesson. Hell's bells, and you wonder why the kid's
anemic? From now on, she sits there until her plate is clean—
one hour, two hours or all night for all I care."

Mommy just kept nodding her head, and softly repeating,
"Okay, okay." The more he talked the closer I scooted my chair
to hers. And when he pounded the table again with his fist, I
clung onto her arm with both hands, folding myself around her
arm as if it were a life preserver. In a way it was. My shoulders
convulsed, choking back sobs as I listened to what seemed like
an endless sermon. He must have had a nicotine craving when
he suddenly stopped talking and pulled a cigarette from the
pack of Marlboros on the table. He flicked open his Zippo,
lit it, sucked in the smoke, blew it out his nostrils and left the
room to go watch the Huntley-Brinkley News Report on TV.

No one had ever laid a hand on me before, but now when
someone did no one stopped it. It was 1959.

CHAPTER 2

THE HAPPY DAYS

My name is Stefanie Luna and my mother's name is Marjorie Van Ness. We have different last names because she took back her maiden name after she divorced my father.

I wasn't quite two when my mother and I moved into the two-bedroom craftsman style home on 58th street in Los Angeles with my grandparents, Betty and Charlie, which is how I addressed them, by their first names. Betty was my mom's mom who married Charlie after Mom's real dad died of TB. 'Step' or not it made no difference to me, the bond was there. Charlie was not only my grandfather, he was my best friend.

Everyone in our household worked, except me of course. Betty and Charlie owned a dry cleaners and Mom worked at the phone company running some sort of adding machine called a comptometer.

Professional babysitters were brought in to take care of me five days a week, none of them lasting very long.

Mary was the worst, she was overly strict and every time she arrived for work, I would greet her by saying, "hi Mary, bye Mary" and then when she didn't leave, I made a beeline for the back door. After she quit, they hired a German woman with a thick accent, whom they fired after 30 days for stealing Betty's linens and silver.

Betty appreciated having nice things and was always saying, "I'll take quality over quantity any day. I'd rather have fewer nice things that will last, than a lotta chintzy stuff that falls apart." Along with a decent collection of linens and silver, there was a houseful of fine furnishings, nothing fancy, but well cared for by Betty.

The solid mahogany Duncan Phyfe drop leaf dining table had so much polish that you could see your reflection in it. The matching chairs were covered in an elegant burgundy striped silk that Betty said was imported straight from Hong Kong. The living room furniture all matched and the upholstered pieces were all draped with lace doilies over the arm rests to protect the velveteen fabric from handprints. We didn't have actual doors to the bedroom entrances either; instead covering the doorways—as well as the windows— was bark cloth tropical printed drapes. They not only added some splash, but privacy.

The household furnishings reflected Betty's philosophy, so when the babysitter helped herself to her cherished belongings, it created a fuss.

Betty caught on to the German sitter after a couple of things happened. First she noticed some of her lace tablecloths were missing. And on several occasions—when Mom arrived home from work—she found that my cheeks and hands seemed cold. After she mentioned it to Betty, it was easy to figure out what was going on. It seems Helga was grabbing the valuables and then dragging me along with her on the bus back to her house where she would stash the goods and then bring me back before everyone got home. In an attempt to catch the woman in the act, Charlie came home a little early one night only to find the house empty. Just before five o'clock, when Helga walked in the door with me in tow, he busted her.

She was unflappable, sticking to her story that she took me to the park. But then as Charlie waved her off in a dismissive gesture, it must have given her the impression that she got away with it. Helga was making a show of tidying up before she left when Charlie turned his attention toward me as he bounced me on his knee. He spoke in a casual tone. "Hey Steffie, what did you and Helga do at the park today?"

Helga knew she had underestimated this three year old's above average communication skills when I responded without hesitation. "No park today Charlie, we went on the big bus to Helga's house, so she could take her stuff home."

That was the end of strangers coming into the house. Mom called upon her former mother-in-law, my other grandma, to help out until an all-day nursery school could be found. Charlie pitched in too, arranging his schedule so he could pick me up after lunch.

My fraternal grandparents lived just a few blocks away on 52nd street, and Grandma who was home all day, was thrilled to have me all to herself. She spent most of her time in the kitchen cooking and baking and I was always standing on a chair next to her watching whatever she was doing. She even bought me my own child size rolling pin so that we could make tortillas together. She didn't drive, so we went everywhere on the streetcar or the bus. We had to make daily trips to the grocery store because without a car, she could only carry so much on the public transportation. I didn't care where we went, I was just happy to be away from those sitters and with my grandma.

Charlie couldn't wait to shut down the presses and call it a day. Pitching in to help with my childcare needs was his ticket to freedom. Now Betty wouldn't be able to find reasons to keep him at the cleaners. The best part of the arrangement for me was tagging along everywhere he went. No place was off limits. If he felt like stopping off at one of his watering holes on the way home, having me along didn't hold him back.

Every time we pulled up to the curb there was always one of the regulars foraging in the gutter for a half-smoked cigarette before making his way into the tavern. The first time I saw it happen, I asked Charlie why the man was looking for cigs in the gutter. "Well, heck, people do it all the time, like if they run outta smokes, they can usually find 'em in front of bars and restaurants," he explained. I waited for him to continue. "And since it's dark inside no one really pays attention if someone lights up a used butt that they had just scrounged."

I nodded as if I understood.

The bartender was a hammy sort, always making a big production whenever I came into the bar. With his Irish brogue, he would pretend not to know me. "Well now, Charlie M., and who might this young lassie be?"

Charlie would play along. "Well, sir let me introduce you. This here is Miss Steffie, my best gal, that's who." Everyone would laugh. Then Sean, the bartender would take my order. "What'll it be little lady? Never mind, don't tell me, I've got something special coming right up."

Before I could say "lickety-split," a Shirley Temple with extra cherries was sitting in front of me. I alternated between taking sips and spinning myself in circles on the red vinyl swivel stool.

With Charlie, the journey was half the fun, the car rides in his white Chevy wagon became an educational experience. Practically as soon as I could talk, he taught me about the cars on the road. Now every time we were driving around he would use it as an opportunity to do his best to stump me on all the makes, models and years. Charlie would say, "Hey Steffie, what kinda car is that blue one over there?"

Without hesitation, "It's a Buick."

"What year?"

"1950."

"How about that black one in the next lane?" He would point with his thumb.

"Oh it's just an old Ford," I would say if it were a really old car.

Charlie guffawed whenever I did that.

The fun continued on once we arrived home. Charlie and I created our own games out of nothing. I would close the doors on the television set while he was relaxing on the sofa watching the news. Pretending to be annoyed, he would roll up the newspaper and smack his hand with the paper. As he got up from the couch to open the doors he'd bark at me like he was fit to be tied. "God almighty, Steffie, I was watching that—I'm gonna tickle you crazy if you do it again."

With hands on my stomach, I would roar back with laughter and then run out of the room. After a few minutes I would peek around the corner to check if Charlie was engrossed in his show before tip-toeing back in and sneaking up behind him so I could do it all over again. He was my big playmate and he loved every minute of it, but by the time Mom and Betty called us to the dining room for dinner, he was grateful for the break.

Betty was a whiz in the kitchen while Mom was in charge of setting the table and pouring the drinks—milk for Charlie, milk with Ovaltine for me and coffee for Mom and Betty. Since Betty and Mom were from Oklahoma, southern cooking was a staple in our house. We ate lots of cornbread with black-eyed peas, yams, collard greens and fried pork chops, commonly referred to as Okie food. I went for the cornbread first before it got soggy from the soupy black-eyed peas, never mind the greens, they never made it onto my plate.

The food was served family style where everyone helped themselves from serving dishes placed on the center of the oval dining table. It was a good kind of noisy with everyone talking and passing dishes of food back and forth while the phonograph played in the background. Tonight it was Les Paul and Mary Ford's, "Bye bye Blues."

I had grown accustomed to the nightly dinners that had become part of living with my grandparents for the past three years, so when Charlie and Betty made the decision to move, it was a blow. Since I was almost five and about to start nursery school that meant Charlie would no longer be picking me up from Grandma's either. To ease my anguish they promised that I could come and spend the night every weekend, which made it sound like a new adventure. They wanted to live closer to their business so they sold their house to Betty's newly married brother, Stuart and his wife Amanda. Stuart worked at the Herald Examiner and Amanda was a professional waitress at the Bullocks Wilshire Tea Room.

CHAPTER 3

JUST THE TWO OF US

Mom and I didn't have far to move, just to the studio apartment in the backyard that had been used as storage up until then. Fortunately for us, it came furnished since the storage items were mostly old pieces of furniture that Betty brought from Oklahoma.

The front house was still accessible for me to come and go—since Stuart and Amanda didn't have kids of their own—they welcomed my company. One of my favorite reasons for visiting was so I could brush Amanda's thick, curly, red hair. I would climb up on the couch and situate myself on top of the high back so I would be able to reach her hair better. She had a flamboyant way about her, the way she expressed herself in her high-pitched sing-song voice with her arms flapping like a bird ready to take flight. I thought that she was fun to be around and also a good sport about letting me play beauty shop.

The new living quarters may have been small, but it never seemed cramped. It felt warm and cozy and safe.

Mother and I slept side by side on a trundle bed that served as a sofa by day; my side was solid dark green and Mom's was the printed side embellished with a tropical plant pattern.

I was in all-day nursery school by now, so I had to get ready to go in the morning same as Mom. First things first, every morning after we got up we would press our feet on the metal bar and lower my half of the bed enough to slide it under the other one so that we could have room to move around, converting our bedroom by night into a living room by day.

The clothes that my mother wore during the 1950's were intriguing to me. The top of her full-length lace slips could be seen through her sheer blouses, which were always tucked neatly into straight pencil skirts. The blouses buttoned up the back and I would stand on a chair so I could button the ones she couldn't reach. She wore garter belts to hold up her seamed nylon hose.

She always wore high heeled shoes, either brown or black, that had a little peep hole so you could see the big toe that was always polished in red. Her shoes were the first thing that came off when she got home from work, and first thing that I put on. I loved the clanking sound the shoes made on the wood floor as I clomped around the little studio apartment.

There was a nice patch of grass below the wooden porch that stretched along the entire side of the house. We had our own gate that connected to the alley so that when the milkman delivered my order of orange drink and chocolate milk it would be waiting right outside the door.

The galley style kitchen was a separate room with a small wooden table where we ate our meals. The layout was a bit odd with the placement of the fridge in a separate enclosed back porch that connected to the kitchen. One time a mouse was back there and we couldn't eat anything that came from the ice box for two days until the exterminator showed up because of Mom's fear of mice.

The only good thing that came out of not eating in for two days was eating out for two days. We went to the Ontra cafeteria where I could see the food on display and pick out whatever I wanted. The rainbow jello squares that they were famous for were always on my tray along with a chicken drumstick and chocolate pudding that was garnished with a wreath of whipping cream.

I couldn't seem to get enough chocolate pudding. Making our own became a Saturday ritual between Mom and I. Nothing got past me though. As soon as the porch was cleared, I started in, "Mommy, now that the mouse is dead, can we get the milk from the fridge so I can make chocolate pudding?" She always said "sure," and a few minutes later, I scooted up to the kitchen table where I would kneel on a chair and began the process of churning the crank on the beater croc.

It was an eggbeater with a splatter guard that was attached to a brown croc bowl and it took a lot of time and effort with my little arms to create pudding. Sometimes, I simply couldn't wait until the pudding cooled to eat it, so Mom would dish up a helping of the warm chocolate for both of us.

Since it was now just my mother and I living alone, she became my world. She was tall and slender with long blond hair that she wore in a ponytail and to me she was the most beautiful creature in the world. She had light brown eyes that were deep set and kind of small but her arched dark eyebrows made them look bigger. She had well-defined cheekbones and she wore red lipstick that was applied over her natural lip line because she said her lips were too pointy. That, and it may have been a fashion statement during the 50's.

I on the other hand, didn't inherit the blond hair or the ponytail, just the opposite. In fact my hair was dark brown and cut short, typically known as a Dutch boy cut. I had dark brown eyes and wore thick coke bottle type glasses because my eyesight was not only bad, I also had a lazy left eye. Mom took me to an eye specialist every week and sometimes I had to wear a patch on the good eye as therapy to help strengthen and straighten the weak one.

I hated my eye therapy because it interfered with "I Love Lucy." I cried, I begged, I bargained. "But Mommy it's my favorite show, I promise I'll wear it after it's over." I did everything possible to negotiate not wearing the patch, but always in vain. Mom would say, "I'm sorry Steffie, but Dr. Nesburn said three hours a day and we have to follow his orders. You don't want to have to wear glasses forever, do you?"

I shook my head and lowered the black patch across my right eye as I flipped on the TV. I plopped down on the floor and scooted myself as close as possible to the TV so that my nose practically touched the black and white screen.

Wearing the patch every night was non-negotiable and as easy going as Mom was, she put her foot down on that one. The doctor's hope was that the combination of therapy and strong corrective lenses would prevent eye surgery and eventually strengthen the muscles and straighten my left eye, so it would no longer wander off. I always felt self-conscious because of the glasses though, especially after I started nursery school because nobody else wore them. Kids want to blend in. I didn't.

CHAPTER 4

COD LIVER OIL
AND ICE CREAM

Day care was long and regimented; we had to take naps on cots and were given a daily spoonful of cod liver oil. The kids would line up before snack time every morning and wait their turn to have a spoonful of the putrid smelling foul tasting substance poured down their throat. The sight of the used stainless steel spoons that accumulated after each child got their dose will be forever etched in my brain.

This was the first time that I had ever been around other kids my own age, adults had been my playmates up until then so it took some getting used to.

I made friends with a girl named Myrna, who was also an only child and lived alone with her mom too. She and I spent hours playing dress-up in the playhouse section of the classroom where they had a trunk full of garments. We would prance around the make-believe kitchen wearing the long skirts and stoles and then take turns serving each other pretend meals. Myrna was easy to be around and she never argued whenever I wanted to be the hostess instead of the guest. She knew how much I liked to play with the pretend stove and dishes. Our moms met each other when they came to pick us up and after seeing what good buddies we were, even arranged some Saturday play dates.

The boys weren't as nice. Once a mean boy threw handfuls of sand in my eyes after he called me four-eyes. When the school nurse was unable to remove such a large amount of sand by flushing my eyes with water, she called my mother. I was screaming with pain by the time she got me to the doctor. The extraction process that I had to endure—using some sort of special suction hose placed inside my upper and lower eyelids that sucked out the grains of sand—was excruciating. Fortunately there was no permanent damage.

Another time when I was on the swings, a bully called me names because of my glasses and my last name. He yelled, "Four-eyes and tuna-Luna." I got singled out because I was different. I wore glasses and my last name wasn't Smith or Jones.

I couldn't wait to get picked up from Hyde Park School and climb inside Mother's Studebaker, where I would stand beside her for the ride home. Whenever she came to pick me up at school I wanted everyone to know that she was my mother. She was everything that I wasn't and everything I wanted to be. She didn't wear glasses, she had long blond hair and a better last name. I wanted to show her off thinking, maybe kids would be nicer to me if they could see how pretty my mom was.

One day, along with my milk money, Mom gave me an extra dime so that I could buy the orange colored ice cream on a stick, like the one I had seen kids eating the day before. It was the first time that I had eaten a 50/50 bar and it was so delicious I wanted to share it with my mom, so I went back with the extra nickel and bought one for her too.

Later that afternoon, during free playtime, there was a commotion in the cloakroom. The teachers were running back and forth between the sink and cloakroom with armloads of wet jackets and sweaters. The closet sized room attached to the classroom was where we children hung our jackets and stored our belongings. After the teachers finished cleaning up, one of them came out and began questioning everyone about the mess that an ice cream bar had created after being placed on a shelf and melting onto everyone's clothes. By the time they got to me I figured out what I had done probably wasn't a good idea. Shifting from one foot to the other, and gazing at the floor, I confessed. "I wanted to save an ice cream for my mommy so I put it on the shelf so she could have it when she picks me up."

The teacher slowly shook her head as she took my hands in hers. "Oh, Steffie, you can't save ice cream, it has to stay in the freezer otherwise it melts, just like it did today."

How was I supposed to know that? I never knew ice cream came in bars, I had only had the kind that was served in a dish. Maybe the bar kind was supposed to stay frozen?

I was sitting by myself at one of the back tables drawing pictures of heads and coloring them in with crayons, tears rolling down my cheeks and onto the paper smearing my artwork. I was feeling ashamed that everyone would find out that I was the one who did it. I just wanted to runaway and never come back.

I felt even sorrier when I saw all of the damage to everyone's clothes, but by the time my mom picked me up the coats and jackets had been rinsed and packed into paper bags labeled with each child's name across the front. After the teachers told my mother about it, she made her way over to where I was sitting and kneeled down so that she was at my level. She swiveled my chair so I was facing her and put both hands on my knees.

"Steffie, honey, that was such a thoughtful thing to do, but please, please do not do it again."

I managed to apply some logic. "But, Mommy it was so delicious. I've never tasted anything so good, I wanted you to have one too and now you won't be able to."

She delivered a stiff smile in spite of her eyes watering up and then she stood and scooped me from the chair and carried me from the room.

My fears of being outed were for nothing, the incident was quickly forgotten and the kids, who weren't that concerned to begin with, were never the wiser about who the culprit was. It's a good thing because I was stuck there for three years considering the elementary school was next door and all the other students with working parents just like me would be shuffled back into after-school care until six o'clock at night.

CHAPTER 5

THE BOMB

Whenever she wasn't working, and I wasn't in school, Mom and I were always together. She even took me along when she went on dates.

Usually we all went to dinner and the movies. I especially enjoyed going to the Wich Stand restaurant. It looked like a space ship and served fancy desserts that were displayed in a glass case behind the counter. One time though, what appeared beautiful on the outside was a dud on the inside. Mom tried to talk me out of ordering the cake, that she called cheesecake. It looked different from all the others in the case because of the decorations. The smooth cake was covered with rosettes circling the outer top and bottom edges and in the very center on top was a pile of jumbo strawberries. She kept warning me that I wouldn't like it, but I ordered it anyway, and after one bite, I scrunched up my nose and spit it out. How could such a masterpiece of a dessert not taste as good as it looked?

The movies were another story. They were grown-up films filled with drama, like *I Want To Live* and *Imitation Of Life* with famous stars like Susan Hayward and Lana Turner. Sometimes they became a little heavy for a six or seven year old child, so we would have to leave before the ending because of my loud crying in response to the onscreen emotions.

The one guy that she saw a lot of was Joe, who happened to be the one I liked the least. He drove a beater car, a Ford Anglia that had primer patches and he had wispy red hair and his face and arms were covered with freckles. I couldn't explain beyond the superficial reasons why I didn't like him. Kids just know the good ones from the bad ones, and there was something that didn't feel right. He was friendly enough, but it seemed unnatural. I didn't worry about it too much because putting up with him a night or two a week didn't change the status quo.

Then my world turned upside down. Joe had just dropped us off after seeing *North By Northwest* and that's when my mother sprang the news on me. "Steffie, Joe and I are getting married." Just like that, no prior discussion.

"Oh nooo!" I blurted out. "Don't marry Joe, I don't like Joe. Why can't things stay the same? Or if you're gonna get married, why can't you marry Gary instead? He has a convertible." It was a red, shiny Ford Crestline and he was a nice guy too. He always let me push the button to make the top go up and down.

A moment of silence passed before Mommy, explained her reasons. "Because I don't love Gary, I love Joe, and guess what, you get to be in the wedding too as my flower girl."

I wailed and stomped my feet. "I don't care, I don't want to be in your stupid wedding and I don't want to be a stupid flower girl!"

"Oh but Steffie, you'll get to wear a beautiful new dress and carry a basket full of flower petals."

Pouting, I folded my arms across my chest and planted my feet firmly on the floor. "No, I won't go!"

"It will hurt my feelings if you're not in the wedding," Mom announced. "I want you to be a part of the wedding and walk down the aisle right ahead of me."

My protests fell on deaf ears, her mind was made up and I was mad. Why wasn't she listening to me? She hardly ever said "no" and now she wasn't budging. No amount of foot-stomping and temper tantrums made a difference this time.

My wants didn't matter and neither did anyone else's. I picked up on the vibes and learned that Betty and Charlie weren't exactly thrilled and neither were my dad's parents. My dad just knitted his eyebrows and chewed on his bottom lip and said nothing when I told him.

When I talked to Betty and Charlie about Mommy marrying Joe, they hugged me and told me everything would workout. But, later when they thought I was watching TV, I heard Betty talking to Charlie. "Out of all the men out there how'd she ever get involved with that deadbeat, Joe Hoskins? I'm gonna call her right now and tell her just that."

My other Grandma just shook her head. "She should have stayed married to your dad."

Sadly, after the wedding I didn't get to visit my dad's parents every week like I used to. Joe made sure of that. He was always nice to them to their face, but behind their back he would make disparaging remarks to my mom about my dad and his family. "What'd you ever see in that twerp of a pencil pusher?" When there was no response, he would continue. "Why you lettin' Stefanie go over there so much? This is her home and family, besides they just pump her for information, and it's none of their business what goes on under this roof." I did like carrying information back and forth.

The only time I saw them now was whenever my dad came to pick me up for his visits. He traveled a lot and didn't have a set visitation schedule, so every couple of months was the average. I could tell how much my grandparents missed me by how happy they were to see me the minute I walked through the door. Grandma had a thing about matching socks, and as soon as the hugs were finished, she sat me on a chair and proceeded to remove my mismatched socks and replace them with brand new matching ones. She and my aunts loved buying me new dresses too. I was not only the first grandchild, I was the only grandchild.

Joe couldn't get rid of Betty and Charlie quite so easily. They picked me up every Saturday so that I could spend the night. They regularly took me to work with them at the dry cleaners where I would sometimes be put to work myself. I got paid a penny per hangar to "make hangers," meaning I slipped the paper covers over the top of wire hangers or the cardboard cover across the bottom part for trousers. When we got home, we spent the evening watching *Roller Derby* and *Gunsmoke* on TV while eating Red-Delicious apples and chocolate chip ice cream.

The cleaners was located on the corner of Western Avenue and 47th street in Los Angeles. The mostly black clientele who lived in the neighborhood were loyal customers. Betty knew all of them by name and made them feel special. The buildings on the street were dingy and run down and many of the businesses were boarded up because of the climbing crime rate. There was talk of street gangs moving into the area, but Betty didn't care, as long as the money was rolling in.

The cleaners was Betty's home away from home, she worked twelve hours a day, from seven in the morning to seven at night, six days a week. Since she was up by four in the morning she required a nap, which was taken on a cot that was shoved under the plastic covered clothes along the back wall. At naptime, she would say, "I'm just played out," and then she would disappear for an hour.

By the time she got home from work and then cooked dinner, she could hardly stay awake to eat. She would sometimes fall asleep at the table to the point of falling face down into her plate of food. It wasn't a pretty sight to watch.

Charlie would grumble at her when her head would begin to bob. "Christ-almighty, Betty, for God's sake go to bed if you're that tired." He would then escort her from the dining room and put her to bed.

During the daytime, she was a dynamo, when she wasn't waiting on customers at the counter, she sat at the Singer sewing machine doing the alterations with a bean bag ashtray close-by that was overflowing with butts. I don't think she ever smoked an entire cigarette from start to finish—she mostly let them sit in the ridged metal clip that threaded across the top of the ashtray like a little bridge—until the ash grew so long there was no more cigarette.

She was more than just a sewer; my Grandma was an expert tailor. She could design and sew anything from a man's suit to a fully lined woman's wool coat. She made most of my clothes until I was around nine. She was also a perfectionist—unlike my mother—who Betty used to say, did everything half-assed. Betty was always laying into her about not doing things properly. She would harp on my mother about her lack of housekeeping skills. "Marjorie Ann, you call that dusting? You gotta remove everything from the table before you dust, not just leave 'em in place and push the cloth around them." Mommy would feign ignorance, nod her head and then continue on in her same lackadaisical manner.

Charlie on the other hand was carefree. He was no slacker, but when the job was done so was he. Charlie was fun loving and knew how to enjoy life.

At the dry cleaners, he ran the presses and usually called it quits by early afternoon after enduring the constant steam that produced a sweltering environment. He ran errands and socialized at the local bar or the coffee shop, like Virgie's across the street. Virgie, the owner, had short gray hair that was teased on top and tucked behind her ears and she wore a waitress uniform of the same color. She made a mean milk shake when she wasn't on the phone placing bets. According to Betty and Charlie, she was also a bookie. I didn't know exactly what that meant, just that people called and gave her money to place bets on stuff like horse racing.

During the time that we lived together, I was Charlie's constant companion. At the end of the day, we would come back to the cleaners and pick up Betty and then stop at a drive-in hamburger stand like McDonalds, where a waitress would come to the car with a metal tray of food and clamp it onto the window. All three of us would be in the front seat munching away on the burgers and fries.

Charlie was also an alcoholic. I never saw him drunk and the only reason I knew was because I pretty much saw and heard everything, even though I didn't know what most of it meant. Mom would just say, "alcoholics can never have a drink," and leave it at that. There were times when Charlie would disappear to a hospital to dry out and then Betty would have to hire a temporary presser. He was never gone for long, maybe a week and then everything would go back to the way it was.

Even though Betty and Charlie owned their own business, they always managed to take a vacation every summer and I always went along. We visited the redwoods at Sequoia National Park, where we drove through a giant redwood tree, and on our way to visit Charlie's parents in Arkansas, we stopped off at the Grand Canyon. We stayed in a cabin at Big Bear Lake, and one night when Betty and I were walking back from the restrooms in the pitch dark, she suddenly tightened her grip on my hand and began running. When we got back to the cabin, she told Charlie that she felt a bear rub up against her leg. Of course we couldn't know for sure, since you couldn't see your hand in front of your face, but what else would it have been? From then on out, Charlie escorted us, along with his flashlight to and from the public bathrooms.

Since we all loved the beach, we sometimes rented a beach house in Long Beach right on the sand, so we wouldn't have to drive back and forth. There were always day trips too, which were usually on Sunday where we visited the orange groves in Orange County, the Pomona Fair, and El Porto beach.

The carefree childhood that I enjoyed came to a screeching halt when Joe entered the picture. My environment went from a safe haven to a reign of terror. The prevailing circumstances created a dispiriting sense that I had never felt before.

CHAPTER 6

CHANGES

From the studio apartment, Mom and I moved to a one-bedroom single story apartment not far from the studio. Amanda wanted to move her ailing mother closer to her and the studio was the perfect location, so we had to leave. The new complex was referred to as "court" apartments where single level units faced each other across a common walkway. They resembled a motel, just a row of units, no grass, no trees no plants, just concrete. It was slightly bigger than the studio but not much. The only difference was that there was a separate bedroom. The inside was dark no matter what time of day because of the attached walls on both sides, unlike the freestanding studio that had windows on all four walls this felt like a tunnel. Once Joe moved in, about six months later right after they got married, I got booted to the sleeper sofa in the living room while he took over my portion of the bedroom. I didn't like sleeping alone in the living room where I could hear the people walking along the sidewalk on the other side of the front door. Instead of listening to the outdoor sounds, I distracted myself by listening to the wheezing sounds that I produced from Asthma. The symptoms appeared right around the time Mom got engaged to Joe.

The wedding was held on a Friday evening at a small

church in Los Angeles. Mom, now sporting a 'duck tail' haircut, wore a pink three quarter length fluffy dress with an organza wrap that covered her shoulders. Since I became the flower girl after all, I wore a matching pink dress with a ruffled hem. It was a long walk down that aisle tossing flower petals on the floor but I made my way to the alter performing my duties without a glitch.

The only good part about the wedding besides the new dress, was the lemon filled wedding cake.

Mom and Joe's honeymoon consisted of a long weekend in Ensenada. I had so much fun staying with Betty and Charlie I didn't have time to think about missing my mom or fretting about the recent marriage. When they took me home on Monday, I was sad to leave them, but happy to see my mom.

That was the night before the spanking. Little did I know the relevance of the sadness to leave my grandparents and the limitation of the happiness of coming home.

I was instructed by my mother not to tell anyone about the spanking, but the next time I saw Betty and Charlie a couple of Saturday's later, I spilled the beans. They were livid. Betty was wringing her hands and pacing to the point of carving a path onto the kitchen floor. "I knew it, I knew it," she repeated. "When Marjorie Ann ended up in the hospital with a broken eardrum, last January, I told you Joe was responsible."

Charlie, smearing jam on a piece of toast said, "I never liked the guy, and you're probably right about him punching Marjorie in the ear, but she's a grown woman, and we need to stay out of that part of it."

"When it comes to my daughter, I have every right to voice my concerns, grown up or not!"

"Yeah, well leave me out of their problems, except I am gonna have a word with Joe about him hitting Steffie. He better not ever lay a hand on that child again, or he'll have hell to pay."

"Be careful, Charlie, he's proven that he's got a bad temper."

"He's also proven that he's a coward, picking on women and children, gall dammit."

They must have remembered that I was sitting at the breakfast table, because all of a sudden they cut the conversation short.

The kitchen got quiet except for the sound of utensils scraping across the plates, as we ate our breakfast. When I finished my eggs, I tapped Charlie on the arm, and asked, "What's a coward?"

"Uh, it's a person, who, uh, well… it's a scaredy-cat, that's what it is, except they're not afraid of someone littler than the are."

"Oh." Pause. "Is that what Joe is?"

Before Charlie could respond, Betty interjected. "Steffie, Charlie and I don't like Joe spanking you, that's all, now let's forget about it, OK ?"

"OK."

CHAPTER 7

THE BIKE

It had been a little over a month since the wedding when we all moved to a rental house in Hawthorne. It was a nondescript one-story washed-out gray stucco that had a yard and a second bedroom where I would have my own room, at least for a few months anyway. Mom announced that I was going to have a little brother or sister soon and the baby would be sharing my room. Once again, I had big ears and whenever I visited picked up on the snickers amongst my grandparents and aunts about the sudden pregnancy

The neighborhood was made up of minimal traditional style single-family homes with big front and back yards. Our block had mostly boys, except for one girl, Carolyn, who lived next door. She was two years younger than I was, but since it was the beginning of summer and would be a while before school started, I didn't know where to find the girls my age so I played with her. Carolyn had two older brothers that were one and two years older than she and all three of them were kind of dirty and still talked baby talk. They all had black crud under their fingernails, and their faces and necks had smudges of dirt mixed with sweat that formed rings of grit around their neck. Their clothes had holes and frayed hems along with food and dirt stains and all three kids had kind of a ripe odor.

Joe worked at a lumberyard and sometimes it included Saturdays. I looked forward to having Mom all to myself even if we were just home doing nothing in particular, it didn't matter as long as we were together. I preferred to spend time with her instead of the kids next door.

Life was different now, instead of just the two of us, there was Joe, occupying Mom's attention. I didn't like how he monopolized the TV, either. We watched Wanderlust adventure shows because that was what *he* wanted to watch. We ate what *he* wanted to eat, which was mostly some kind of meat usually served with fried potatoes floating in bacon drippings. Whenever, I asked Mom to help me make chocolate pudding, she said she didn't know where the beater croc was, claiming it must have gotten lost in the move.

Joe was a big presence and not easily ignored. He had to be the center of attention, which meant life revolved around him. Always. And he had to know everything. You didn't whisper in his presence. "If it's worth sayin', it's worth sayin' out loud," he harped. "Y'all tryin' to keep secrets from me?"

A verbal greeting wasn't enough, he wanted—demanded physical affection. I trembled every time he came near me.

The man couldn't keep his hands to himself. He'd walk up to just about anyone, wrap an arm around their shoulders and start chatting away. Boy, could he pour it on thick. He sure loved playing the part of the good old southern boy, which I suppose he was, being from Texas and all. Women ate it up, thought he was charming, but both sets of grandparents saw right through him and cringed every time he would throw his arm around them. Small children were easy targets, me included He would say—and this would make my skin crawl every time I heard it: "Come here and give me some sugar." Even though I didn't want to be hugged or kissed by him, he forced me.

My room became my sanctuary where I could retreat and feel safe at least for a little while. It was spacious with natural light coming through the two corner windows that provided a view of a banana tree's overlapping leaves waving in the breeze like giant fans. There was plenty of room for me to spread out, in fact it felt like two rooms in one and it was in a way, with the crib against one wall and my twin bed on the other side of the room on the opposite wall.

This was my private world where I could escape into my head whenever I needed to. I entertained myself for hours engaging in long conversations with my dolls. I especially loved playing with paper dolls, many of which were likenesses of movie stars like Natalie Wood and Elizabeth Taylor. One of my favorites was Mary Hartline from TV's "Super Circus."

But it was conceiving stories from my sketchpad drawings that brought me the most fun. I would bring to life the characters that I created on paper by means of role-playing out loud. Mom always made sure that I had plenty of drawing materials, like pencils and sketchpads. She even said that I had natural talent for drawing. I liked drawing figures, mostly women wearing fashionable clothing. They would be sitting at a table having lunch together on one page, where one would tell the other, "I'm going out tonight with a new guy and he has a shiny red Cadillac," and the other one would respond, "Oh you're so lucky, I have to babysit."

Once I exhausted that dialogue, I kept the momentum going by creating a new scene. I moved on to the next page, where the characters would be standing in front of a store window shopping and making plans to get their hair done. This escape from reality brought me great pleasure.

Joe saw things differently, he thought kids should be outside playing not inside drawing pictures and talking to themselves. I heard him say to Mom on a few occasions, "Marjorie Ann, tell me sump'n. Why in the hell is that kid holed up in her room on a nice day like this?"

Mom would defend me. "Well, she hasn't made many friends yet, and besides she likes to play by herself."

"I'm sure she does, but it ain't normal, and how the hell she gonna make friends stayin' inside all day?"

"Oh, I think it's perfectly healthy to use your imagination instead of always needing to be entertained."

"Shows how much you know, kids belong outside," he declared. "When I was a kid we played outside all day and didn't come inside till dark."

That afternoon, he decided that it was time for me to learn how to ride a bike. At almost eight years old my royal blue bike that I named after my favorite candy, "Tootsie Roll" still had training wheels.

In my defense, it's not uncommon for kids living in urban neighborhoods not to know how to ride a bike. My "Tootsie Roll" was mostly for show, since I barely rode it, and when I did, it was back and forth a short distance on the sidewalk.

Joe removed the training wheels and demanded that I get on the bike. I inched my way backwards and shook my head. "But I don't want to, why can't I keep the training wheels on?" I quibbled. "I like it that way."

With his thundering voice he laid down the law. "You're too big for training wheels, whaddaya' a baby? Eight year-olds don't use training wheels. Get on the bike, I'll be right behind you holding the seat."

I hate you.

I began sniveling and calling out to my mother—who

had by now waddled across the driveway wearing a black and white polka dot smock over a black skirt that had a cutout for the tummy. She was pressing one hand on her back and the other was resting across her pregnant belly as she watched from the curb.

The bellowing grew louder. "Nooooo, Mom, I don't want to."

A stiff smile that was plastered across her face looked forced, along with her upbeat tone. "Steffie, it's OK, Joe's not going to let go," she said. "He'll be right behind you the whole time honey, I promise he won't let go." *Liar.*

He snatched me from where I was standing and plunked me down on the seat and before I could climb off, he started running behind me, pushing the bike by the back of the seat. I held on for dear life, the handlebars swiveling back and forth. Farther, farther, he ran behind pushing until we were clear down on the next block. Never having ridden a bike in the street, I focused on the broken glass and dirt clods that covered the asphalt. The thought of making contact with the menacing terrain frightened me. Sure enough, with all the weaving I was doing and my inability to keep the bike straight, I lost my balance and the bike slid out from under me. I skidded across the asphalt, missed the glass, but my knees were covered with dirt and gravel. I was sobbing by then, but he didn't care, he grabbed me by the back of my shirt and deposited me back on the bike.

"Stop your cryin' or I'll give you somethin' to cry about." One of his favorite sayings.

He didn't care about the pebbles and dirt embedded on my bloodied scraped knees. After an hour and a half of him pushing, shoving, letting go, and me weaving, wobbling, and falling, I was finally steady enough to stay up. For a brief moment I stopped thinking about how miserable I was and embraced the sense of accomplishment that I felt. Mom was clapping and Joe was so tired from running, all he could muster was an, "I told ya so." In the end it felt good to be able to ride on two wheels, but the way I got there felt like torture.

CHAPTER 8

LOST SATURDAY

One Saturday in October I was sitting on the cold cement porch, breaking open the milk filled stems on the large pink hydrangea bush to pass the time. I was waiting for my mom to take me shopping for new shoes for school. I had just started second grade in a new school a few weeks before and my saddle shoes no longer fit. Of course I was excited to have something new to wear but the best part about it was that I would have my mother all to myself.

Hearing footsteps, I started to get up, but instead of Mom coming out, it was Joe, who swung open the scroll grilled aluminum screen door and broke the news.

Judging by the sweat that was dribbling down his face and his accelerated breaths, I would say that Joe was in a panic. "Sis is comin' over to pick you up," he announced. "Momma's water just broke and we're goin' to the hospital."

Tilting my head back so I could see him better, I frowned. "What's that?"

"Never mind, you wouldn't understand," he replied.

"Will she take me shopping when she gets back?"

"Nope, she's having the baby and has to stay in the hospital. Just stay outside and wait for Aunt Gloria."

"OK, but why can't I come..." He slammed both doors and I heard the lock click. Now I couldn't even go into my own house. What didn't they want me to see? I was mulling the situation over when Gloria pulled up to the curb, scraping her tires while she was at it.

She jumped out of her car and made a beeline for the front door, nearly tripping over me as she climbed the steps. Almost like an after thought, she looked down. "Stay here a minute, I'll be right back," she ordered.

After two short buzzes of the bell, she disappeared inside as soon as Joe opened the door. Minutes later, all three of them came out. Joe was practically carrying Mom, his arm wrapped tightly around her waist as he cradled her elbow with his other hand. Gloria, now clutching a small suitcase, ran ahead and opened the car door for them, tossing the suitcase in the backseat.

Mom leaned over and barely brushed the top of my head with her hand as she hobbled to the car. "Go with Gloria and I'll see you soon," she said over her shoulder. "Love you."

"I love you too, bye Mom," I answered weakly. Gloria and I went back inside and she cleaned up the dirty dishes that were in the kitchen sink as I packed an overnight bag.

"Make sure you include some clothes for school in case you end up staying longer than a night or two," she called from the hallway.

What? More than one day? One was enough, anything more was unbearable. Why couldn't Betty and Charlie pick me up? I already knew the answer. I had school and Gloria lived closer, besides Betty and Charlie had to be at work early in the morning. I was a goner.

I hopped in the front seat of Gloria s station wagon and pressed my forehead against the window. As we pulled away from the curb, my eyes on the now empty house, tears began streaming down my cheeks.

Gloria and Walt owned a three-bedroom home that was located on a cul-de-sac in a neighborhood called Westchester, a Los Angeles suburb that encompasses the LAX airport.

They had three daughters, one a year older, one a year younger, and the youngest being three years younger.

Gloria wasn't much of a hands on mom, everyone fended for themselves. I wasn't used to scavenging for my own breakfast so when I sat at the round kitchen table and all that was there filling the Lazy Susan was Trix, Alpha Bits and Frosted Flakes cold cereal, I was a little baffled. My mom had always cooked a hot breakfast, oatmeal, eggs, toast.

That night, Joe came over with a handful of cigars, giddy over the birth of his baby daughter. I can't say that I shared his excitement; I just wanted my mom to come home. This was all too much for me to make sense of, first she gets married and now seven months later there's a baby.

My new cousins and I didn't have much in common, they mostly liked watching TV and I liked playing with dolls and drawing. Without my dolls and drawing tablet, I had to go along with their program. Three days later Gloria brought me back home. Not a minute too soon, either.

When I walked in, Mom was sitting on the couch holding Sheila, my new half sister. I had never seen a real baby up close before and she was so tiny all swaddled in a pink blanket. "Come and sit next to me and you can hold her, just keep your hand under her head," Mom explained. She carefully transferred the bundle over to me and placed her on my lap. It was sort of fun, like holding a real live doll.

"She looks so small, but she's kinda heavy," I said.

"Oh that's because she was actually kind of a big baby at

nine pounds," Mom replied.

The newness soon wore off once all of the baby chores began. It didn't take long for me to become Mother's little helper. "Go grab me a diaper." "Here, take this dirty diaper and throw it in the pail." "Oh, Steffie, can you come here and hold Sheila while I go heat up her bottle?"

What would they have done without me? Mom seemed overwhelmed with all of the extra work it took to care for an infant and Joe wanted no part of the diaper changing and midnight feedings, but he was great at playing with her.

Having to share my mother with another child was hard and when it came time for me to go to school, I cried and didn't want to go. Mom wasn't working and I wanted to stay home with her and the baby. I guess I was afraid I was going to miss something.

One morning, a neighbor saw me outside sitting on the curb weeping and after she asked me what was wrong, she escorted me back home. I told her that I had a stomach ache. Mom let me stay home that day even though she knew I really wasn't sick. When I tried to stay home the next day, she got mad and made me go to school. The neighbor ended up walking me part way down the next block where she stood and watched until I was out of sight. She was a nice older lady from Massachusetts who lived three doors down. She was heavy set, with a Boston accent and reeked of strong smelling perfume, which Mom said was called Tabu. Her husband was the opposite, small and wiry and a funny guy. They reminded me of Fred and Ethel Mertz from I Love Lucy, in fact his name was Fred and hers was Elma.

Once they got wind of the new addition to the family, Fred and Elma couldn't stay away. They became like grandparents to Sheila, always stopping by, bringing knitted baby blankets and booties and offering to babysit. They didn't have any grandchildren of their own, their only son had died in an automobile accident at a young age and hadn't had the opportunity to marry and start a family. Their two cats were their children now.

A couple of months after Sheila was born Fred and Elma stopped by for a visit. They thought nothing of popping in without an invitation, and even though it bothered Mom and Joe, they never said a word to their faces. This particular Saturday evening, no one noticed when one of their cats followed them into the house. Everyone was in the living room, when Joe heard a noise and bolted to the back bedroom. He could be heard shouting about finding one of the cats in the crib where Sheila was sleeping. Then everyone heard the cat let out a blood curdling yowl. I got up first to see what was going on, and as I rounded the corner of the hallway I saw Joe racing out of the bedroom holding the cat by it's neck. I made a u-turn and followed on his heels. He darted toward the back door screaming his usual profanities, which by now had everyone on their feet. Fred and Elma caught up with him just as he completed his wind up—now holding the cat by its tail—swinging it around in circles above his head maybe four times, before he let it go and flung it over the backyard fence. It happened so fast, it looked like roadkill flying across the sky.

No amount of reasoning could have made a difference; Joe was on the warpath. Enraged and shouting, "You think I'm gonna allow that Goddamned som'bitch to suck the breath out of that baby?" He bellowed. "To hell with the fuckin' cat—it has no business being in my house."

Fred was furious, shaking and swearing right back at Joe, "For the love of God, what the hell's the matter with you Joe?

You coulda just picked him up and put him out, you didn't have to do that."

"The hell I didn't, how else they gonna learn? You and those fuckin' cats. I'm sick of em' following you every time you come over here. It's bad enough to have to hear em' when they sit on our front porch, whinin' and carryin' on till you come out, but comin' in my home that's another thing," he fumed. "And just to be clear, I ever see either of em' near my property, it'll be the last time."

They both stood there staring in disbelief. Fred promptly ushered the sobbing Elma out the door so they could go find their beloved cat. They never did.

I later asked why cats suck breath from babies. "Why, cats are jealous of newborn infants and they somehow smother and suffocate them," Mom explained. I was stunned, but Mom and Joe believed it to be true.

CHAPTER 9

BEHIND THE CURTAIN

Just like the falling out with Fred and Elma, friendships came and went with Joe. He had a mean streak that was hidden behind the curtain of congeniality.

My friends would say, "Oh your step dad is so funny." I would roll my eyes because no one would ever believe that it was all a facade to hide the monster beneath.

In public, he was Mr. Nice Guy. He drew people in with his wit and charm. One who never knew a stranger, he engaged everyone that he came across. The waitresses would swoon, the salespeople would giggle and blush at the attention. He would call them by name if he saw a name tag, otherwise he'd get them to tell him. Then, he would pour it on thick as syrup, with more Texas drawl than usual. "Myrtle, now tell me how did you get so good lookin'?"

It was all good until the switch flipped. It didn't take much to set him off either and when he got that way most people bolted after witnessing a scene of his explosive temper. Just like with the cat episode. He had a short fuse. If anyone crossed him, there were consequences. He struck first and talked later. Mom never learned that lesson.

She had a way of getting under his skin. Sometimes it was her nagging about little things around the house, like using an ashtray. Sometimes it was accusations about bigger things like money or coming home drunk. Depending on his mood and alcohol level, he would either haul off and slap her across the face or he would fire off a round of verbal assaults. "For god's sake, woman, would you shut the fuck up, if you are so worried about my ashes, then you can go fetch me an ashtray." She didn't hit back, she didn't yell back, she didn't stand up for herself.

What she did do, though is keep score. Her retaliatory actions could be described as subtle. There were little lapses and passive aggressive behaviors like the burnt toast, charred bacon and forgetting to buy shaving cream so Joe would have to use soap to shave. Every time it happened, it irked him. He would say, "Marjorie-Ann, is it too much to ask to cook my bacon rare the way I like, instead of charred? Jesus Christ, can't you do anything right?" She never apologized or took responsibility, but she always had an excuse ready. "I thought the stove was on low," she would say and then it would happen again.

She couldn't be trusted either. I had a hard time facing that. If I confided in her she would tell Joe, but she would never admit it. If I told her about being scared to raise my hand in class, the next thing I knew, Joe was lecturing me about being a wimp. "Ya'll can't just sit there like some spineless shrinking violet, stick that arm up there like you own the place, God-dammit. People are gonna think you're some sorta weak numbnuts."

Mom was sneaky about money too and Joe was always scolding her for buying stuff. She lied about the cost of getting her hair done and she was careful about buying food, stretching the dollar by serving variations of the same piece of meat. A pound of ground beef was reincarnated for days, there were hamburger patties, tacos, mystery casseroles and finally Joe's military specialty, S.O.S.-shit on a shingle. It was white glue-like gravy, highly seasoned with an over abundance of salt and pepper, poured over ground beef and then sopped up with slices of Wonder bread. Even worse was the chipped beef version. It was by far the most wretched plate of food that was ever put in front of me. It truly did live up to its name.

With Joe's eagle eye watching where every cent went, Mom couldn't afford to buy me new clothes. If my real dad didn't come through, Mom would put me up to calling Betty and asking her to buy me things. She always said yes, but there were usually strings attached. She expected Mom to help her out at the cleaners in exchange for the gifts, favors and money that she doled out for this and that. None of it set well with Joe.

He would get mad whenever Mom worked at the cleaners because it was located in a typically dangerous part of town. He was always making racial slurs about the people who lived in the neighborhood, who were Betty's loyal customers.

"There's nothing but niggers around there, you better watch your ass settin' foot in that ghetto," he would rant.

Mom would give him an, "Uh, huh... I know, I know, but I'm careful and Charlie is always there."

"Yeah, well, he ain't no match for them coons they cater to."

"Well, so far they get along fine with everyone, their customers love them, and no one has ever stepped over the line with me."

"There's always a first time, you dumb shit, and I think you're askin' for it even drivin' down that street with all them jigs roamin' around."

It was always the same, he criticized the cleaners and she defended, yet he never objected to the extra cash that appeared whenever Mom needed it.

In front of people Joe was the big spender, but behind the scenes he was cheap. Money slipped through his fingers, like water, he couldn't hold onto a penny to save his life. He spent it as fast as he got it. We lived hand to mouth, paycheck to paycheck. Spending money suited him as long as it was what he considered important. Picking up the tab at restaurants, booze, guitars, anything showy to make him look important to others was the only acceptable form of consumption. He wanted attention and to be the big shot. Behind the scenes, the hand-me-down furniture, unclaimed clothes from the cleaners, frayed towels and chipped dishes didn't make a bit of difference to him.

He thought nothing of emptying my piggy bank. He would come into my room, walk directly to my chest of drawers, where he would simultaneously be pulling the rubber stopper from the underside of the polka dot ceramic pig as he spoke. "I'm gonna borrow a few bucks, I need gas for the car: I'll get it back to ya on Friday." He never asked, he just did it, and I watched as he fished out whatever was in there with his fat finger.

That was why Mom had to go back to work at the phone company two months after Sheila was born, we needed two paychecks to survive and it was cheaper to hire a sitter. I liked having her home, though. Every morning she would pack a lunch into my Roy Rogers lunch pail after we ate breakfast. She made sandwiches with little Vienna sausages cut in half or sometimes deviled ham with lots of mayonnaise. I also liked having her there when I came home from school, even though she was always preoccupied with taking care of the baby. A lot of times I felt like there was no room for me. I wanted things to be back the way they were so I could be near my mom and not have Joe or Sheila around. It felt like the three of them were a separate family from me, and they were in many ways, same last name, mom, dad, and kid. I was the outsider.

As if I didn't already feel like an alien, they were always making me go places by myself, even to church. I walked the six blocks to the neighborhood community church where I would see all the other families attending together. I had no choice. I was forced to go to church. Mom went occasionally and Joe never attended. He booted me out the door every Sunday to attend Sunday school. His usual response, "do as I say, not as I do," was the reply when I asked him, "How come you never go?"

It was a small non-denominational neighborhood church that was always having incentive contests to keep the congregation growing. Eventually I grew to like it after I won a clock radio for memorizing the books of the bible.

CHAPTER 10

DOUBLE SPANK

A proud parent, Joe never missed an opportunity to show off his new baby. Joe's sister's house was the destination this time. As usual the grownups gathered in the family room oohing and aahing as they passed the baby around. The room was decorated in early American colonial maple furniture with knotty pine paneled walls, milk glass lamps and lots of dark green plaid. Only "family" didn't seem to use it, just the adults. While they got comfortable on the tartan plaid sofa and chairs, the kids played outside or in their own bedrooms. Unlike the integrated household that I was accustomed to living in, this place had boundaries between adult and child. Anytime we visited I never saw Mom and Joe again until it was time to leave.

My new cousin, Katie, the middle one, and I were playing with jump ropes outside when she got the idea to go exploring. I was hesitant at first, but what else did I have to do? Her sisters weren't home and I would have been sitting there alone otherwise. "Are you sure it's OK to leave the yard?" I asked.

"Yeah, I do it all the time," said Katie.

"Shouldn't we ask first?"

"Nah, c'mon let's go."

She lifted the latch and opened the wooden gate that was attached to the fence that ran along the back yard. Once we were on the other side of the gate, Katie led the way down a steep embankment behind their house. I followed her along the narrow dirt path that was mostly covered with plants and weeds. We spent so much time navigating the steep hill, slipping and sliding, and trying to keep from falling, that I guess we strayed too far from the house. We finally ended up at the lower level of the development on a street that I'd never seen before. We were sitting on the sidewalk resting, when here comes Joe running down the street waving his arms and yelling. "What the fuck are you two doing all the way down here? Do you guys know how far away you are from the house? Who the hell told you it was OK to take off?"

Katie and I eyed each other as we stood dusting the back of our pants. "It's OK, my parents don't care if I climb the hill," she said.

"The hell they don't, who do you think dropped me off?"

No answer.

"Your dad that's who, we've been drivin' around for the last half hour lookin' for you guys, now git."

He came up behind us and started pushing us with his hands to go back up the way we came as punishment, and when we didn't move fast enough he unbuckled his leather belt and whipped us both across our butts all the way home.

Whack, run, whack, run all the way up the embankment. We were using both hands to grab onto handfuls of ice plant to keep from slipping, so we couldn't protect our backsides with our hands. We were both bawling from the stinging pain that the belt caused as we tried to scale the steep hill, which was a lot harder going up than down. "Get going, move it, get back up the hill, you know better than to go down that hillside." He kept hollering. "We didn't know where you were, don't you ever pull that shit again, now get your asses home."

Katie and I both wet our pants, which Joe probably didn't notice since it was outdoors where the weeds and plants were tall and thick. When we finally arrived back at the house using the same gate that we used to escape, we headed straight to Katie's room, where we stayed until dinnertime. We rinsed my pants out and hung them in the bathroom to dry and in the mean time, she loaned me a pair of underpants and peddle-pushers.

Joe stepped into the bedroom about thirty minutes later. "Y'all can come out now, dinner's ready."

Katie and I just got up from the floor where we were playing cards and followed him down the hall. We sat at the kitchen table squeezing Bosco into our milk as Mom and Gloria placed the burgers on our plates and then Gloria said with a smirk, "looks like you girls got tarred and feathered for runnin' off without tellin' anyone." Katie spoke up hoping to get some sympathy. "Yeah, Uncle Joe spanked us all the way back up the hill till we got home."

"Well let that be a lesson to stay in yer' own yard next time," Gloria barked. "You guys aren't even eight years old yet and shouldn't be runnin' off like that. Shame on both ya."

Mom now heating Sheila's bottle on the stove, said nothing, even though she was within earshot. Typical.

Katie and I exchanged looks before we started slathering mayonnaise on our buns and placing cheese slices on our patty. Once we were alone, I questioned her about the spanking. "Has Joe ever hit you before?"

"Uh-uh", Katie replied shaking her head.

"He sure was mad, how come you said we could go down there?"

"Cuz I've done it before with my sister."

"Yeah but she's older, did your mom know?"

"I think so, she's seen us play on the hill before."

"We shouldn't have gone, my bottom still hurts," I said as I rubbed my backside.

Katie nodded, "I know, mine too."

The adults could be heard from where we sat in the kitchen, talking and laughing in the dining room as if the spanking incident had never happened. Mother was so busy with Sheila I don't think she even knew the details. Katie's parents must have thought it was all right that Uncle Joe was corporally disciplining her because they didn't object to the paddling either.

CHAPTER 11

ALL IN YOUR HEAD

Mom and Joe had been married a little over a year and so far I had had two spankings. I was about to get another one.

It was the middle of summer and I wanted to go swimming at the high school pool during public swim time. Since I couldn't find a friend to go with me, I resorted to asking my next-door neighbor, Carolyn. Since she was nearly two years younger, along with the fact that I had made new friends in school, I had lost interest in her. But I was desperate.

Mom usually stayed and swam in the adult lanes but this Saturday Joe was working and couldn't stay with Sheila. Hawthorne High School was just under three miles from our house and that Saturday, after Mom dropped us off at noon, she promised that she would be back by 2 o'clock, instructing us to wait out in front. We waited and waited and Carolyn kept asking, "Where's your mom?" And I replied the same thing every time, "I don't know, maybe she forgot us."

When she didn't show up after more than an hour, Carolyn came up with an idea. "I know, let's start walking."

"We can't, we don't know the way," I replied.

"I do! I know the way home."

"You do? Are you sure? Have you ever walked from here before?"

"Yeah lots of times with my brothers."

I believed her that she knew the way home, which she didn't so we got lost.

It was hot and we were tired and thirsty and nothing looked familiar as we trudged along the busy street. I should have known better than to believe a seven year old.

"How much farther?" I asked.

"I think just a few more blocks," Carolyn answered.

"We've been walking for a long time." I was getting a bad feeling. "Are we going the right way?"

She hesitated. "I think so."

I gave Carolyn a look that was cold and doubting. "You think so?"

It was when I saw a sign that said we were on El Segundo Blvd. and we spotted a small market, that I decided it was time to ask for help. The man behind the counter let me borrow a dime so that I could call home. Mom answered the phone after the first ring. "Where are you? I came to pick you up and you weren't there, I even went into the pool area. I've been frantic, it's nearly 4:30!"

I told her what happened. "We waited and you didn't come. I thought you forgot us. We started walking because Carolyn said she knew the way home, but she didn't, so now we're in a store."

"Let me talk to the owner, and don't you dare leave, stay there do you hear me?" She screamed. "I'll come and get you. I was about to call the police, I was so worried!"

A short time later, Joe and one of the teenage boys from the neighborhood showed up and when I asked for money to buy a Dr Pepper, he said no. On the ride home Joe and Dave were deep in conversation about sports and never once said a word to Carolyn or me. I thought it was odd that they didn't want to know more about us getting lost. Once we pulled in the driveway, Carolyn and I started to mosey over to her yard, when Joe called out. "Where do you think you're goin'?"

I circled back to face him. "Next door to play."

"No, you're not, get in the house."

I was confused by the scowl on is face. Why was he so mad, I didn't do anything. I thought he'd be glad to see me.

As I was walking toward the door, he stepped inside right behind me and told me to go to my room.

I started to turn and ask "why," but I thought better of it. I was now afraid, so I kept walking. As I made my way across the living room, Mom came out of the kitchen and said, "I was so worried when I couldn't find you, don't you ever take off like that again."

I whirled my head her way and shot back, "I thought you forgot us, you said two o'clock and it was three-fifteen, according to the pool clock when we started walking."

That's when Joe pounced. "You don't speak to your mother like that! I don't care if you have to wait two, three or four hours or even all god-damned day! You don't leave! Ever. When your mom tells ya to wait, you wait! Got that? Now get in your room!" He shouted as he gave me a shove with his hand.

His command gave me a jolt, the kind that triggered the urge to pee—because I was now crying. The next words out of his mouth, as he followed me into my room were: "You want me to give you somethin' to cry about?" Before I could respond, he grabbed my hairbrush from the top of my dresser, sat at the foot of my bed and yanked me by the arm to turn me over his knee so he could paddle me. It hurt so bad, with just a swimsuit between me and the brush it felt like my bottom was on fire. I was howling and trying to wiggle away, but he had me pinned so I couldn't move. When he finally stopped, as I was getting to my feet, he saw the wet stain on the rug.

"What's that?" He demanded.

Sobbing, I lied, "I d–d–don't know? Something spilled."

"Is that pee?"

I shook my head quickly and that's when he twisted my arm and slung me back across his lap and spanked me some more. "That's what you get for peein' all over the rug and lyin' about it. Clean it up and stay in your room!" He left the room, slamming the door behind him.

The rug was an ugly multicolored blue and pink woven area rug that lay directly onto a concrete floor with no padding. It was uncomfortable to sit on because the fibers were plastic coated and made indentations on your legs. The colors were were so dark I'm surprised he even saw the stain where I had peed. I needed to go get a towel from the bathroom in order to clean up the pee, but I feared that if I left my room, I would get in more trouble. Instead, I grabbed a baby blanket and tried to rub the stain out, but then Mom came in with a wet rag and helped.

I could barely speak in between the hiccups. "Mother, he, he b-b-beat me with a brush, I couldn't help it, the pee just came out, it's your fault that I got spanked."

Somehow she justified the beating. "Do you understand we thought someone kidnapped you guys?" Avoiding eye contact, Mom continued blotting the rug with the wet towel. "I was driving up and down the streets between here and the high school like a madwoman."

"But we thought you forgot us!" Like a goalpost, my arms spread upward. "Why didn't you come when you said?"

No response, more dabbing at the spot.

Mom shook her head, gathered the rags, and then closed the door and left without another word.

The next day, when Carolyn came to the door she asked why I couldn't play and I told her that I got in trouble for walking home. She scratched her head and seemed to mull it over. "How come? I didn't."

I wondered about that. If we both did something wrong then how come only one of us got in trouble?

Maybe it was because Carolyn and her brothers did pretty much anything they wanted. The kids roamed the neighborhood and came home when they were hungry.

Our household wasn't quite so mellow. Joe was always on my case. It seemed like he was looking for excuses to punish me. Since he never hid his dislike for my dad, I wondered if he was jealous because Mom had been married before? I was, after all a constant reminder.

One night after dinner, when I was in the living room watching TV, I overheard Joe and Mom having a conversation about my dad while they were in the kitchen. I turned the volume down lower so I could hear better.

"He's just an office clerk, dunno what you ever saw in him? He's a deadbeat; the man can't keep up with child support. Hell, half the time his checks bounce."

Joe continued to rake the poor man over the coals. "But he sure likes to show off with gifts. Shit, the way he spoils Stefanie at Christmas and her birthday, with all that excess. I ain't never seen anything like it, loadin' up one on top a the other 'til the presents reach the ceiling! Disgusting spectacle, if you ask me!"

"I know, it's his way of making up for the money he's supposed to pay and for not being around, I guess."

"Why doesn't he just let me adopt her and be done with

it? It's not like he's here every weekend, shit his parents see more of Steffie than he does."

"Always a sob story, sez the same thing, 'I'm broke.'" Mom added. "And whenever I broach the subject of adoption, he refuses to discuss and hangs up on me."

They concluded that since my dad refused to give up his rights, they would go ahead and change my last name to Hoskins, so that all of us would have the same last name. I liked the idea, but my dad and his side of the family didn't.

Joe wanted to adopt me, yet he still seized each and every opportunity to pick on me. He would snicker and mock me. "You trying to get sick," whenever I was sick, including a bout with pneumonia.

As for my Asthma condition, anytime I had an attack, he made derisive comments. "It's all in your head." I didn't know what that meant, it sure seemed like I was sick when I was gasping for breath.

I would lay in bed at night listening to the wheezing sounds that felt soothing at times because I pretended that they were fairies singing. That help put me to sleep, but it didn't last long because I would jolt out a deep sleep screaming my head off. The bad dreams were so scary, and felt so real. During the dream, I would be asleep in my bed and all of a sudden the bogeyman would be standing at the foot of my bed holding a knife and then just as he would begin to lunge at me, I would start screaming and wake myself up. Mom would come running in, and try to calm my fears. And she did, until the next time.

There was no question, Joe's temperament was volatile there was no in-between. The aggression alternated between the gregarious and explosive. When he was in one of his chipper moods, he was affectionate with everyone. He would force himself on me to give him a hug and kiss, and make me say "I love you" when I really wanted to say, "I hate you." Then came, "Come on give me some sugar." I wanted to vomit. It felt so fake, couldn't he see that I didn't mean what I was forced to say? If he could, he didn't let on, and Mom seemed to stick her head in the sand during the whole performance. Any way he could get attention was all that mattered.

Whenever I tried to talk to Mom about Joe, she usually just nodded and would say, "I know" and in the same breath, she would add a "but", "He does so much for you." She would then, tic off all the ways that Joe supported me, like paying my Brownie dues, then came the food, clothing and roof over my head. Before she was finished she would take another swipe at my real dad. "All Jerry cares about is Jerry, he hasn't given me a dime in six months. He's supposed to help me with the things you need, but since he doesn't, then Joe has to do it, so he's not all bad."

I had seen my dad hand checks to my mom, but I had no idea how much he was supposed to pay for me.

CHAPTER 12

THE FRIEND

Either I got smarter at age ten or the leash was so short I had little opportunity to screw up because the spankings seemed to have stopped. It also helped that by now we all knew who was boss. The verbal barbs, and yelling however, continued. "Look at me when I'm talkin' to you." "Do as I say, not as I do." He got in my face if I said or did something that could be construed as smart-alecky; no shoulder shrugging, eye-rolls or "don't ask me" responses.

Every time he raised his voice it triggered an involuntary pelvic response in me, making me feel like I wanted to pee. I lived in fear every day of my life that I was going to get whacked or screamed at. The only way to survive was to walk on eggshells whenever he was around and live by his rules. "Do as I say, not as I do" resonated like a broken record in my head.

His parenting style was heavy-handed and authoritarian, whereas Mom had a gentle demeanor and was permissive, never yelling or hitting. It was a mixed up place and it was oppressive. Joe was a tyrant who maintained tight control, giving no one much of a voice, or much in the way of autonomy. Mom and I went along with whatever he said and Sheila was too young to know the difference.

Whether he walked in whistling or swearing, there was that impending sense of doom every time he came through the door. He had a way of sucking every bit of air out of the room by his mere existence. It was like living at the foot of Mount Vesuvius—you knew the volcanic temper outburst was coming, you just didn't know when. I hated it when he was home. I felt so discontented and tense. I couldn't be myself, either. My emotions and words were all locked up.

Joe's friend, Glenn, however, provided a welcome reprieve whenever he came over. They met at an office machinery company, where Joe was now working after getting fired from his construction job for getting in a fight. I think he was the only friend of Joe's who stuck around, partly because of Joe's sociability and also being new to the area without many friends. Since he was single, Joe brought him home to have dinner and cocktails at least once a week. He was so different from Joe both in looks and personality. Glenn, who was from Alberta Canada and of French descent, was very handsome. He was much shorter than Joe, maybe 5'6" to Joe's 6'4" and had black hair, deep blue eyes, an olive complexion and no freckles, only a mole on his cheek.

I always looked forward to seeing him and I think he liked seeing me too. He was especially nice to me, and actually talked to me like I was a person. He was such a happy guy and had the best belly laugh, kind of high pitched, almost like a woman's. His bubbly personality and infectious laugh felt like a breath of fresh air had been pumped into our house whenever he came to visit.

Every time he came over he tucked me into bed with a bedtime story. He would take a seat on the edge of my bed waiting for me to get comfortable before he began. "Once upon a time there was a beautiful princess, cowgirl, circus performer, dragon slayer, named, Steffie." He made up a medley of adventure stories that always included me as the leading lady and when he finished his story, he pressed his two fingers on each of my eyes and made me close them and then he kissed me "good-night" on the forehead.

Eventually he got married and moved away. I missed the joy and laughter that he brought into our house and the bedtime stories. But most of all I missed my friend.

There would be more so-called friends coming and going. None of them like Glenn; he was one of a kind. Joe was always schmoozing someone to see what he could get and our house was a revolving door of new friends. Never my mom's, only his. The latest was an attempt to get in good with this older man who remodeled homes. Joe didn't like selling office machines and wanted to get back into construction and Hal Harper was his ticket.

He was always hanging around the Harper house, trying to get hooked up in the old guy's business and socializing was one way to get his foot in the door. The Harpers started coming over to our house for dinner and sometimes just to play cards. They became a foursome in spite of the age differences; the Harpers were a good 25 or more years older than Mom and Joe who were both 30. I remember the woman had mounds of curly black hair with threads of silver coiled throughout and huge breasts that bulged out of the top of her scoop-necked dresses. Her name was Wanda and she was extra nice to me. She invited me over to her house once to see her antique doll collection and then she made me lunch and afterwards she also let me brush and style her long curly hair.

Their neighborhood wasn't too far from where we lived, maybe fifteen minutes but it was a lot nicer than ours.

Just like Wanda's house, many of the houses on the street

had wood siding painted white, with green shutters and trim around the doors and windows. They all had manicured lawns with rose bushes and rows of towering shade trees that lined the sidewalks. The inside of Wanda's house was fussy and looked more like a parlor, with fringe and beaded trimmed lamps, frilly pillows, and doilies. Then there was her doll collection that occupied an entire bedroom. Most were locked up in a glass cabinet—like the original Madame Alexander ones—but she did let me handle the less fragile ones.

I liked her, but for some reason my mom got quiet whenever I brought her up. Then one night I understood why, when she packed Sheila and I into the car and proceeded to drive by Wanda and Hal's house. "I need to see if Joe is over at Hal's house," Mom said.

"Why can't you just call," I asked.

"I did and Wanda said she hadn't seen him."

I thought about that and frowned. "I don't understand, if she said he wasn't there, then why are we going over there?"

"Never mind, I just need to check for myself."

But when we got to the street, there, big as life was Joe's truck parked in the driveway, but the strange thing was, Hal's truck wasn't there. Mom first drove past the house and then made a u-turn, and parked across the street.

She said, "I'll be right back."

"What are you doing, the lights are out and it looks like nobody's home."

No response.

She slipped out of the car and ran across the street. From the passenger seat, I watched her march up to the front door and begin knocking. Within seconds her knocks turned to pounding. Then, I saw her pacing back and forth on the porch waiting for the door to open. It didn't.

When no one answered, she gave up and side-stepped, as if in slow motion, one step at time easing her way across the lawn and never taking her eyes away from the house, until she got back to the car. Just before she opened the car door she paused and instead of getting in, she pivoted on her heels and darted back toward the house.

"What the heck?" I asked myself.

This time she approached the driveway, where she stopped dead in her tracks at the sight of the padlocked chain link gate. I saw her jiggle the lock a few times and when it didn't open she just stood there like a statue before she wandered back to the car for the second time.

When she slid into the driver's seat, I asked what was going on. "Looks like Joe and Wanda have something to hide," she said in a sarcastic tone. "I don't want to talk about it. Just be quiet and keep it to yourself." And then she started sniffing and wiping her nose with back of her hand as we pulled away from the curb.

"What do you mean, something to hide?" I asked. "Do you think he's inside the house, with the lights out?"

"Sure looks like it, two-timing bastard," she muttered.

I turned in my seat so I could face her. "I don't understand, why didn't they answer the door?"

Mom's hands were gripping the steering wheel for dear life. "That's a good question, now be quiet, I need to think," she said through clinched teeth.

We rode the rest of the way home in silence.

When Joe finally came home some time during the night, I heard them from my bedroom, yelling at each other and then I heard something break. The next sound was their bedroom door slamming followed by the bathroom door, which was located in the hall right outside my room.

I thought it was strange that Joe and Wanda were in the house alone with all the lights out, and up to no good, according to Mom. She was old enough to be his mother and she was also friends with us. It didn't make sense to me, Mom was so young and pretty, and Wanda was so old and wrinkly.

Another night Mom woke me up around eleven o'clock and made me get out of bed along with Sheila who remained asleep. She packed us in the car once again and all she would say is that she couldn't find Joe and wanted to check someplace. We drove to a bar in Inglewood and then circled around the back to the parking lot where she spotted Joe's white pickup truck. We sat in the car for awhile and then she turned to me and said, "I want you to go inside and see if Joe's there."

I didn't completely understanding her request. "Wait, you want me to walk into a bar by myself?"

She did her best to persuade me. "Steffie, please, just run in there take a quick look no one will notice you, then you can run back to the car."

Shaking my head like a windshield wiper in a rainstorm, I refused. "But Mom, he'll see me and then he'll come after me, nuh uh."

She kept nudging me, practically pushing me out the door. "No one's gonna notice you, everyone's too busy drinking and talking, now c'mon, just go."

I slid across the seat and climbed out of the car, looking over my shoulder as I slowly crept my way to the back door. Standing there for what seemed like hours, I wrapped my head around the corner, snuck a peek, and then whipped my head back where it was safe from view. I caught a glimpse of Joe sitting at the bar laughing with a bunch of people. That was all I could handle, so I ran as fast as I could to the car and told Mom he was there.

She fired up the engine but the car didn't move. She began quizzing me for details. "Did he see you? Who was he with?"

"No he didn't see me and I don't know who he was with," I told her. "Now can we go? And I'm not going back in there!"

"Okay, okay."

As soon as Joe got home, Mom started in on him and all I could hear was his booming voice slurring apologies and then he must have passed out because the argument stopped.

CHAPTER 13

FITTING IN

Mom finally quit working when Sheila was two and I was ten. She was home all the time and thankfully Joe was working until dinnertime and sometimes on Saturdays, which gave me a small window of time to be with her.

I made lots of friends at York Avenue Elementary and began to feel like I belonged. First there was the school safety program, where I got to wear a white cross-body belt with a badge attached whenever I was on patrol duty, which made me feel super important. My job was to help the first and second graders cross the street.

The teachers were nice, especially Mrs. Thompson, my third grade teacher. One time, when she asked me to fetch the stapler from her desk, I noticed her high heels sitting on the floor under the desk. I kicked off one of my shoes, and pretended to look for the stapler so I could slip my foot into her shoe for just a second. She was never the wiser, and it soon became a little game for me, whenever I had the opportunity to come near the desk.

Fourth grade wasn't as fun since I had to share a double desk with Billy McDougal. He constantly picked his nose and wiped his buggers on the underside of the desk. It was disgusting, especially when I would accidentally brush up against one of them with my fingers. Fortunately we rotated desks every other month. After that experience my hands never ventured to the underside of any future desk.

I was active in Brownies, and then Girl Scouts along with all of the school activities, of which there were many. The school was always having special events for the students and their families, where all the grades were integrated. The May Day parade and school plays were also a chance for us fourth grade girls to mingle with the sixth grade girls that we looked up to. One girl in particular, whose name was, Sue-Nae, was the one that we all wanted to emulate. Her teased blond hair fell just below her shoulders and was garnished with bright colored scarves. She painted her lips with fuchsia pink lipstick and applied powder and rouge to her face. Her circular skirts were inflated by conspicuous stiff crinoline slips bearing layers of ruffles. I couldn't wait to be in sixth grade so I could be just like her.

At least I no longer had to wear glasses full time. My eyesight had improved enough so that I only had to wear my glasses for TV and reading. And with the Dutch boy haircut long gone, there was a glimmer of hope that someday I may just turn into a swan like Sue-Nae.

Almost every weekend my girlfriends and I traded spending the night at each other's houses. One time my friend Patty and I got to sleep in her parent's camper—that was parked in the back yard driveway—as part of our Girl Scout nature badge requirement. It had an overhead bed above the truck cab and that's where we slept. We felt so grown up having it all to ourselves. We cooked our own hot dogs and beans on the stove and stayed up late giggling and playing card games.

Another friend, Paula, who lived on the next block, had wooden stilts that her dad had built for her. They were a blast to walk around on and soon became our go-to activity whenever I visited. We took turns climbing onto the corral fence that circled her yard, where we would push off from a seated position before tromping around the paved portion of the yard. I could've spent hours walking around on them, but because her mom was super strict, she wouldn't let her play very often or for very long. If I had had my own set then Paula and I could have made better use of our stilt walking time. Joe said that he would get around to building me my own set one of these days. He never did.

Most of my friends lived within walking distance, so there was never a shortage of people to play with. Those social relationships that lasted throughout the five years of elementary school were my lifeline.

I finally looked forward to going to school, not only to be with my friends, but learning was becoming less of a struggle once my vision became stronger. Except for math. I couldn't even catch a break with my homework. Instead of helping me understand, Mom would just look up the answers in the back of the workbook and fill in the answers because she didn't understand it either. I squeaked by with C's and D's.

I used to get eyestrain from reading, but with the extensive treatments and exercises, including the patch, I was now able to read with minimal effort. I wasn't a fast reader by any means, but discovering books opened up a new world for me. Mom hardly ever read, except for magazines but Joe always had his nose inside a thick book with a black swastika on the cover—that sat in the center of our coffee table. My books came from the school library, my favorites being, the Oz books, and Nancy Drew. I especially enjoyed biographical stories and anything to do with travel and fashion. Two of my most cherished books were *Mrs. 'Arris Goes To Paris*, about a cleaning woman who saves her wages for a year so that she can go to Paris and buy a Dior dress and *The Dress Doctor* by Edith Head. I wanted to be a costume designer when I grew up after reading Edith's book about getting to work with all of the famous movie stars designing their clothes for films. *Wings On my Feet* by Sonja Henie inspired me to ice skate.

However, I didn't have to wait until I grew up to learn to how to ice skate. Twice a week, I took lessons at Margaret Parker's Ice Skating Rink, in Culver City, where I became proficient enough to take part in their twice yearly shows. It was great fun for two years but once I graduated from elementary school, I began to lose interest.

My friends and I were excited and also kind of nervous to be transferring to Hawthorne Intermediate School following our sixth grade graduation. This was big stuff, no more single classroom with one teacher for the entire day, now we would have six periods where we would be changing classes.

I was in my second week of junior high school when Mom and Joe informed me of their decision to move to Orange County. It might as well have been the moon. They were so sneaky the way they went about it, never an inkling that something this important affecting all of us was in the forecast. Mom and Joe had apparently signed on the dotted line while Sheila and I were in school because now it was a done deal. I was beside myself. Every chance I got, I pled my case to Mom whenever I could get her alone. Today she was taking a nap, I didn't care, I went into her bedroom anyway and seated myself at the foot of her bed. She was a light sleeper and opened her eyes the minute I walked in. Without delay I started in. "Please, Mother, why do we have to move?"

"I told you, honey, we want to own our own house and Orange County is more affordable than here," she said.

"But, Mother, I'm twelve years old and I've been with the same kids since second grade when I was seven, can't you see how important they are and not only that I just started a new school, and now I won't know anyone."

"It won't be that bad, you've only been in junior high for a couple of weeks, plus your York school friends are all scattered in different classes now."

"Yeah but I still see them at nutrition break and lunch, besides I like my classes and I'm settled now."

"Steffie, I know it's hard to move during the school year, but the new house wasn't going to be ready by the time school started."

My eyes teared up, "this isn't fair, what am I gonna do? Do you know how weird it's gonna be to be the new kid after school's started?"

Mom busied herself propping herself up on her pillows, probably trying to buy some time while she thought up a response.

She switched gears and tried to sell me on the positives. "Listen Steffie, the house we're buying is brand new and we're the first ones to live in it. And don't forget, you'll have your own room!"

"Humph." I gave her a sour look, sprung to my feet and stormed out of the room slamming the door behind me.

CHAPTER 14

BEAN FIELDS

Huntington Beach had been nothing but bean fields until 1964. Now there was a crop of newly built housing tracts replacing the farms and fields one by one. The giant billboard standing at the entrance of our soon to be neighborhood had an image of a Dutch girl in full costume with yellow braids extending from a winged Dutch cap publicizing homes at a price of $14,000.

The Dutch Haven tract of one-story houses all looked alike with a choice of three exteriors. In keeping with the Dutch theme, the most popular was the gingerbread ornamentation that included a scalloped A-frame trim across the front of the house. It was a big change from the densely populated urban neighborhood that was part of Los Angeles County with older, architecturally diverse homes and where everything was convenient and close by.

There wasn't any landscaping or fences just cookie cutter one story houses sitting on flat dirt lots. Our three-bedroom house was the most basic of all of the exteriors. It had light brown tinted stucco set off with dark stained wood trim and a curved asphalt driveway that encompassed the front of the house and led to the attached garage.

Inside, the floor consisted of ivory colored linoleum stamped with a pattern of some sort. The walls were white, and the ceilings textured. The living room had beige wall-to-wall carpeting and also a whitewashed brick fireplace and large metal framed sliding windows that provided a view of the street. Toward the back of the house was the kitchen. It was square shaped with avocado green appliances, and there was a gold-flecked Formica breakfast bar that divided the kitchen from the dining room. Mom found some unfinished wooden barstools at a lumberyard and spray painted them orange.

Then, there was our furniture, which sort of threw a monkey wrench into the brand new environment. The biggest eyesore was our dark brown tattered sofa, a collage of bald spots where the burnout fabric had worn away, mostly on the arms. The hand-me-down wooden dining table wasn't much better. The top was both scarred and coated with water rings and had to be made level with a book of matches under one of the legs.

My room on the other hand, had all new furniture, thanks to my dad. I had a bright orange slip-covered trundle bed with orange and brown striped bolster pillows along the back so it could serve as a sofa by day. I also now had a desk where I could do my homework. It had a cool looking black and white gooseneck lamp that sat atop the wood veneer surface along with a white plastic molded chair to match. The best part of having my own room—other than no more sharing—was having the freedom of decorating it anyway I wanted. The wall space was now all mine, where I could hang posters of Ricky Nelson and Elvis. Now that I had my own record player, all my money went toward buying records. Every time I went to the grocery store with Mom, I bought a new record with my own money that I had earned doing chores. Spending time in my room singing along with my rock and roll idols to their hit songs—"Hello Mary-Lou" and "Love Me Tender"—took my mind off the bleak surroundings.

From the back of our house we could see a farm in the distance with a big red barn, other than that there was nothing but dirt and fields as far as you could see and when the Santa Ana winds blew all of that dirt blew our way and seeped inside. It was like that for six months until the next phase of houses was built behind us. The nearest grocery store was in the next city of Westminster. On the plus side, the beach was only four miles away and as I kept reminding myself, I did finally have my own room.

The biggest bombshell though, was when Mom tried to enroll me in junior high school and discovered they didn't have one. Suddenly, I was demoted back to elementary school. It seems that the population of the rural community didn't warrant a junior high school yet. We were in one of the first new housing tracts in a brand new growth area.

When I saw the school, I freaked out. "Mother, this school looks like something out of the dark ages; talk about a step backwards from the schools in Hawthorne." It was a combined school of kindergarten through eighth grade. The seventh and eight grade classrooms were only separated by a low-slung chain link fence that ran along the inside perimeter between the buildings, otherwise we were all sharing the same real estate.

"I'm sure it's a very good school and since it's so small it will be easier to make friends," Mom said.

She was right about it being small and the rest I would think about.

The good news about Rancho View was I wasn't the only new student. With the influx of home building and migration to the suburbs of Orange County there were lots of families moving into the area. This made making friends easier. The other two new girls, who enrolled the same week I did, were just as scared as I was and the three of us instantly became friends. The student community was spread out well beyond traditional district boundaries because the population hadn't justified a demand for school construction, but that was rapidly changing with the real estate boom.

As a way to ease my distress from leaving my friends, Mom and Joe allowed me to plan a slumber party shortly after we moved. We mailed invitations to five of my best girlfriends from Hawthorne about a week before the Saturday party. I could hardly contain myself when the day finally rolled around. I was so excited to see them after a month and show them our new house. I kept running to the front window every time I heard a car.

We went all out with food and decorations. There was a red and white checked paper tablecloth with matching plates along with the red, yellow and blue balloons that we tied to the wrought iron light fixture that hung from the dining room ceiling. For dinner we bought three large square shaped frozen sausage pizzas, three bags of potato chips, two kinds of dip, onion-garlic and ranch, and three large bottles of soda pop, Bubble-Up, Nehi Orange Soda and Dr Pepper. For dessert we picked up a sheet cake from Safeway. The cake was chocolate marble and the frosting was chocolate buttercream decorated with sprinkles.

Everything looked perfect, all the food was laid out on the table and the house was even tidy. The invitation said 3 o'clock, and when an hour had passed without any guests, Mom said for me to start making calls. I called Betsy first. "Hi Betsy, it's Stefanie. I was just wondering when you were coming to my party. You got the invitation, didn't you?"

"Hi Stefanie, umm, yeah, but my dad said it's too far to drive," she replied.

"Oh no, how come you didn't call?"

"I couldn't, it's a toll call."

"Oh, um… well, couldn't you get a ride with Gayle and Lori?"

"No, they're not coming either."

"But we bought all kinds of extra food cuz I thought you guys were gonna come."

"I'm sorry Stefanie, I wanted to but you live so far away."

The answer was the same after I called everyone. No one was coming. They explained that all of their parents said it was too far to drive. I cried and cried. I was inconsolable as I stood in the dining room brooding over all of the food and decorations that none of them would ever see. I was having a party and not one person was coming. Even Joe felt bad for me. It was a cruel thing to do. I said to Mom and Joe, "They didn't even have the courtesy to call and say they weren't coming. They just don't show up?"

I kept repeating. "I don't understand, I thought they were my friends, how can they just not come, what are we gonna do with all this food?"

Mom stepped forward and held me close, and then she abruptly pulled away, placing her hands on my shoulders.

"Well, we'll just have to have our own party; come on don't cry."

Pouring himself a glass of Dr Pepper into one of the red party cups from the table, Joe chimed in. "You got new friends now, you don't need them little piss asses, and their dumb ass cheap parents. Summa bitch, who the hell do they think they are? Can't even say they're not comin'—what kinda chickenshit thing is that to do?"

I never saw any of them again.

Mom and Joe were right; my new friends took their place. There was Joni, my new best friend, who came from South Gate and now lived just a few houses away from me. Carla, from Louisiana moved in about a week after I did and lived at the far end of the block. She had a thick southern drawl and smoked cigarettes. She was fun to hang around with, because she seemed so worldly, but before long she had a steady boyfriend, so she was mostly tied up with him.

Most of the native boys surfed and played guitars and wore their sun-bleached hair long—well past their ears. You could spot the new boys though; they had short hair and wore high waisted pants with collared shirts.

It didn't take long to forget my old friends, with all of the new families arriving in droves. We were all in the same boat and eager for relationships, making it easy to connect.

The kids came from all over, other states, and far away cities in California, so there wasn't much in the way of predisposed notions, no one knew anything about anyone. The old kids accepted the new kids and eventually everyone blended with the Friday night dances at school being the icebreakers. Everyone went and mixed together.

While the school part of my life was going well, home life was tough. Joe was always on a tangent about something and money was always the root of it. I started babysitting for a couple of families in the neighborhood, so that I would have my own spending money, and also to get away from the house for a few hours.

I got so sick of hearing him bitch, mostly to Mom and me. "Can't you turn off the lights when you leave the room? How much did it cost to get your hair done? Is that a new sweater? I've never seen it before." His unreasonable rules went so far as to calculate toilet paper usage. "You girls don't need to use the whole damn roll of paper every time you wipe your ass. When I was in the Marine Corps we were only allowed five squares." He would even barge into the bathroom if the door was unlocked to make sure we weren't wasting paper. It was humiliating, especially for a pre-teen going through puberty.

CHAPTER 15

SNEAKING TO SEE GRANDMA

Joe continued to be a pain to live with. It was always something with him, as if he thrived by creating havoc. He seemed to be looking for reasons to get pissed off. This time it was Mom's poor housekeeping. Never mind that he got a pass, his mess didn't count.

She never cleaned up after meals. Her excuse: "The dishes need to soak." By the next morning the dishes were still sitting in the sink, the suds vanished, the water now cold and milky with bits of bloated food scraps floating along the top. Dishwashers were luxury items that cost extra and we didn't have one. If we had had one, she most likely wouldn't have loaded it anyway.

There was a blanket of dust that coated every piece of furniture, from tabletops to lampshades. Cigarette butts filled ashtrays and stayed there for days. Mom was also a messy smoker. She frequently let her cigarette ashes grow to the point that they dropped to the floor and instead of sweeping them up, she simply ground them into the floor or carpet with the toe of her shoe. Joe, who ate just about anything, was always criticizing her cooking. He was right; Mom's cooking was lousy. She didn't inherit the southern cooking skills—growing up in Oklahoma—that Betty had.

When we lived with Betty and Charlie home cooking meant just that, everything was made from scratch. Betty's sweet potato pies were heavenly and she even turned spaghetti into a southern baked casserole with yellow cheese and green bell peppers mixed in. Mom had little interest in cooking and always took the easy way out. She threw things together, a little of this and a little of that, never measuring or referring to a cookbook. Her standard of operation was, if it could be made in one pan that was dinner.

Joe's biggest pet peeve though, was her not making the bed. One day he had reached his boiling point, and was shouting at her about the unmade bed. "Marjorie Ann, for Chrissake', why can't you make the goddamned bed after you get up in the morning? It takes all of five minutes." Then he hollered my name summoning me to their room. "I'm sick of this unmade bed bullshit! If your mother can't seem to make the fuckin' bed, then it's your responsibility to make sure she does," he barked. "And if the bed isn't made by the time I get home, I'm gonna beat both your asses, got that?"

My eyes grew wide and I just stared back at him. He repeated his order, tapping my chest with his index finger for emphasis. "Do! you! un–der–stand?" I nodded. "Then say it, goddammit, 'I will make the bed if mom doesn't.'"

I did. But, I wanted to scream, "I hate your guts, what do I have to do with it? It's not my bed!"

I was always sweating bullets that I would forget to check on the bed situation. I remained vigilant, never knowing what he would do next. I checked the bed daily as soon as I came home from school and found that I had to remind Mother a few times to make it. Sometimes she would do it just before dinnertime. Her reasoning was that since she liked to take naps, it didn't do any good to make it sooner.

About a year after we moved to Huntington Beach my beloved, Charlie got sick with leukemia and needed a bone marrow transplant. He died in his early fifties when he didn't get one. He had been hospitalized for about a month waiting for a match from the donor list after his only living relative, a sister, refused to help him.

Mom took me to visit him at the Los Angeles County General Hospital that was located downtown on State Street, also known as a place for indigents, which didn't make sense why Charlie was there. Betty had placed him there, claiming it was because of the top doctors, but Joe and Mom said it was because it was cheaper. It was a massive million square foot art deco white building with a maze-like interior that reeked of antiseptic blended with decay. Charlie was in a ward with lots of other sick men. He just laid there on his back dressed in a hospital gown and covered by a pale yellow sheet. The first thing I noticed when I saw him was his swollen foot that had been uncovered. Although he looked pale and tired, he seemed to be in good spirits—but that was who he was, never one to complain. That was the last time that I saw him alive.

When he died, my world died right along with him. Just because I didn't see him as often after we moved from the LA area, knowing he was there was a comfort. And now that he wasn't, there was no getting over losing him. The joyful memories of all of those Saturday nights together watching Roller Derby, eating crispy Red Delicious apples followed by a bowlful of chocolate chip ice cream, were both beautiful and painful. His voice too, would stick with me forever and the way he put his own twist on pronouncing words, like Los Angeles. He would say "Loss Ang–less." I looked up to him and loved him more than anyone and I know he felt the same. The bond will last forever along with the grief.

At his funeral, with her body draped across the open casket, Betty was so bereaved her intense sobs grew into wailing.

Her loud wailing then triggered a flow of sobs from me as I reflexively imitated her behavior. Standing beside her, I slowly turned my gaze toward Charlie's lifeless body and noticed how peaceful he seemed, just like he was asleep only he was wearing his Glen plaid suit instead of pajamas. This was the first time that I had ever seen a dead person and I simply couldn't process any of it. I tentatively raised my hand to rest gently on his shoulder and then I touched his chest as if I was hoping for a heartbeat and willing him to wake up. When he didn't, I tucked an old photo of the two of us sitting side by side on the sofa just inside his suit lapel. I leaned over and whispered in his ear, "I love you Charlie, please come back." I was grief-stricken and all I wanted to do was remain in that spot and never leave the casket where he rested.

It was my dad who finally took me out of the church, wrapping his arm around my shoulders. Come on Steffie, come on, lets go." I was inconsolable as he ushered me back down the aisle past the pews filled with, customers, friends and relatives until we reached the door. He led me to the waiting limousine that had driven us there and sat me inside the back so I could settle down. He stood watch from there until it was time to leave.

Betty ended up staying with us for a few days and during that time she wanted to keep going back to the cemetery, which was in Glendale. Since she had given up driving, she needed to be driven there by Mom or Joe. She kept coming up with excuses to go to the mortuary office, a signature was needed, a bill needed to be paid, which were all a ruse to ensure a gravesite visit.

About a week after she had gone back home to her apartment in L.A., she began asking again to be taken to the cemetery. It was a Sunday afternoon and Joe reluctantly agreed to take her. We all piled into the car and off we went. She must have stayed too long because by the time Betty, Mom and I came back to the car, where Joe was waiting with Sheila, he was fuming. Joe banged the dashboard with both hands and then began to chew her out. "What in god's name were you doin' in there this time? We've been sittin' out here for an hour."

Visibly shaken by his outburst, she began digging in her purse and then once she found the wad of bills, she reached across Mom, sitting between them, to hand him the money. "Here this should take care of the gas," she said.

He ignored the money and replied in a sarcastic tone. "Oh yeah that should solve the problem." Leaning forward he shot her a sour look before he craned his head to the right so he could look over the seat to back out of the parking space. His voice grew louder. "All you care about is yourself and that goddamned cleaning shop. I am not one of your nigger slaves!"

Betty leaned forward, turning her face in Joe's direction as she spoke. "Listen here Joe, I just buried Charlie and I have business to tend to with the mortuary, you could be a little more tolerant. After all I've done for you, paying your utility bills and buying groceries, and you treat me like this? I Just lost my husband for God's sake. Can't you have a little compassion?"

"You fucking bitch, you think you can buy everyone!" He shot back. "I don't need your money, Marjorie shouldn't be asking for your help, in fact I'm so sick of you, and your preachin', and bellyachin' about how hard you work. I don't ever want to see your face again! Not only are you a bad mother, you are a bad grandmother! Stay away from my house, stay away from my family, don't call, don't write, don't come over!"

"What's gotten into you? How can you be so cruel? How dare you speak to me that way!"

"What's gotten into me is you and your crazy behavior—poppin' pills left and right—nigger lovin' old battle ax. Marjorie and Stefanie, she's outta yer life! I forbid either of you to have contact with her again. That means no calls, no letters no goin' to see her, no more cemetery and I better not find out about either of you goin' behind my back."

Mom just sat there, her head bent forward looking downward and of course saying nothing. I watched the whole thing from the back seat, not quite believing my own eyes and ears. Betty didn't even try to talk to Mom, she knew better than to expect her to get involved when Joe was on one of his rampages.

He pulled up to the curb in front of her house and told her to get out. She was dabbing her eyes with a hankie as she let herself out of the passenger door, and then slammed it.

He continued on his rant all the way home, cursing Betty and warning Mother and me to never contact her again.

I was devastated by his outrageous behavior and the stuff he said about pills and Betty being a bad grandma didn't make sense, but now all I could think about was how I was going to find a way to defy his orders and see her.

The next time my dad came to pick me up, a few weeks later, I told him what happened and he took me on a secret visit to see Betty. She was so glad to see me and she was even nice to my dad for bringing me. The three of us went to DuPars for lunch where we hashed over the cemetery incident. I continued to call her collect whenever Joe wasn't around, that way there would be no phone record.

My mom knew about it, but she was still too scared to disobey Joe's command. It took her a couple of months to finally work up the courage to call Betty. The feud ended up lasting about six months. Mom used the upcoming holidays as an excuse to bury the hatchet and by the time Christmas rolled around, Betty was back in the family. We never went back to the cemetery, though.

CHAPTER 16

BLACK EYE

Joe was busy working in construction—mostly doing painting and clean-up—all over Orange County during the building boom, which was good because that meant that he wasn't home as much. He left at six in the morning and came home around dinnertime. Huntington Beach continued to be the prominent locale of the growth and development, bringing new families into the area everyday. Among them were Mary Jo and her dad.

Her mother had died and she and her dad had moved from Palos Verdes to Huntington Beach about half way through the school year. She was streetwise, had kind of a stocky build and looked like a surfer chick, with bleached blond hair that hung over one eye. She was nice enough and tried to fit in; so much so that she offered up something wrapped in tin foil called pep pills to some of us kids. Some of the girls didn't like her because she was kind of a tomboy, but I knew what it felt like to be the new kid, so I made friends with her.

One Friday night before our weekly school dance I was talking to Mary Jo on the phone about my upcoming slumber party the next night and we were kidding around that if Sheila, who was six at the time, started bugging us, we would give her the opposite of pep pills, like a sleeping pill. I was in my room getting ready to meet up with Carla and Joni, so we could walk to the dance together, when I heard Joe summon me to the dining room. He was still wearing his work clothes caked with paint, so he must have barely walked in the door from work, when he started calling my name. I had scarcely stepped into the room when he shouted from the bar stool where he was perched. "Are you doin' drugs?"

Not understanding where this was coming from, I calmly replied, "No."

He continued on with the interrogation. "Who's Mary Jo?"

"A girl at school." I could feel the sweat dripping from my armpits and soaking my shirt, accompanied by that feeling like I was about to wet my pants.

"You and she planning on doin' drugs and giving some to your sister?" More probing, his eyes cold and penetrating. "Don't lie, your mom heard the whole thing."

I looked helplessly at my mom who was standing on the other side of the breakfast bar refusing to make eye contact with me. What a sneak, she was listening in on the extension. I wondered when she started doing that?

It was just the three of us in the room. Sheila was at her friend's house across the street.

"We were just kidding." Hoping to diffuse the situation, I forced a weak smile and pumped my hands upward, shrugging my shoulders.

"Have you tried pep pills?"

"No, we were just kidding."

In a flash, the next thing I knew he was on me, he grabbed the front of my white oxford cloth button down shirt with both hands and within seconds he let go with one hand long enough to land a punch on my left eye.

The force caused me to lose my balance and fall backwards onto the floor near the dining table. My eye was burning with pain.

He stood over me, spit spraying from his mouth as he shouted, "I said…have–you–tried–pep–pills?"

I tried to scoot backwards on my behind to gain some distance, but he reached down and grabbed me by the shirt again this time punching my other eye and face with the back of his hand. Once again I fell back onto the floor this time landing near the sliding glass door.

He was screaming at the top of his lungs, "I said, did you take pep pills? Goddammit!"

"I–I only tried them just one time." I admitted, hoping my confession would put an end to the beating. I was wrong. He began alternating between shaking me and hitting me so hard with his fist across my face that I skidded across the linoleum floor knocking over all three bar stools.

Another pop. "That's what you get for lyin' to me!" I tried to block his punches by raising my arms but it wasn't much of a defense and only made me lose my balance as I flew across the room in the opposite direction, this time toppling a dining room chair and sliding head first into the hutch. I was sobbing hysterically as he came at me again. He flung me across the other side of the room where I landed under the breakfast bar taking the fallen stools with me. My ears were ringing and I felt dazed when I heard him say something about hanging around people who were a bad influence, then I could hear Mom's raised voice, pleading. "That's enough, Joe you're going to kill her. Stop!" He did.

Once the dizziness cleared, I noticed that there was a puddle on the floor which I discreetly sopped up with my skirt as I made an effort to stand up. Joe then ordered me out of the room. "Now get outta here and go to your room, I don't wanna look at ya!"

I stopped off in the bathroom to clean up, which is when I saw blood smeared on my face and clothes. There was a cut on my cheek and I had a bloody nose. My hair was sticking straight up as if I had stuck my finger in a light socket and my eyes were red and practically swollen shut. I dabbed my face with a wet washcloth as best I could, but it hurt to touch. It was when I entered my room to remove my wet underpants that I heard knocking on my window. I looked out and saw Joni and Carla standing there. They jumped back and put their hands over their mouths at the shock of seeing me. I quietly slid open the window, and they told me that they had gone to the front door after I hadn't shown up to meet them on the corner and that my mom explained to them that I was on restriction and couldn't go to the dance. They were curious to find out what had happened, so now they appeared at the window.

We spoke in soft voices through the screen. "What in the hell happened to you?" Carla asked.

Feeling embarrassed and still sobbing. "Joe hit me because of the pep pills Mary Jo gave me. I just flushed the rest down the toilet. He thinks I'm a drug addict now."

Carla could barely find her words. "Your shirt… I can see the wrinkles where his hands musta been holding the front. That's sickening, it gives me chills to look at it. It looks like he beat the shit out of you." Joni was crying by then and I told them to get going before we all got caught.

After a couple of hours Joe called me to come out and began lecturing me about drugs, and then made me hug him and tell him I loved him. I gaged on every syllable. I hated him to the core. He was Satan. It was his way to assuage the guilt I suppose, forcing me to say those fake words. It was like a sick game.

Mom brought me a washcloth with ice in it and told me to hold it on my eyes. I snatched it from her and glared at her for what she had done.

That night as I lay in bed I wished him dead.

On Monday, besides having to go to school with two black eyes, Joe further humiliated me by marching me into the principal's office so that he could announce that there was a drug problem at the school.

I wore sunglasses but when I removed them, the principal did a double take and then quickly averted his eyes and turned his attention to Joe who was doing all the talking. "I'm here to tell you, ya'll got a drug dealer in this school, and ya better take care of it."

Nothing much came of the meeting. Principal Crane took it all in and promised to have a talk with the alleged drug dealer, Mary Jo along with her dad, which seemed to pacify Joe.

I was the talk of the seventh grade. The kids were stunned to see a girl that beat up. Most of them came right out and asked me what happened, others stared and kept their comments to themselves. As for the teachers, they all seemed to be wearing blinders. Mary Jo said that she didn't get in trouble with her dad and the principle gave her a light sentence: write a paper about the evils of drug abuse. After that, I wasn't allowed to hang around with her anymore.

When I told my dad what had happened, he was fit to be tied, and said that he was going to have a word with Joe. The next day, the two of them were standing in the living room screaming at each other. My dad was a good ten inches shorter than Joe, but he held his own. The scream fest ended with parting threats; Joe warning bodily harm to my father and my dad threatening a custody battle.

CHAPTER 17

CAMP

The following summer, I went to camp in Canada for one month. Every summer I was sent off to some sort of camp, usually for a week or two, but this time it would be for a whole month.

I actually wanted to go, it was my second year and I was looking forward to the freedom camp brought and to seeing many of the same kids from the year before. I had never kissed a boy before until we played spin-the-bottle in the barn that first year at the co-ed camp. I decided I liked it.

The kids were from all over California, ranging in age from twelve to sixteen years old. Friendships were developed and correspondence continued once camp was over. It was a unique experience writing to and receiving letters from my new distant friends scattered all over the state.

Cherie, who was from Palo Alto, had the most beautiful scented stationary. It was thick lavender paper with a matching envelope and had her initials embossed across the top. My stationary was of the industrial sort, college ruled notebook paper stuffed into white letter size envelopes. As soon as I saved enough money I upgraded to a boxed set of mod floral designs that I found at the drug store—not as chic as Cherie's but a definite upgrade from the notebook paper.

With many of us returning for the second year, and being a year older, we were ready to raise the bar on fun. We all smoked cigarettes and played kissing games, which turned into necking and heavy petting.

The camp was housed in an old estate, which was part of a working farm on Salt Spring Island, British Columbia, a small island that is tucked up against Vancouver Island between Vancouver and Victoria. The owners were a young couple with three small children. They ran a nursery school in Hawthorne during the school year—where Sheila had attended when we lived in Hawthorne. It was the two of them and a cook who ran the camp and they were outnumbered.

Most of the fifteen or so campers were sneaky and resourceful. The property was vast, a couple of hundred acres, with too many places to hide and get into trouble. The curriculum was pretty laid back and what few planned activities there were, consisted of swimming in the lake that was on the property, going for hikes and camp outs, shelling for oysters and clams and doing chores.

The chores were minimal, like milking the cows and helping in the kitchen, and afterwards we were free to roam about as long as we were back in time for supper. Since everyone knew one another on the small island, we were allowed to hitchhike into the village to buy candy at the one and only general store.

Once we camped out overnight on a pocket-sized neighboring island, called Chocolate Island. There were no inhabitants, just nature. We cooked our weenies and marshmallows over an open fire that we built by gathering driftwood. When I asked Cherie if she knew where the bathrooms were, she rolled her eyes and pointed her finger in the direction of a clump of bushes in the distance. "This is whatcha call roughing it," she snickered.

"No way, there has to be at least an outhouse someplace, let's go do some exploring," I said.

Cherie and I explored the island in its entirety—which took us all of ten minutes—and sure enough there were no facilities.

The sleeping accommodations were equally primitive. We had to sleep in sleeping bags—out in the open—on the beach that was varnished in crushed shells. I woke up in the morning to the sensation of cold wet toes. The rising tide had caused the lapping water to soak through my sleeping bag along with a few other campers, who dared place their bags that close to the sea.

I matured a lot over the summer, which didn't go unnoticed by Joe. At thirteen, I had shot up to almost 5'5" with expanding breasts and curves. It was going to be a big jump going from a junior high housed in an elementary school to high school, but I was more than ready to leave the juvenile environment, both physically and emotionally.

What I wasn't ready for was private car rides with Joe. They seemed to come out of nowhere. He would come into my room and make the command. "Come on we're goin' for a little ride." I would use the homework excuse, and he would insist that it wouldn't take long, giving me no way out.

He would drive to a remote area near the dump and away from the main road, park the car and then light up a cigarette. Why did he have to drive me to a deserted area to talk to me? There was nothing but open fields of dirt and weeds, not a person in sight. I was in a vulnerable situation that made me feel frightened and helpless. I scooted as close as I could to the door where I tucked my left arm under my right out of sight so it would be close to the handle in case I needed to get out. I willed myself to become invisible.

He would just sit there making a big deal of enjoying the silence and chain smoking. Then he would start his lecture. This was his idea of imparting some sort of coming of age type wisdom with sexual significance and conveyed in a vulgar twisted way. Rude and crude was all he knew. A male had a cock and a female had a pussy. I stared straight ahead out the window, praying that time would accelerate. He would say things, like, "gotta watch them boys sniffin' around, only after one thing and that's playin' grab ass, ya get what I'm sayin'?"

"Uh, huh."

"Any of em wanna play tickle the pee pee?"

I shook my head. "Nuh uh." *Please God, make this stop.*

He continued the one-sided conversation for about an hour and then without a word, he would put the key in the ignition, start the car and head home. It was embarrassing listening to his version of the birds and the bees. Playing song lyrics in my head helped me block out the details but not the fear.

I couldn't stand to look at him the whole time he was spewing his raunch. It happened maybe two times and each time was torture for me—the terror that I felt was that he was going to rape me. The second time he drove me there, a group of dirt bikers came by, much to my relief, cutting his lecture short.

My mother never said a word and neither did I. I had learned my lesson about how much to confide in her or saying the wrong thing and having it get back to Joe. I wondered how she could not be a little more curious about what he was doing?

Had it been the other way around, Joe would have been all over it. Everything that went on under our roof was Joe's business. He stuck his nose where it didn't belong as a way of ruling the roost. Nothing got past him. He noticed everything. He would taunt both Mom and me with his critical remarks about my physical appearance. "Look at that little mouth," he would say to Mom. "It looks like a bird's mouth; when is she gonna get fuller lips?" He even took a swipe at me for wearing glasses. "Hey Steffie, you were sooo ug–leee. Man those glasses you used to wear, were as thick as coke bottles and that eye of yours goin' off into no man's land." No one laughed but him. His words stung, yet oddly enough, I still wanted his approval.

He was quick to point out that I was developing breasts when I first entered puberty. He thought nothing of grabbing a squeeze. "Hey Mama, lookee here, is that baby fat or is she getting' titties." His crass assessment was demeaning. Mom would make a feeble attempt to stick up for me—saying how pretty I was becoming and that my development was normal—talking about me like I wasn't even there. It all made me want to fade into the background. In some ways that's exactly what I appeared to do.

Mom was always reminding me to stand up straight because I was hunching over so that no one would notice my breasts. No, that's not right, so that Joe wouldn't notice. I was actually ashamed of my body for fear of more ridicule.

I went through a phase of hiding myself inside oversized hooded cardigan sweaters. They were all the rage and were so long that they hung below the hemlines of our skirts, making us all look like a bunch of robed monks.

By the end of my freshman year, though, boys were coming around, which Joe loved. He'd always wanted a son, and this way he could strut his stuff, especially with the boys who played guitar. It was great fun for him to whip out his guitar and play tunes with them. Or demonstrate how he could literally crack the whip. He bought a black and white woven leather bullwhip in Tijuana and snapping it in the yard was one of his favorite pastimes. I was always embarrassed by him, but the kids thought he was funny. He even bought me a little Honda motor scooter so he could show off what a generous guy he was.

That summer, I was about to have my first girl-boy backyard party. My friend Gary, who lived down the street, came over to help me with the guest list and that's when he began pitching his friend's band as the entertainment.

"Hey Stefanie, you need to have a band at your party."

"Yeah, right! Bands cost money," I replied. "Besides, what's wrong with just playing records?"

"Nothing, but there's this groovy band, Vance And The Surf Cats, and I know they'll come and play at your party for free," Gary proclaimed.

"How do you know they won't charge," I asked.

"Cuz they need the practice."

"That would be sooo cool if I had a real band!"

"That's what I'm tellin' ya."

"Okay, okay, I'll ask."

"Outa sight, everyone could dance and rock out to surf music, they're really bitchin' too!"

He was right. They were a big hit, a real live band in my back yard. What I wasn't expecting was that the lead guitar player, Vance De Luca would be such a babe.

He was the bandleader and played the electric guitar really well. He was also cute and he kept making goo goo eyes at me during the gig. When they stopped playing at ten p.m., he took a seat near where I was standing and the next thing I knew, he pulled me down on his lap and really started flirting. I started to squirm away.

"Hey, don't run off, I want to get to know you," he said, tightening his grip around my waist.

"I've never seen you in school before," I replied, forgetting about moving after I looked into his hazel eyes framed by thick lashes and dark expressive eyebrows. With his sun-bleached hair and olive skin, he was the handsomest boy I had ever seen, and the most charming.

"That's because I've been in Catholic school which goes through ninth, but in September we'll be in the same high school."

"So, that would be Marina High School, right? Since Huntington Beach High is closed for remodeling?" he asked, and then answered his own question. "Yeah, all the boundaries will be combined for two years, I guess, and then after that, who knows where everyone will be after they re-open the 1908 relic downtown."

"That's where I wanted to go, instead of a high school with a moat around it!"

Vance, laughed. "Yeah I've heard about that."

Although he wasn't particularly tall, he seemed physically mature. He had whiskers and chest hair that I could see peeking out from the collar of his pinstriped shirt, where the first two buttons were unbuttoned. He told me he was an only child and that his parents had come from Italy, attributing his olive skin coloring to his Sicilian heritage.

Vance was the last one to leave at eleven, but only after he kissed me goodnight in the front yard just before his dad picked him up.

We were both fifteen by then and allowed to date. Sort of. Since neither of us was old enough to drive, either his parents or mine drove us places, but we mostly got around on foot and sometimes on my scooter. He would ride his bike over to my house after school and we would do homework or make out if no one was home. I turned sixteen just before he did and whenever I got to use the car, we went to the drive-in movies. We never watched the movie, we made out instead.

I don't know what happened, some stupid argument over nothing, but we broke up after being together throughout our sophomore year at Marina High School. I was sad for a long time, I really loved him and kept thinking he would call. He didn't. I never saw him again because we ended up at different high schools when we moved up to eleventh grade. When Huntington Beach High School re-opened I had to leave Marina along with about half the kids who had been temporarily housed at Marina.

CHAPTER 18

STORM THREAT

At home I never knew when the next storm was going to hit, just that it would. There was always tension. Joe was always looking for a fight and Mom continued fanning the flames. God how she loved to nag.

Joe thought he was a good cook, but mom nitpicked about the ingredients and the mess that he made. "Joe, not so much salt and pepper." No response. Five minutes later. "Did you go easy on the salt?" He filled the skillet to the top until it spilled over, and when it did, she jumped right in. "Joe, why didn't you get a bigger pan, it's spilling over the top." She had a way of pushing his buttons and knowing no other way to communicate, he would inevitably lose his temper; sometimes it was a shove, sometimes a slap and sometimes it was a punch.

In this case his response involved a projectile. He threw the saltshaker across the kitchen where Mom was standing, but it hit the cabinet instead, shattering the glass and spilling salt all over the floor. "Goddamnit, quit yer naggin' and get off my back, woman!" He shouted. "Sonnabitch', Marjorie Ann, I've been makin' my gravy my way for over ten years and no one ever complained cept' you. Now shut the fuck up."

One night he started beating on her after she questioned him about coming home late with alcohol on his breath.

Sheila and I had both been asleep, but the ruckus woke me up. I just laid there listening to the two of them carrying on, he cussing at her to get off his back, glass breaking and then slapping noises and her screaming for him to stop. The neighbors apparently called the police when they heard the screaming.

When the police came to the door, I slipped out of bed and crept part way down the hall so I could hear better. "We got a complaint from a concerned caller saying she heard screaming coming from your house," the officer said. "It appears that this isn't the first time we've been here."

Then began the same old story. "Hey, it's nothin', had too much to drink, lost my temper, sorry for the noise officers, it won't happen again." Joe apologized.

The officers then asked to speak to Mom. Joe hollered, probably toward the kitchen, "Marjorie Ann, get over here and tell these policemen yur OK."

I caught a glimpse of mom through the louvered door as she made her way to the front door. From my point of view, she appeared to have visible scratches on her face and her robe was torn.

Her reply sounded shaky, "I'm OK. He just had one too many—it's all my fault I started it—but we're fine, really."

The police asked her how she got the scrapes on her face and she told them that she hit a table when she slipped and fell.

The next thing I heard was the police telling them to keep the noise down and then they left.

I snuck back to bed and before I closed my door all the way, I heard Joe say to mom, "Listen up, bitch, a man's home is his castle, and don't you ever forget it. The law sez' I'm free to do whatever I want in the privacy of my own home."

The next day Joe's sister stepped into the fray when Mom asked her to come and get Sheila for a couple of days. Gloria made Sheila wait in the car, and then she laid into Mom with me standing a few feet away. The two of them were in the dining area and I was making sandwiches for Mom and me in the kitchen.

Gloria was in a huff. She got in Mom's face, and in a scolding voice with her hands planted on her hips, she started in. "What seems to be the problem here? Can't the two of you behave like civil adults?" She appeared to be oblivious to the bruises and welts on my mother's face. She never acknowledged them, and acted as if she didn't care. Instead, she placed the blame on both of them, her voice notching up in decibels. "Y'all need to grow up and learn how to solve your problems without violence. I don't care about that one," she said, with her left hand aimed toward me while her eyes never left Mom. "I only care about what happens to Sheila, so you both best figure it out or I'll make arrangements to take her away from you." With that she turned on her heels and stomped out of the house.

I couldn't believe what she had just said in front of me. It was cruel and insensitive. My lower lip began to quiver and tears spilled onto my cheeks. That's who she was I suppose, a woman who said what was on her mind no matter the consequences.

It stung at first, hearing those words. She spoke the truth—a truth that I would have been better off not knowing. I never really felt like I was a part of Joe's family and maybe deep down I really didn't want to be, but her words confirmed any uncertainty that I may have had about acceptance. Mom made excuses—chalked it up to Gloria's personality. "Oh you know how she is, they're all so emotional about everything. Just ignore her, she didn't mean it."

I knew different, she'd meant every word of it.

CHAPTER 19

RUNNING AWAY

The beatings continued, yet Mom stayed. I wondered how much more she could take.

One afternoon when I got home from school, no one was home except Joe, whose truck I had seen parked outside. I headed for the kitchen for a snack, when I heard him holler from upstairs. "Is that you Steffie?

"Yeah, I'm getting something to eat," I responded.

"Bring me a cup of coffee, will ya?"

Oh crap. "OK, I'll be right up."

I took a couple of sips from the Diet Rite that I had just opened and decided that I no longer had an appetite for a snack. Shit, what's he doing home? I thought I was gonna have the house to myself since Mom was up in LA for the day, now asshole is here. I looked around for a clean mug and found one in the dish-drainer. The Pyrex percolator was sitting on the stove with about an inch of cold coffee still inside. I fired up the electric burner and paced back and forth as I waited for it to start bubbling. I just wanted to get my coffee run over with.

When I entered the master bedroom, Joe was lying on the bed, still dressed in his work clothes and propped against the headboard reading the newspaper. I carefully placed the mug of hot coffee on the cluttered nightstand next to the pack of Marlboros and overflowing ashtray. I turned to leave the room, when he stopped me. "Sit down here a minute," he patted the bed. "I want to ask you somethin'."

I hesitated and felt myself stiffen. I eased onto the very edge of the bed and into a launch position, keeping my left leg firmly planted on the floor, with my right leg bent across the top of the mattress.

He began rambling about how sorry he was for hitting Mom and how crazy she makes him when she nags. I just nodded, more and more vigorously as I began squirming. I was thinking maybe he was a little drunk by the slowness of his speech. When I started to rise, Joe lunged forward and all of a sudden he wrapped his arm around my waist and began to pull me toward him. He was coming closer, about to kiss me, bringing his face close enough for me to get a whiff of his breath wreaking of booze and cigarettes. Stricken with terror, the only thing I could think of was to get away. To avoid making him mad and risk being physically assaulted or worse, I made up an excuse. "I–I–uh–have to go to the bathroom," I blurted.

He loosened his grip as I scooted off the bed and I ran into the nearest bathroom, which was connected to the master bedroom. I shut the door and twisted the dial in the knob to lock it. As soon as I lowered myself onto the toilet, the door opened. *But, I locked it, how did he open the door?* I must not have pressed it all the way closed.

Now he was standing in the doorway. I knew that I could pee if I had to, even with him watching. I had to remain calm. I managed to urinate, making sure I kept myself covered by spreading my dress over my front and also by leaning forward. He came closer and lowered himself into a squatting position so that he was inches away. The way he just stared, with that dopey look plastered on his face, was creepy. If he spoke, I wasn't listening. His hands were pressed against the sides of the toilet for balance. *What the hell was he doing? Why is this happening?* I couldn't think of what to do next, I thought the bathroom excuse would have been enough to deter him.

I knew the minute I finished, he was gonna try to rape me!

God bless Sheila! Like a blast the front door slammed with a thud rattling the house and hurricane Sheila came bounding down the hall hollering, "I'm home!" Joe leaped to his feet and out of the bathroom as he met her at the entrance to the bedroom. I have never felt such relief and gratitude to anyone in my life. I bolted out of the room—not bothering to flush—blowing past Sheila, who was now showing Joe her school papers.

When Mom came home later that afternoon I couldn't get her alone to tell her what happened, between Joe and Sheila grabbing all of her attention. It would have to wait until the next day. I stayed in my room except when I came out to eat dinner. That night, thankfully, there was no face to face dinner table chit chat since it was grilled cheese sandwiches served on TV trays in front of the TV.

My sleep that night was fitful and I woke up screaming about a man crawling through my window as I slept.

The next morning after Joe went to work, I told Mom what happened.

I could barely say the words out loud and by the time I finally spit it out, we were both crying. She said she knew that she had to do something but that she wanted to wait until the right time to confront Joe.

Two days later, when I got home from school, there were two men loading our stuff into a moving van. Mom was in the bathroom frantically throwing cosmetics into a brown grocery bag. When I asked her what was going on, she announced that we were moving. She motioned me to my room to pack my belongings. I started to ask questions, but she said there wasn't time and that we had to leave right away, before Joe came home. The whole thing felt dangerous, but I understood why she had to be sneaky, Joe wouldn't have let her go.

It was with Betty's financial assistance that we were able to rent a place. Mom couldn't have done it without her. Betty never made it a secret that she didn't like Joe. So anytime Mom needed to be rescued, Betty was the one who jumped in.

She had hired the movers so that we could take some of the furniture and all of our personal belongings all in one trip.

The condo was nicely furnished with three bedrooms and the best part about it was that Joe wasn't there. It felt good to have our own place even though it was so close to our house where Joe was. Mom's theory, hide in plain site. "He'll never think to look for us this close by," she reasoned.

I felt such relief to be out from under Joe's thumb. I could now speak freely, I could talk on the phone whenever I wanted, leave food on my plate, watch what I wanted on TV. I could be myself, and best of all, I wasn't scared every minute of every day. Mom seemed more relaxed, but Sheila at eight years old, was confused until Mom made it feel like a new adventure—that and buying her all of the Ding Dongs that she wanted.

We had been there about a week and a half when one night while Mom was cooking dinner the doorbell rang. As I went to answer it, she shouted from the kitchen, "Ask who it is!" I did. A man's voice said, "Landlord" so I opened it. I jumped backwards, my eyes opened wide and just about popped out of my head in shock. It was Joe reeking of booze and cigarettes. He had a smirk on his face as he pushed past me into the living room, his voice ringing out. "Surprise! So you guys think you're pretty smart, huh?"

Every bit of oxygen was sucked out of the room the minute he set foot inside the door. I was now frozen where I stood, as if my feet were glued to the floor. I couldn't believe how stupid I was. My heart was pounding as I stood there rubbing my arms. Up until then, I had felt safe, a mistake that caused me to let my guard down. Hearing his voice, Mom came running out of the kitchen. Keeping a safe distance, she screamed, "Stefanie, I told you not to open the door! Look what you've done!"

"He said he was the landlord. I'm sorry. I didn't know," I said.

"Joe, I don't know how you found us, but you need to leave or I'm calling the police," Mom declared.

He spoke in a flat chilling tone. "Now, now, let's not get huffy, Marjorie Ann." His speech was slow, and deliberate, like he was working hard to keep it together. He eased toward her. "I don't think that's such a good idea. Do you?" It was creepy and unlike his loud obnoxious self. I knew it would just be a matter of time before he exploded.

Mom backed away, and said nothing.

"Whaddaya think they'd say about you takin' my daughter without telling me?"

A moment of silence passed as Mom stood there speechless.

Giving the place a quick once-over. "Nice place you have here by the way," he commented. "Where'd you get the money to pay for it? Never mind, I know. It came from the old bitch."

Sheila came downstairs and ran into his arms. "Daddy, Daddy, I thought you were on a trip." Joe whirled her in circles and then plopped himself onto the sofa where he held her in his lap and smothered her with "sugar" kisses as Mom stood there wringing her hands.

"Is that what your mom told you?"

Sheila nodded.

Pause. "Well, we'll just have to set her straight, now won't we," he said with sarcasm.

"Don't let me interrupt your dinner. Go on girls go ahead and eat." He shooed Sheila into the kitchen. "I'm in no hurry. I'll just relax here in front of the tube." He didn't try to hide the flask that he removed from his coat pocket as he took a pull on what was inside.

We poked at our food and then he sent Sheila and me upstairs to our rooms. "You guys go on upstairs. Your mom and I are going to have a little talk." As I was walking up the stairs, I could hear him. "No matter where you run and try to hide, I will always find you."

About an hour later, when I heard something break, and Mom begging him to leave, I knew something bad was going to happen. I opened the door a crack, so I could listen. "No, no, stop," she begged. "Let go of me, I don't want to go with you."

His voice grew louder, "Shut the fuck up, we're going for a little ride." Then he yelled up to me, "Steffie we'll be right back!" He didn't wait for a response. I heard the garage door open, car doors slam, the Buick motor rev.

It was after nine when they left and Sheila was asleep. I was in Mom's room watching TV and checking the clock every few minutes. It was getting late and I was scared. Not so much about being left alone but about what Joe was doing to my mother.

At eleven, I picked up the phone and called my dad's house. His wife, Rita answered and explained that he was on a business trip back east. I told her what happened and she asked if I wanted her to call the police? I said no, because I didn't know where they were and I was afraid of Joe getting angrier, knowing the call came from me since it wasn't like they were at home fighting where neighbors would hear and call. She asked if I wanted her to come and get me, I did but I couldn't leave Sheila. Plus, she was an hour away and if they came back there would be a confrontation and I would pay the price. We finally decided to give it another hour and then I would call her rather than her call me and risk being caught in case they came back.

It was midnight when I checked in with her. I was scared and didn't know what to do, Rita kept me on the phone asking if she should call the police. I knew they wouldn't do anything, just like before. Then I heard the garage door and whispered that I had to hang up. We agreed that she wouldn't come until she heard back from me.

I raced back to my room and pretended to be asleep. I couldn't quite make out what the noises were. It sounded like they were shuffling around downstairs before I heard the creaking noises on the stairs as they made their way upstairs. The bedroom door closed, the shower turned on. I fell asleep knowing that our freedom was gone.

CHAPTER 20

THE ESCAPE

The next morning, Joe came into my room around seven and told me to get up and start packing because we were moving back home. I did as I was told without question. When I came downstairs, and didn't see Mom, I asked where she was, and he said he already drove her back home and that he and I were going to do all the moving. I was astonished.

We loaded his truck with Sheila's twin mattress, along with a TV, the bicycles and a few other pieces of furniture. Since I now had my driver license I drove the car which would be used to bring the kitchen and bathroom stuff and piles of clothes from each of our closets and we made the first of many trips back to the house.

When I walked into our house it was the first time that I had seen Mom since the night before, she was drying the dishes, and her face looked like hamburger. She was bruised and puffy, her lip was split and covered with dried blood sealing the wound. Her left eye was black and blue and swollen shut. I caught my breath and started to say something but she put her index finger to her mouth warning me to be quiet. I went to her and lightly patted her shoulder and then I asked if she wanted Rita to come and get us? She nodded twice. I told her I would make the call, and then I quickly went back to the task of moving back in, dropping stuff in different rooms as quickly as I could.

He was still unloading the truck when he told me to go back and get another load.

When I got to the condo, I quickly dialed Rita. "I'm at the condo, I have to talk fast before Joe comes back," I panted. "He's making us move back right this minute; he beat Mom up really bad."

"Oh, God, where is she now?" Rita asked.

"She's at the house, he's making her put everything away as we bring it back. I'm supposed to be filling the car with another load right now, when can you come?"

"I don't know, let me make some calls and work on it," she replied. "When will you be done and back at the house?"

"I guess a few more hours. It's just the two of us doing all the moving, Mom is in no condition to help."

"That guy's nuts, he oughta be behind bars!"

"I know, I have to go."

"Wait Stefanie, try to call once you get back, so I know when to come."

"I'll try, but I don't want him to hear me."

"Then call, let it ring twice, then hang up, I'll know it's you."

"OK, that's better." I agreed and then quickly hung up.

It was two o'clock when we finally finished emptying the condo. When we got back to the house, Mom was laying on the couch holding a washrag filled with ice on her eye and Sheila was playing at a neighbors house.

"What the fuck do you think yur doin,' layin' around?" Joe barked. "Get your ass off the couch and get this house squared away, you sneaky, lying cunt."

Mom slowly got up and did as she was told going back to putting away dishes and pots and pans while I put my room back together. About 45 minutes later, Joe went back to their bedroom to get some sleep, making sure he took both sets of car keys along with Mom's purse that contained her wallet.

I made a dash for the kitchen phone, and instead of hanging up after two rings, I whispered to Rita, "he's asleep, please come and get us now." Click.

Once I finished my room and the hall bathroom I parked myself on the couch where I had a view of the street. Mom soon joined me and as we both sat together waiting to be rescued and praying that Rita would show up before Joe woke up. She kept wincing every time she changed positions, an indication that there was more going on beyond what was visible. She complained that it hurt to move her shoulder and to take a breath. We mostly sat in silence, waiting and keeping our voices down so as not to wake Joe.

It was getting close to 4:00 and Joe had been asleep about an hour, when a black Cadillac slowly eased up to the curb and I saw the passenger window roll down and there was Rita, her arm outstretched, signaling me to come. I tapped Mom on the shoulder, and we both hightailed it out the door with the clothes on our backs, no suitcases, no purses, no money. I was so scared that Joe would wake up and catch us that I left my wallet that contained my driver license on the coffee table.

We jumped in the backseat and then realized that it was my uncle, Antonio, my dad's brother-in-law, who was driving and not my dad. Antonio hit the gas as we peeled away from the curb barely giving me time to close the door and then Mom asked him drive around the corner so we could pick up Sheila. Luckily, she was playing outside with her friends. I hopped out of the car and ran across the lawn, shouting. "Come on we have to hurry." I grabbed her arm and pulled her into the car and that's when we sped off. It was a risky move but we managed to escape before Joe woke up.

Once we were safely out of the city, Rita placed her arm on the back of the seat and turned to face us. She said, "Marjorie, what in the hell happened? You look like you've been in a boxing match."

Mom started at the beginning about how Joe pretended to be the landlord and got me to open the door. "He said he wanted to talk away from the kids and then he made me go for a ride with him in the Buick. Once he backed out of the garage, he drove without saying a word for several miles. I could tell he was seething and all I wanted was for him to stop the car, so that I could get out and run for help. As if reading my mind, he pulled over on some remote street, which was when he grabbed a bottle of whiskey from under the seat and started chugging it. With his free hand he gripped my wrist. There was no way that I could get out and besides there wasn't a soul around and I didn't even know where we were. The more he drank the angrier he got; he never let go of my arm between guzzling the whiskey and taking drags off a cigarette. He kept shouting, 'you dumb bitch, are you that stupid to think I couldn't find ya?' 'You can run all ya want but not for long.'"

"Did he ever say how he found us?" I asked.

She shook her head. "I asked him that before we got in the car, and he just laughed, and said, 'wouldn't you like to know.'"

Her voice cracked as she described the violence. "After we sat there for awhile, he started up the car, and the whole time he was driving he had this wild look in his eyes as he pushed his foot down on the gas. There wasn't another car in sight. He would just speed up in one direction and then he'd hit the brakes skidding to a stop and then make a u-turn and go back the way he came, back and forth, back and forth. He was a maniac, like he was on a suicide mission, the way both hands gripped the steering wheel, and his jaw clenched. It was terrifying." I scooted closer to her and placed my arm around her.

Mom was now sobbing as she continued. "Each time he came to a stop he took a swing at me with the back of his hand. 'That's what you get for runnin' off!' He kept this up for what seemed like hours, going over 100 miles an hour, screeching, and spinning the car around and then going the other direction and at that time of night—it must have been around midnight—no one saw us."

Antonio would occasionally glance into the rear view mirror, never saying a word only shaking his head in disgust. Rita, patted Mom's knee. "Marjorie, I really think we need to take you to the emergency room and get those cuts stitched up before we go home."

Mom just nodded and then laid her head back and closed her eyes.

I kept thinking, this was *my* family, and they were sticking their necks out to help my mother and not just me.

Antonio pulled into a small community hospital in La Mirada where he immediately headed to the pay phone and called Aunt Isabel to let her know why we would be late and then he joined us in the hospital waiting room. Mom ended up needing stitches on her forehead and above her left eye; they also taped her ribs and then I saw Antonio pull out his checkbook and pay the bill.

He dropped off Rita, who lived about two miles away and then took us to his and Aunt Isabel's house in Whittier. They had three kids, yet they re-arranged everyone so that we could stay there for as long as we needed to. It was June and school was about to let out the following week for the summer. I would be missing the last week along with final exams, lowering my already slipping grades.

Later that night, Isabel took us to Sav-On Drug Store, where Antonio worked, and used her discount to buy us toiletries, underwear and a change of clothes.

We ended up staying a few days and then Mom came up with a plan for a temporary living arrangement. I would live with my dad in Whittier for the rest of the summer while Mom and Sheila would move to Pasadena where she could work for her friend's husband in his accounting firm and also stay at their house.

Mom had to hire an attorney, who filed a temporary restraining order against Joe, so that we were able to go back to the house and get our belongings. Mom was also able to get her car thanks to Isabel and Antonio driving her back down to Huntington Beach.

CHAPTER 21

TEMPORARY CUSTODY

Living in Whittier was a new experience. Rita was nice to me and my dad was OK whenever he was around but he was gone a lot traveling as a sales representative for an electronics company. I spent most of my time with Rita's daughter, Candy, who was a year older than me and many years wiser.

She was a wild child, who liked pushing the limits and she and her mom went round and round, always bickering about something. It seemed like Rita kind of picked on Candy, and the whole thing made me uncomfortable when they had their fights in front of me. Antonio ended up getting me a summer job scooping ice cream at the Sav-On Drug store in Norwalk, where he was manager. Rita let me borrow her vintage stick shift Rambler, so I could get there. That is, after she taught me how to drive it.

Even with the free ice cream and hot dogs, the job wasn't as nifty as it looked. Standing on my feet for eight hours, wearing a uniform that included a hairnet and an apron and worst of all, trying to master the manual cash register, zapped all the fun out of it. I didn't know how to make change even though I should have at sixteen years old. It was just something I never paid much attention to and never learned. Rita did her best to teach me, sitting me down at the kitchen table where we practiced making purchases with dollar bills and change from the piles of pennies, nickels, and dimes that she accumulated from her wallet and bottom of her purse. It was hopeless. It involved math and I simply had a mental block.

Scooping ice cream and serving hot dogs was the easy part, and whenever there were two of us, I would opt for the food prep and let the co-worker operate the register. But when I was alone and the lines got long with all those ravenous faces staring at me to hurry up, I panicked at the register. Sometimes I would reach into the till with ice cream dripping from my hands, grab a random bunch of coins and plunk into someone's open palm—neglecting to count back—before sending them on their way. Most of the time the customers didn't check, and when they did, I believed them and handed over whatever I had shorted them. Of course, no one ever complained if they made money on the transaction.

On my days off Candy and I got to drive the Rambler down Beach Blvd to Huntington Beach. The big hang out area was the bleachers at the foot of the pier. There was piped in music that played all day, the most played song being, *Shotgun* by Jr. Walker & The All Stars. I was always running into my school friends who congregated on the bleachers, usually with a paper food tray filled with taco strips smothered with hot sauce. No one thought much of me spending the summer with my dad, and I didn't volunteer the details. We chummed around with kids at the beach during the day and at night it was back to Whittier. Without wheels or friends with wheels, we stayed in.

The main form of entertainment in Whittier was to cruise Whittier Boulevard, which was a giant party on wheels. We participated once or twice, usually on our way back from the store or to get ice cream in Dad's Mustang. We would've never considered being seen in the Rambler.

That summer, I started hanging around with a guy from Huntington Beach, who was eighteen and had already graduated high school two years before. His name was Rocky Murdoch and he had a reputation as a bad boy. He liked fast girls, fast cars, cigarettes and booze and I liked him a lot. His cockiness along with the hot looking, fine-tuned car that he kept sparkling, defined his popularity. It was a pale yellow Chevy Malibu Super Sport that had been lowered and had chrome rims and a V-8 engine along with a four-on-the-floor manual transmission.

Rocky was about five foot seven, lean and wiry and wore his black wavy hair plastered with Dippity-Do gel and a load of hairspray that made it stick straight. It never moved, but the look suited him. He was a sharp dresser too, sporting v-neck alpaca cardigan sweaters over white tee shirts. I noticed he was also really good at making eye contact, something I had trouble with, and when he looked at me with those emerald green eyes it was as though he was staring right through me.

One night, I was invited to spend the night with my friend Christie in Huntington Beach, and then we were going to go to a party at Rocky's apartment, which was the part that I left out when I asked my dad and Rita if I could go.

My dad and Candy drove me from Whittier to Huntington Beach and dropped me off at Christie's house. I was excited to have so much freedom, since Christie was older and could stay out past midnight. We got ready together and then waited for Christie's boyfriend to pick us up. All three of us arrived together, but after awhile I lost track of them. It didn't matter, everyone was friendly, laughing and having a good time. It was the first unsupervised party that I had ever been to and the first one where there was booze. Rocky was drinking something called a Screwdriver, and without asking me, he mixed another one for me. It contained mostly orange juice with a smidgen of vodka, it tasted pretty good. If I hadn't seen him add the alcohol I would have never known it was there—except for the heat rush that I experienced after a couple of sips. I was having so much fun hanging out with Rocky and the older crowd that I didn't want it to end. Unfortunately it did and much sooner than I thought!

Rocky and I were in the kitchen kissing, when I abruptly pulled away and stood frozen listening to the sound of unwelcome familiar voices coming from the living room announcing: "Party's over!" It couldn't be, could it? The next thing I knew, my mom and Rita were standing at the kitchen doorway with hands on hips and smirks on their faces, Mom saying, "Party's over, get your stuff, you're leaving."

Rocky and I instantly disengaged, both of us now standing next to each other and staring in shock at the two moms.

"Why? What's going on? What are you doing here?" I asked.

Mom was eying my drink sitting on the counter nearby, "You lied, and is that your drink?"

Without a beat. "No, it was already sitting there," I replied. "And what did I lie about?"

"You said that you were spending the night with Christie, yet here you are at a party instead," she said, with a sweep of her arm. "Where is she by the way?"

"She went somewhere with her boyfriend, and I am too spending the night with Christie."

"Well, her mom sure doesn't have a clue what's going on, we stopped there first."

Feet firmly planted to the floor, I argued. "Christie and Bob will be right back, they went to the store and then I'm going home with her."

"No! You are not," Mom declared. "Come on, let's go."

"Why are you making such big deal, just because I didn't tell you I was going to a party?"

"That's right, Candy told her mom all about it."

Rita had made her way back into the living room and was now socializing with the teens she had just met and trying to be the cool mom.

Glaring at my mother, I lowered my voice through clenched teeth. "So now you're dragging me out of here by my ear, like I'm five years old?" God, I can't even believe this, just because Candy wasn't invited, she snitches on me and everyone makes a mountain out of a molehill!" I groaned. "I hate all of you!"

Mom cocked her head toward the door and calmly said, "C'mon, Rita's waiting, let's go."

"What about my stuff?"

"We already got your overnight bag when we stopped by Christie's house."

I wanted to die. Rocky tried to be cool about it, but even he was stunned.

He attempted to smooth things over, saying, "Mrs. Hoskins, I'll make sure she gets back to Christie's by eleven, honest we're just listening to records and dancing. Please let her stay."

Mom shook her head, cutting him off with a one-word response. "Nope." With that she hooked her arm through mine and escorted me toward the door. "Let's go," she ordered, and we were gone. I was humiliated, literally being dragged out of a party by my mom in front of all those older kids. The whole thing happened so fast, one minute I was in a party mood, laughing, goofing off and having fun and the next I was exiled.

Both moms were so pleased with themselves the way they sashayed across the parking lot to the car. I was lagging pretty far behind wanting to place as much distance as possible between them and myself.

They'd caught me red-handed. All I could do was pout, and that's exactly what I did all the way home. I was gonna kill Candy. I knew she was mad because I went somewhere without her, but she didn't have to rat me out and get me in trouble.

Candy and I hardly ever got into arguments, which is why I was so surprised that she squealed. She could be strong-willed and bossy, but after all, she was an only child and wasn't accustomed to suddenly having a roommate or sharing her things. I thought that she was a good sport about it and she seemed to like having me around. She had a flair for doing hair and make-up and I was her guinea pig. Once she woke me from a dead sleep early in the morning, by plucking my eyebrows. She decided that they were too bushy.

Meanwhile, Mom and Rita pulled into a Norms parking lot for dessert and when they signaled for me to get out, I refused.

Mom said, "Do you want to come? We're getting coffee and a piece of pie."

I shot back with an emphatic "no!" They shrugged their shoulders and went inside without me. I was actually kind of surprised that she was willing to leave me sitting in the car alone. I thought she would at least beg just a little. The longer I sat there the angrier I got. They took their own sweet time, feeling no guilt whatsoever about leaving me confined inside the car after dark. I was fuming by the time they returned.

The remainder of the ride home I was silent. What I couldn't figure out was why those two were together anyway? Why would Mom come all the way to Whittier to partner with my dad's current wife just so she could bust me? They were having a good old time, talking and yucking it up, and listening to some stupid music station playing some old crooner music.

When we got back to my dad's house, Mom announced that I was prohibited from seeing Rocky and that my dad was to follow her orders. Suddenly she's all strict. She left and drove back to Pasadena and I went to the bedroom, where I came face to face with Candy. I refused to speak to her, or look at her. She was invisible. Sensing my furor, she broke the silence with an innocent feint. "They asked me and I told them the truth."

I rolled my eyes. "Yeah, since when?"

She gave me a blank look. "I didn't want to get in trouble."

There were a lot of emotions percolating inside me, so I decided to keep quiet. I felt betrayed, angry and frustrated because I was no longer allowed to see Rocky.

Candy apologized the next day and admitted that she felt left out, which prompted me to admit that I was equally angry at myself for lying by omission. We buried the hatchet and did our best to get along for the remaining three weeks we had left before school started, when I would be going back to Huntington Beach.

CHAPTER 22

THE NANNY

This being the longest time we'd spent together, my dad now wanted me to live with him permanently. Candy tried to talk me into staying and switching schools, which I didn't want to do. My dad felt bad about asking me to change schools, but more important, he reasoned that he didn't want me living in such an unhealthy environment. Mom convinced him that she wasn't returning to the abusive situation because she was getting a divorce. She determined it was in my best interest to remain in Huntington Beach, so I could stay in the same school. I think she was afraid that my dad would go to court and try to get full custody of me, which seemed odd, since I was two years away from legally becoming an adult. He said he understood, but he still seemed sad to see me go.

Mom came up with a temporary living arrangement that suited both of us, well mostly her. I would stay with the Eisenberg's, a family that I babysat for back in the same neighborhood as our Huntington Beach house, until her work contract in Pasadena expired in three months. I wasn't thrilled but it was better than living with Joe, who was living in the house by himself.

At the Eisenberg's, I had to share a large bedroom with their three boys, ages seven, five and eighteen months. Along with two sets of bunk beds and a crib, taking up three walls, there was a full sized pool table right in the middle of the bedroom. With all of the toys and games close at hand, the oversized room also served as a playroom. Both older boys preferred the top bunks, so since I would be sleeping on the bottom bunk of one of the beds, neither boy was inconvenienced. Most of their clothes were folded inside their dressers, leaving plenty of room in the closet for my stuff.

Once I moved in, I went from occasional babysitter to full time nanny. It wasn't too bad, since the kids were well behaved and I still had time to myself. The arrangement worked well for everyone. The parents, Denny and Charlotte, now had a built in babysitter with freedom to come and go without planning and without paying. Mom was relieved because she could work out of town, knowing that I was happy staying in my high school. And, I had a roof over my head, food on the table and a safe place to live.

It was a fairly easy transition since I was used to being around the family, until I blew it. I just couldn't stay away from Rocky, so I cooked up a scheme with my friend Joanne, so that I could see him. I had been with the Eisenberg's about a month when I got permission from Charlotte to have a couple of friends come over to play pool one night which would include Joanne, her boyfriend John and his cousin Marty, who was really Rocky.

The four of us took over the kids' bedroom, while they watched TV with their parents until nine o'clock. We laughed and joked, and never once slipped up by calling Marty "Rocky." John poured it on thick with his overuse of family labels. "Hey cousin, your shot," he joked. "Good shot cousin."

The next day when I got home from school, Charlotte summoned me to her bedroom where she was seated on a stool with her back to her vanity table. She motioned me to sit across from her at the foot of her bed. Her aquamarine eyes narrowed and took aim at me like two missiles about to be launched. Without so much as a blink of an eye she fired off the first question. "I'm going to ask you one time and one time only—and don't you dare lie to me—was that Rocky who was here claiming to be Marty?"

Holy cow, where'd that come from? Picking lint off my sweater, I inhaled and mustered as much bravado as I could. I raised my head and stared right back at her. "Nope, that was John's cousin, Marty."

Now, she was even more pissed off. She called my bluff, "Well he sure looks a lot like Rocky according to your mom."

A pause. No turning back, trying my darnedest to stay calm and more important maintain some sort of eye contact, "I guess so, but it wasn't him."

She glared, staring me down and looking for a tell that I was lying.

Charlotte was a beautiful woman, statuesque, flawless skin, straight teeth, perfectly clipped frosted hair. She had been a role model, someone I looked up to, sort of like a big sister. She let me wear her make-up and borrow her shoes and she always said that she enjoyed having me around to talk to about fashion and female stuff in a house full of males. So when I saw her so angry, I knew if I told her the truth, she would hate me—and all *that* would go away.

Charlotte made sure she got the last word. "Fine, I better not find out that you're lying!" She waved me off. "That's it you can go now."

I guess I hadn't been so smart after all trying to pull a stunt like that. My Marty aka Rocky deception had caused Charlotte to become suspicious which is why she must have called my mom and compared notes about Rocky's description. In reality I did get busted even though I got away with the lie. Things were never the same for me living with the Eisenberg's.

The next problem was a class change that was supposed to be signed by a parent within a deadline and since Mom wasn't immediately available and Charlotte refused, the last resort was to ask Joe. I wanted out of the French class so bad that I set aside my animosity and called Joe. I got Joni to walk over with me and she stood with me on the porch while I explained the school situation to Joe. That was when I told him that I was staying with the Eisenberg's. He had no idea I had been living right around the corner. He agreed to sign the form, under the condition that I tell my mom that he signed it without any problems and that I come back for a visit. I said I would, which was a lie. It was scary enough seeing him for five minutes, I couldn't imagine a return visit with or without a bodyguard.

Once Charlotte found out that I had contacted Joe, she didn't like the idea of him knowing where I was and that he could show up anytime. The Eisenberg's decided that they no longer wanted the responsibility and that it was time for me to leave.

My grades continued falling with all of the turmoil going on. I couldn't concentrate and I hated school. Seeing Rocky during our clandestine brief encounters was the only good thing in my life. He would pick me up after school so that we could spend a few minutes together before I was supposed to be home. He would then drop me off at Joanne's house and I would walk to my temporary home with the Eisenberg's from there.

Mom called me after receiving notice from Charlotte that I had to leave, which is when she broke the news that she was moving back into the house with Joe. I was stupefied and I told her so. "Mother, how can you go back after the last beating? It's only been four months!" I knew that she had seen him whenever he visited Sheila, but she never gave any indication that they were getting back together. "Why can't we find another apartment," I pleaded.

"Stefanie, he's sorry," she said defending her decision. "He really wants to try again."

"He wore you down, sweet talking you all nice and begging for forgiveness," I said with sarcasm.

"He promised never to hit me again. He's a changed man, he's now attending AA meetings and he's learned his lesson by living alone."

"And what about what he tried to do to me?"

"He denied it was all his fault, he said you were the one who went to the bathroom in front of him."

"Oh my God! I told you why I had to do that!"

"Let's just try to forget about it, OK?"

"Forget about it! How can I ever forget something like that?" I shouted. "You know what? I just want to go home!" I conceded and slammed the phone so hard it fell off the desk.

Back to him she went and all of the bad stuff got swept deeper and deeper under the rug. Things were quiet and peaceful mostly because Joe was working a lot and was making some money. He wasn't in our faces as much and he did seem grateful to have his family back. Maybe the meetings were helping? After a month had gone by without any blowups, he decided that we were going to move into one of the new tract developments where he had been working as part of the construction crew. Several of the workers had gotten good deals on their home purchases and Joe wanted in.

Mom liked the idea of a bigger and newer house and so did I. Sheila, on the other hand, didn't want to leave her friends who lived in the neighborhood. I didn't care about leaving the neighborhood since I had made new friends in high school and everyone was mobile now that we were all over sixteen.

Our house sold quickly and by the first of the year we moved. The new house was a two story, much larger than the old one and of course we didn't have enough furniture to fill it. Our old tattered living room sofa and coffee table with the mosaic top that Mom had crafted, fit into the family room whereas the so called formal living room was completely empty, and would remain that way.

The house had Kelley green shag carpet everywhere and in a large room with no furniture, it looked more like a fairway.

CHAPTER 23

A BUDDING ARTIST

Joe's abstinence from alcohol was short lived. The construction business after work happy hour was far too much of a temptation. Joe was out drinking most every night with his cronies. He had even let it slip about drinking on the job once when he referred to his thermos as a container for firewater.

The more Joe drank, the more Joe hit Mom. It took less and less to set him off. He would pound on her and she would take off with Sheila and I to a motel. Betty always came to the rescue, Mom would call in a panic and Betty would immediately wire money to the Western Union in the grocery store where we'd pick it up. It was humiliating to ask my friends with cars for rides home from school when home was the Surfrider Motel or the Sheraton on Pacific Coast Highway. I would tell them flat out. "My mom gets mad at my stepdad, so she takes off for a week or so and then they kiss and make-up." That seemed to satisfy their curiosity and derail the questions. I never told them about the physical abuse.

True to form after about a week or two, back we went to the house and to Joe.

The spring semester of my junior year, Mom was summoned by my guidance counselor to discuss my grades and test scores. Since my scores were so low, college most likely wasn't an option. "Just tell her to stick with art," he suggested. "She'll never get into college." When my mother relayed the information it stung at first and I felt stupid, then I reasoned to her that it must be because I didn't do well on tests? Mom tried to make me feel better by saying, "I got low grades in everything but art too. All that other stuff was boring, so I guess we're a lot alike." I decided that it didn't matter and I hated school and wanted to do my art anyway.

My art classes were fun and my straight A's reflected my enthusiasm. This semester I was particularly immersed in my craft class where we were learning how to make objects out of Paper Mache'. My project was to create jewelry. I ended up working on it day and night until I became proficient. All I wanted to do was design and construct, and a one hour art class wasn't enough to devote the time and energy required to accomplish my goals. I loved the challenge of bringing my own ideas to life with my own two hands, so working on it at home never seemed like homework. My first item was going to be a bracelet and I used one that Mom had purchased in Tijuana as my model. I played around with different forms to be used as a base, until I settled on cardboard tubes that a neighbor had cut into one inch sections with his saw. From there I began the process of tearing newspaper into strips and soaking them in wheat paste until they were wet and sticky so I could easily wrap them around the cardboard circles until the edges were rounded and began to resemble a bracelet. Once the rings dried in the sun, I painted each one with a base color before adding designs. I hand painted flowers of all varieties, sizes and shapes in vibrant colors like orange and hot pink, making each design different and unique. They became hand-made one of a kind pieces of wearable art. Once I was satisfied with the design, I shellacked the entire bracelet and hung them to dry on outstretched wire coat hangers. Each bracelet was better than the previous one until the perfected pieces looked professional.

I got an A on the project, and of course Mom loved the end result. "Steffie I can't tell the difference between your bracelets and the one I bought," she gushed. That was nice to hear, but she liked everything I did. I decided that if they were that good, maybe I could make some money selling them? What I needed was an unbiased opinion.

One day after school, I borrowed the car and decided to try my luck selling the bracelets to Roxanne's Boutique on Beach Boulevard. I thought they looked pretty good, but what if Roxanne hated them, or she thought they looked homemade? The fear of rejection was getting the best of me. I pushed the negative thoughts out of my mind and mustered up the courage to walk in the door.

Roxanne did in fact love them, but rather than give me an order, she requested that I deliver a dozen on consignment in a week. Not exactly a typical purchase order, but I was still thrilled that my creation was good enough to be displayed in a store and hopefully good enough to buy.

Practically sprinting to the car I could barely contain my excitement. I burst into the house, shouting, "Mom, Mom, guess what, I sold my bracelets to Roxanne's Boutique!"

Placing her coffee cup on the kitchen counter, "Oh Steffie, that's wonderful!" She clapped her hands and jumped up and down. "See, I knew they were good."

"She wants them in a week, but she's not exactly ordering, she wants them on consignment. So what's that mean again?"

"It means she doesn't pay you until after they sell, instead of before, which gives her a longer time period to send the money. But that's OK, they'll sell. At least you got your foot in the door. I'm just so tickled!"

I was on cloud nine, someone was actually willing to give me money for something that I made. Mom and Joe let me use the downstairs fourth bedroom as a studio, which up until now only had Mom's sewing machine in it. I didn't have to worry about getting paint on the floor, since it had the same white tile looking linoleum floor as the kitchen and bathrooms. They put together a make shift worktable for me, using a couple of paint splattered wooden sawhorses that supported a piece of plywood. Milk crates served as supply boxes, holding the cardboard rings, bags of wheat paste and shellac. Pie tins along with recycled aluminum Sara Lee coffee cake trays held my brushes and tubes of acrylic paints and provided a palette where I could mix the colors.

I worked non-stop to make sure my order was completed on time. Mom bought me a receipt book so that I could provide an accounting to the retailer. Five days later, I proudly delivered my first order to Roxanne. After she meticulously examined each one, she gave me a satisfied smile and signed the receipt. Mom suggested that I should follow up with her in about a week to see how they were selling.

One week later, I called Roxanne and she said that she had sold eight, and wanted another dozen. I couldn't believe it. "You did, oh wow, thank you… of course I will bring another dozen in a few days."

I was ecstatic. I had just started my own jewelry business and all by myself at age 17. This was only the beginning. I was off and running and decided to venture out to try my luck at some other stores in the area.

I got the same positive feedback. Everyone that I showed my samples to placed orders, mostly on consignment since I was a newbie. I didn't care as long as they said yes.

Once the orders started coming in a little more steadily, Mom and Joe jumped on the bandwagon. They wiggled their way into my operation by suggesting that my stuff could sell on a wider market, offering to give it a go pitching to department stores in Los Angeles. Joe saw an opportunity to bring in more cash, and suddenly he wanted to help little Steffie. "Hey Mama, I betcha if we drove up to Beverly Hills we could sell this stuff to some of them swanky big stores," he announced. "Forget about these little mom and pop places, I'm talkin' big orders, like a gross."

The two of them were standing in the doorway of my newly claimed studio as I sat at my worktable applying paint to one of my bracelets as they began planning my future.

Mom was downright giddy. She squealed, "I know just the stores, but maybe we should call ahead and make some appointments with the buyers."

What could I say? They knew best, or said so.

Mom and Joe went into town one day when I was in school and came back with a stack of orders of several dozen each from Joseph Magnin, Bullocks Wilshire and some others I'd never heard of. The big stores also wanted me to make paper mache' pins to go with the bracelets, which were becoming all the rage. I came up with a creative design for oversized flower pins, adding rice to the centers and gluing the pin attachment to the back; a little more work intensive, but worth the extra sales. I ended up hiring one of my friends from art class to help me with the production so the orders could be filled on time.

Mom and Joe then drove back to Beverly Hills and hand delivered the orders, stopping along the way to sell to a few more stores.

It was an exciting time, but their motives weren't exactly altruistic; they grabbed a chunk of my money from the proceeds, explaining that I had to pay them a commission. After all, their time was worth something, not to mention the money they spent on gas, therefore, they should be compensated. What money I made, after paying them, I either re-invested in the business in the way of buying supplies or deposited into my savings account. The only thing I treated myself to was a powder blue princess phone so that I could have my own phone in my room.

This was the way the business operated: I designed and manufactured the product, and they did the selling. Everything was happening so fast; all I did was keep my nose to the grindstone so I could keep on top of things.

Once summer rolled around I wanted to expand on my art courses beyond what high school had to offer, so I enrolled in a ceramic class at Orange Coast College.

The instructor, Mr. Grayson took me under his wing and inspired me to push my limits. I was always the first to arrive and the last to leave and it was beginning to show in my skill level. Mr. Grayson allowed me to use the potter's wheel after hours and on Saturdays if he was there. The jewelry business had slowed down and now all I wanted to do was throw pots.

That August he invited me to help out here and there in his booth at the Laguna Beach Art Festival. Besides being a cool teacher he was a talented ceramicist with a fine reputation. One afternoon as I was dusting his large vases displayed in the booth, he asked me if I wanted to bring a couple of my small weed pots to display and sell. "Listen Stefanie, I'll have to mix yours in amongst my pieces because it's a juried show," he explained.

I couldn't believe it and could barely contain myself. "You're allowing me to actually put some of my creations next to your exquisite art?"

"Yes, but you can't tell anyone," he emphasized. My little weed pots were unusual in that I didn't glaze them. Instead, painted them with whimsical flowers in the same style my jewelry had been done. No one else was doing that sort of ceramics at the time, which is why Mr. Grayson thought they would be a nice addition to his booth.

A national sales representative from the gift mart in Los Angeles, visiting the art festival, saw my work in the booth and offered to represent me as one of his clients. Up until then I had just begun showing my pots to local gift shops, but this was a whole new ballgame. Soon, I would be able to afford to buy my own potter's wheel.

CHAPTER 24

OUT OF STATE

Joe and Mom continued helping themselves to the extra funds that my small but steady income provided. Now that I had a rep, they could no longer claim commission, so they justified their payments as loans, which in reality should have been called gifts, since they never paid me back. Scraps of paper with I.O.U. $10.00, or $20.00 would appear in my cash box. Did it bother me? You bet, but I mostly kept my mouth shut.

Whenever I did say something to Mom about the loans, she had a way of insinuating that I should be indebted to them for living there. Then she would slip in a plug for Joe, "you know, if it wasn't for Joe, you wouldn't have…".

She never missed an opportunity to rag on my dad to me, either. "He's late again with his check. Your dad doesn't know how lucky he is that Joe's here."

"Mom you talk to him as much as I do," I replied. "Why don't you call him and remind him?"

Flicking her wrist as if to swat an imaginary fly, she said, "Oh it doesn't do any good reminding, he's always got an excuse. It's not like he doesn't know! He'd just rather spend it on the ponies and himself, it's always been that way."

"I know," I responded and let it drop.

In the mean time, Joe's work in the construction industry slowed down to the point that Mom picked up the slack by going to work on Saturdays at Betty's cleaning shop.

Despite the seedy location on Western Avenue, the shop did a booming business, all cash and "Grandma" Betty was quite comfortable. Joe and Mom knew it and she became the money tree with deep pockets whenever they ran low. In exchange for the financial help Mom became her helper—drive her to the doctor, drive her to the mall and drive her to work. I don't know exactly how much money Betty gave them but it was enough to keep the lights on and food on the table.

The deteriorated area where the shop was, in South Central LA was becoming an even bigger crime magnet than before and Mom was becoming more and more apprehensive each time she drove into the decaying neighborhood. There were drugs, shootings, robberies, and even though Mom did her best to persuade Betty to sell and get out, she wouldn't hear of it. A lot of the surrounding businesses were closing and moving to safer sections of town, yet Betty stayed, claiming her loyal customers wouldn't have anywhere else to go.

Mom was always bringing the clothes that people didn't pick up home for all of us to pick through. She and Betty acted like all of the free stuff was a huge perk of the job. I hated it. Most of the stuff was pretty bad, and probably why the owners didn't bother coming back for them. I didn't care how many times the clothes had been cleaned, they were still hand-me-down cleaning shop clothes.

Joe and Mom fought all the time about money. It was a scary time. Whatever work there was, was scattered all over the county and sometimes he would travel as far away as the high desert.

Then like a miracle, Joe followed a lead that there was work out of state. Hallelujah! He would now be heading to

Seattle looking for work. It was going to be the best time of my life with him gone and only one year left of high school.

The construction business hit a snag in several parts of California during the latter part of the 60's and Joe had to go where the work was, which in this case was Washington state. His good friend construction foreman Jim, who lived down the street, was packing up his family and moving north along with some of his workers. Joe seemed enthusiastic about re-locating where he would have a job and a built-in network of friends.

I was so relieved to have him be gone and maybe Mom was too—although she would never admit it. Sheila was a little upset until they explained that it was temporary. It was decided that Joe would get settled first and make sure he had plenty of work before he uprooted everyone.

With the money I had earned from my jewelry business, I bought a potters wheel and saved enough to buy a used kiln from Mr. Grayson.

The jewelry making mostly went on the back burner and the pottery making became my new passion. My entrepreneurial spirit continued with the distribution of my little painted weed pots along with a select few jewelry items, which now included earrings. It was becoming a serious business with a professional sales rep and me occasionally peddling my wares to local stores in the resort communities, like Corona del Mar and Laguna Beach.

My weed pots were soon in stores both locally and nationally. All pre-ordered—no more contingency sales.

With Joe out of the way life was peaceful. I concentrated on my art and business, spending hours in the garage throwing pots. Mom helped me load them into the kiln and then she supervised the gas firing process. I had to help pay for the extra gas but at least she wasn't nickel and diming me like before.

I had a nice little operation going for a high school kid and Rocky, the real one, was back in the picture now too. He and I had kind of cooled it for a while, only occasionally seeing each other covertly. Now, everything was out in the open since I was able to convince Mom that Rocky wasn't such a bad guy. I begged her to please give him another chance because I cared for him. She did. He was also handy to have around to help with things around the house since Mom wasn't exactly a do-it-yourself kind of person. She always had an excuse that she couldn't lift anything, it was her pleurisy, her bad back, her shoulder, her everything.

Joe came home for the Thanksgiving weekend and two days at Christmas without any casualties. I was so busy running my business and dating Rocky that I rarely interacted with either of them.

My senior year in high school was boring and attending half day made it somewhat bearable. Thanks to all of those summer school classes, I had enough units so that I didn't have to stay all day. I had one art class during my last semester that was new to the curriculum and taught by a rookie teacher fresh out of college. He was young and had just moved to the area. Since he didn't know anyone, I thought it would be nice to invite Mr. Tanner to dinner. Mom barbecued the steaks that I had bought and his eyes popped out when he saw them.

The fact that we didn't have living room furniture caused me some embarrassment, so I got the bright idea to borrow the next-door neighbor's sofa and matching chair for a few hours. They were both in their 20's and were our friends as well as neighbors, Greta was a college student and her husband Kent was a pharmacist. Kent was out of town, which made it easier to borrow the furniture.

Mr. Tanner turned out to be a pretty interesting guest. He talked and talked about his traveling the world before he became a teacher. Mom and I were his captive audience, motivating him to recount more stories. The evening had been a success until the doorbell rang and Greta was standing there, frantic and on the verge of tears. "Oh, I'm so sorry to bother you," she said. "I forgot that you had company. It seems that I've locked myself out of the house and I don't know what to do."

Seeing a damsel in distress, Mr. Tanner immediately jumped to her rescue, hopping off the borrowed couch. "Can I help?"

Mom opened the door all the way and invited her inside. "That's OK, uh, Greta, come in. This is Stefanie's teacher, Mr. Tanner."

"Hi Greta, listen, don't worry, if there's an open window, I can get in," Mr. Tanner offered. "Marjorie, do you happen to have a ladder?" She did, so he followed Mom down the hall and grabbed the stepladder from the garage. Then all of us traipsed next-door to Greta's house.

Mr. Tanner assessed the situation, and found an open window in the back of the one story house. We all gathered around to watch him crawl through it. Within seconds, he opened the nearest door, the slider, for all of us to enter the house. Greta profusely thanked him and everybody laughed about it. As she walked us through the house turning on the lights, everyone stopped short practically colliding with one another like a scene from a Three Stooges movie. It was the sight of the coffee table sitting all by itself, on a throw rug, placed several feet from the wall and closing in on the middle of the room that caused the momentary gridlock. The obvious bare spot where a sofa had once sat was the clincher.

A look of horror swept over Greta's face, and then Mom's and finally mine. Thinking quick on my feet, I jumped into action. "Oh my goodness gracious, where's your furniture?" I asked, playing dumb. "Oh I remember you told us it's being cleaned…um how much longer do you think it will be?"

Playing along, Greta momentarily pressing her finger to her chin as she gazed toward the ceiling—trusting an answer would come to her. "Well, it should be any day now, uh, please excuse the mess."

The teacher was a smart guy, I'm sure he didn't buy it.

After he left, Greta was still upset for blowing our ruse, but in the end we all had a good laugh.

CHAPTER 25

THE SLEEPOVER

With Joe gone I felt a huge weight off my shoulders. The spring semester of my senior year was as pleasant as school could be. No more Joe and I was out at noon. It gave me time to run my jewelry and pottery business.

Orange Coast College provided me new opportunities to expand my artistic interests in ceramics and Mr. Grayson continued to make himself available whenever I needed advice, or just to talk about pottery techniques or anything else. He was sort of a mentor to me. He appreciated that I was motivated and talented enough to be able to qualify for college classes while still a high school student and he liked advising me about selling my art.

On a couple of occasions when Mom picked me up from school she had the opportunity to meet Mr. Grayson and I noticed an instant connection between them. He seemed impressed that she had some knowledge about art. They really seemed to hit it off. So much so, that he invited both of us out to dinner. He was a bachelor with a bunch of free time, which explained why he was always so accessible after class.

The three of us went to Don Jose, a casual Mexican restaurant in Huntington Beach. As I sat there watching the two of them chatting up a storm, I could only dream… what if? Mr. Grayson was such a nice man, soft spoken, kind and gentle, and only a few years older than Mom. He was the complete opposite of Joe; what's more, he definitely had eyes for Mom.

In early April Mom and Sheila flew up to Seattle for a three-day visit to see Joe. I refused to go and Mom didn't push it, so I stayed home alone. Little did my mother know that I wasn't entirely alone all those nights. Rocky, at age twenty-one had far outgrown his curfew so staying out all night wasn't an issue for his parents. He wasn't in the habit of answering to anybody since he had lived on his own in an apartment for two years after he graduated high school. I had only been there once when he had that party before we started going steady. He moved back in with his parents shortly after that, so he could save some money and attend college.

Rocky and I had been together for almost two years and marriage was the likely next step. He was working part time in an internship program at an architectural firm while he attended junior college. We loved each other and despite all my crazy family drama it didn't scare him away.

I was on the pill to regulate my periods but obviously there were other reasons that were never discussed. Rocky was the first boy that I had been intimate with. We either went to his house before the parents got home from work, or mine if no one was home. Being together overnight was a big deal and too good an opportunity to pass up.

The neighbors were used to seeing me occasionally driving Rocky's car, which was now a VW bug. When I pulled in and out of the garage in the morning and at night, no one paid attention, or at least I didn't think they did.

Rocky huddled on the floor in front of the passenger seat, which is how I was able to smuggle him in and out of the house in the morning when I left for school and at night when I returned. "It's a good thing I'm small, and wiry otherwise you'd have to pry me loose with a crowbar," he laughed

Looking in my rearview mirror, I slowly backed out of the driveway, trying to speak out of the corner of my mouth without moving my lips. "Shh, don't make me laugh or make me talk in case someone sees me, I'm supposed to be alone—remember?"

Once we got around the corner he surfaced from his hiding place and we went merrily on our way, breathing a sigh of relief for pulling it off.

The three days of playing house went by way too fast. He would drop me off at school, go to college, pick me up at lunch, I would drop him off at work until 6 pm, and then we would go out to dinner and return to my house for the night. On our last night together, we were laying side by side reminiscing about the last couple of days. "I don't want to go home," Rocky said. "I wish we could be like this forever."

I sighed and whispered, "I know, me too. It went by way too fast."

Raising up on one arm he looked down at me. "When do you want to get married?"

With a deep exhale I said to the ceiling, "The sooner the better." Then I caught my breath and turned to face him. "This summer," I said. "Right after graduation."

The streetlight cast a stream of light into my room so that we could make out each other's expressions. I could see the wheels turning the way Rocky's eyes darted back and forth. He began ticking off all of the reasons it was going to work. "I should be working full time by then, and with the money I've got saved by living with the folks, we should be fine," he reassured. "And, I think I know where we can live for not very much rent!"

I had a more pressing reason. "I'm just afraid if we don't make plans right away that Mom may move to Washington," I explained. "And since I refuse to go, I won't have a place to live."

"Oh wow, do you think she'll move there?

"Who knows. Either way, I wanna get out of this house."

"And I want you away from them, especially if Joe comes back." Rocky wrapped his arms around me. "Whadda ya think your mom's gonna say?"

"What can she say? She got married at eighteen and had me at nineteen."

"A small wedding, right?"

"Yes, the smaller the better, but yeah, I do want a ceremony."

"If that's what you want, then that's what you'll get," he stated. "I love you."

"I love you too."

We held each other tight and kissed as we sealed our plans for the future.

CHAPTER 26

FREE AT LAST

I sensed something was up right after Mom returned from her visit to Seattle, but of course she said nothing. She had been home two days, when Mr. Grayson called and invited us to have dinner again at Don Jose's, this time Sheila came along. She was a complete brat, blowing bubbles with her Coke and running back and forth to the restroom so she could play with the foamy soap. Mr. Grayson didn't seem bothered, he was too focused on Mom. It was a week later when she casually mentioned that she had accepted a dinner invite from Mr. Grayson, only this time neither Sheila nor I was invited. I had great fun teasing her about it, but she wouldn't crack.

They ended up going back to Don Jose's. Not sure if it was the food or the Margaritas that was the attraction to that place, but whatever it was, it was definitely a date.

"So, was it a date?" I asked when Mom walked in the door a little after ten that evening.

"It's nothing Stefanie," she replied nonchalantly. "We enjoy each other's company, that's all."

"C'mon Mom, tell me what's going on," I pleaded.

Shrugging, she said, "Steffie, I don't know, we just have a lot in common."

After some arm twisting, she shared that they'd strolled along the beach, dawdled on the swings a bit and that he gave her a quick peck on the lips when they parted for the evening.

Boy, I didn't see that coming, nevertheless, I was pleased and had to know more.

I continued quizzing her. "Yeah, I can tell you like him, don't you?"

"He's a nice friend, let's just leave it at that."

"Uh huh, OK, if you say so, but I wish you'd leave Joe and get together with Mr. Grayson."

"Steffie, I don't know what's going to happen with Joe. It seems like he wants to stay up there, and I'm not sure I want to move."

"Well, then ask him for a divorce."

"It's not that easy and not something I can ask over the phone," she declared. "I'll talk to him when he comes home next time."

"Sure, whenever that will be."

I didn't know exactly what was going on with Mom and Joe's relationship; he had been gone for so long that they had only seen each other maybe eight days in the past eight or nine months. She was always so tight-lipped whenever I asked her if they were getting a divorce.

The next several weeks were a busy time for me as a senior with the end of school projects and graduation details. There were photos, rehearsals on the football field and of course final exams.

Mom planned a graduation party and invited all of my relatives.

My dad attended by himself along with my paternal grandparents, and my Aunt Isabel and Uncle Antonio. Joe didn't show up and neither did Betty, who was too busy working. The next door neighbors came and of course,

Rocky. It was a fun party with hot dogs and hamburgers and graduation gifts for me to open. I mostly received cards with money inside and a watch from my mom. I had secretly hoped for a car from my dad, but instead I got a new stereo. I noticed how everyone seemed more at ease. For once my family could enjoy themselves at our house without the prickly atmosphere that was present when Joe was around.

At eleven that night Rocky and I boarded the school bus for Disneyland and the all-night party that was a long standing tradition for the school.

It had only been a week after my graduation when Rocky and I set our wedding date for the following month. Mom wasn't against the marriage, just the timing. Between Mom and Aunt Isabel, I think the two of them were in cahoots. At first Mom tried to talk me into waiting because she thought there wouldn't be enough time to plan a decent wedding. Then when I called Aunt Isabel to tell her, she offered to give me a nice wedding if we waited until the end of summer.

I wasn't having any of it. It was my decision and I wanted to get married and leave before Joe came back, which could be any day. There was nothing they could do to talk me out of it. Rocky and I decided we wanted a small wedding of family only, in Santa Barbara on Friday July seventh, which was a little over three weeks away. Our thinking was that if we had the wedding out of town, it would keep the expenses down because less people would attend.

No longer discouraging me, Mom was now fired up. It was her idea to accompany me to look for a dress, and to pay for it. Instead of a wedding dress, I chose a simple crisp white cotton pique suit; it was in the junior department of I. Magnin and fit me perfectly. The three quarter sleeves and short straight skirt made it look stylish and youthful.

Mom spent some time calling various churches until she was able to locate a non-denominational minister who was willing to travel to perform the ceremony at the Biltmore Hotel. We ended up inviting thirteen guests, Mom, Joe, Sheila, Betty, and my dad, who now would be coming alone, since he and Rita were separated. My grandparents, along with Isabel and Antonio and both sets of Rocky's parents, his mom and step-dad, and his dad and step-mom would also be there. His sister lived in another state, and my dad's other sister, Anna didn't attend many functions.

Anna's excuses were always vague and were never challenged by anyone in the family. If she did attend it was always alone or with her kids. Her husband, who was black, did not accompany her, mostly because Grandpa did not approve of the marriage. They lived in San Diego, so I wasn't as close to her as I was to Isabel. It's too bad, because she was just as sweet and kind as Isabel, but it was no surprise that she wouldn't come.

Everything was falling into place and magically it all got done within the matter of a few days. My dad offered to pick up the tab for the banquet room buffet, along with the cake and champagne and my mom was going to buy the flowers, and my outfit. Rocky's parents agreed to pay for our hotel stay at the Biltmore.

CHAPTER 27

THE DARK CLOUD

About a week before the wedding, Joe showed up one night unannounced. He had flown back from Washington and then taken a cab to the house without telling Mom. Now that he was back, it was as though a dark cloud appeared out of nowhere and hovered over our house. He just walked in the front door whistling that same old stupid jingle, "Whistle Here." The message: "Here I am everyone drop what you're doin' and come a runnin'." Every bit of joy was sucked out of my life within a matter of seconds. Not so for Sheila, she was delighted to see him, throwing herself into his arms. My greeting was that of a brief dutiful hug and Mom put on an "OK" performance with her lengthy embrace, but it looked to me like she seemed anxious by his surprise visit.

Thankfully, the reunion between Joe and me took all of 30 seconds.

"So, I hear yur gettin' married," Joe stated.

"Yes, in a little over a week in Santa Barbara," I replied.

"Rushin' it ain't ya? What's the big hurry?" He inquired. "Ya'll ain't pregnant are ya?"

I felt my face warm. "Nope. We're ready, that's all. I gotta go, I'm having dinner with Rocky and his parents."

"C'mere' and give me a kiss before ya go."

Gag, I did.

Later that night as I was getting ready for bed, I heard Joe quizzing Mom about her activities during his absence. His voice was booming so it wasn't much of a strain to be able to hear what he was saying. His tone was suspicious and accusatory. "I hear you went out to dinner with that teacher of Stef's."

"Uh, Stefanie and I met Mr. Grayson at Don Jose, as kind of a graduation celebration for her," Mom answered back.

With sarcasm, Joe began to bait her. "And did you think he was good lookin'?"

"What are you talking about? He's her teacher."

"Don't play dumb with me, Marjorie Ann you know what I'm talkin' about, how he has the hots for you."

"That's not true, he's always been a perfect gentleman."

"And how the hell would you know?" Joe set the trap. "Have you been out with him more than once? How about Alone?"

"No, just that one dinner," she lied.

Joe repeated, "I don't believe you, and you didn't answer my question, darlin'. Do–you–think–he–was–good–lookin'?"

I could hear the tension in her voice. "I never thought about it."

"Bullshit! I think this teacher fella is the friend that you supposedly met up with too," he sneered. "In fact I think you've been fucking him."

I couldn't believe what I was hearing, and how did he know about those dinners? Sheila! That little troublemaker.

Their voices started to fade, so I eased my way down the hall pressing myself against the wall, so I could hear more of what they both were saying.

It sounded like they'd moved into the kitchen. I could hear water running, drawers opening and closing.

Joe was getting worked up, his voice escalating.

"Don't walk away from me when I'm talkin' to you, Marge. It just makes you look like you got summin' to hide." The conversation was turning into a full-blown interrogation.

"I–I have nothing to hide and I don't know why you think something's going on?"

"Yeah, well even Sheila thinks so." And there it was.

"She's wrong, she's ten years old for God sake."

"And knows what she sees and hears," he snickered.

What had I done? Introducing my teacher to my mom. And now that Joe found out she would pay dearly. I was scared, anxious and fuming.

It's OK for him to screw around all he wants, but the minute Mom so much as talks to another man, he blows his cork. Asshole. Hypocrite.

Still hugging the wall, I made it to the landing where I remained safe behind the wall but within earshot.

I heard glass breaking and then Mom started to cry.

"Joe, you're hurting my arm," she begged.

"I'll do more than that you cunt."

Tears streamed down my cheeks and I felt that fear in my pelvic area that triggered the urge to pee. After nine months of living in a peaceful environment, now he was back with a vengeance.

I heard cupboard doors slamming, bottles clanking, then ice hitting glass. He was probably hitting the booze. He continued to interrogate, accuse and drink. Mom kept her voice low and calm. I heard her say she was going upstairs to make sure Sheila was asleep, but he wouldn't let her, telling her it could wait.

I slipped back to my room, called Rocky and told him what was going on. He offered to come over, but I said not to. It would only make things worse. He wanted to call the police, but I explained that they wouldn't do anything, just like all the other times. I told him I would call back if it got out of hand.

Around one o'clock in the morning, I was woken up by my mother's screams. Then they suddenly stopped and became muffled cries begging for Joe to stop hitting her. By the sound of the smacks the beating continued. I was almost finished dialing Rocky's number when I heard their footsteps on the stairs.

I was afraid to get on the phone again out of fear that someone would hear me now that they were upstairs in their room across the hall. They didn't even have the courtesy to shut their door because the next thing I heard sounded like sexual noises coming from him. I did my best to block out the noises as I laid there trying to figure out what to do. The answer that came to me was... get out. At eighteen, I was a legal adult and no longer required to live under their roof, even if it was for another week.

I got up by eight the next morning and noticed their bedroom door closed when I went to the bathroom. When I came out I smelled coffee coming from downstairs. I was hoping it was Mom, but what I didn't expect to find was a brutally beaten version of my mother. Her back was to me when I entered the kitchen and she was hunched over the sink rinsing out a cup. When she turned around, I gasped. "Oh my god, Mom you have to go to the hospital."

She gently shook her head and whispered, "I can't right now."

Her left eye was completely swollen shut, her face was purple and swollen, there were cuts with dried blood on her cheeks and forehead. Her lip was cut open and swollen. This reminded me of the car beating. There was hardly an untouched part left of her face, even her hair was matted with blood, all I could do was stare in horror. My blood was boiling; it was all I could do to keep from screaming. Through gritted teeth, I voiced my anguish. "He did this because he thought you were messing around? Because stupid Sheila blabs everything she sees. Why do you put up with this? You have to leave!"

"I know, I know." She struggled to light a cigarette from the corner of her mouth, mumbling, "I'm too afraid."

"I can't take it anymore," I cried. "I don't have to stay and watch this ever again, I'm calling Isabel and Antonio to come and get me."

"Uh, I… think… uh… maybe you should," she replied.

I began walking in circles with my fists clenched. "Mother, what am I supposed to do?" I blurted. "I'm getting married in one week!"

"Have Isabel come and get you. Go now, before he wakes up."

"Everything was fine until he came home." I declared. "He's ruining my wedding, he's ruining everything. Look at you, how are you gonna get away? You have to be there, but how can you?"

"Shhh, hurry, go on," she whispered. "We'll talk later."

I ran upstairs and called my aunt and uncle and they agreed to pick me up in a couple of hours. I packed my clothes and my wedding suit, since I knew that I wouldn't be back before the wedding. I had to leave a lot of my things, but I managed to grab my record player and as many of my personal items that would fit in their car. It was just after noon when the doorbell rang and I ran down to answer it carrying an armful of clothes. Isabel and Antonio quickly took the bundle from my arms and started loading the trunk of their car. I ran up and down the stairs several more times until their car was almost full.

Just before we were ready to leave, Mom came out from wherever she was hiding and thanked them. They were speechless even though they had seen her like this before; it was something you never got used to.

I was finishing up in my room, when Mom tiptoed in holding something behind her back. She moved like a frightened animal. Trembling and cowering she handed me a wad of clothing. "Hide this under your bed."

I took the blood soaked shirt that she had worn the night before and stashed it deep under my bed. "What are you gonna do with the shirt?" I asked. "Show the police?"

Silence.

She appeared disoriented and kind of out of it. No wonder she was barely functioning, after being so severely battered. Maybe she was in some sort of shock? And when I said as much. She shushed me.

"I can't talk, just go," she said. "I'll call when I can."

I hugged her, picked up the last of my stuff and scurried back downstairs. When I reached the bottom I nearly skidded into Joe, who was now talking to my aunt and uncle as if he and Mom had had a minor tiff. "Yeah, that's good that you're takin' Steffie. Marge and me need to work a few things out," he justified. "Probably a good idea to get her away." Isabel and Antonio, clearly looking uncomfortable, couldn't wait to get out of there. Backing away towards the front door, and nodding, they said their good-byes. My arms were full with my last load, and all I could eek out was, "bye." And with that we were gone.

In the car, Isabel was beside herself with worry. "Did you see the way he acted after what he did to her? I think this is worse than the last time. Her eye was so swollen she couldn't even open it. I wonder if we should call the police?"

"They won't do anything because Mom is too scared to press charges, just like before," I explained. "I will call Betty when we get to your house, she'll know what to do."

From the backseat window, I regarded the house and the neighborhood for the last time. As we rode along, I began to worry about my wedding. "I don't know what to do about my wedding either, how's Mom going to get away to go? She can't go anywhere in that condition. Should I postpone it?" My eyes watered up from a mixture of anger and sadness. "I hate him, he's the one who should have the crap kicked out of him."

"We just wanted to get you out of there." Isabel tried to calm me. "I know your mom will try to make the wedding, try not to worry."

CHAPTER 28

THE WEDDING

When we got to Whittier, I called Betty and told her what happened. She was livid. She revealed that she had been making the mortgage payments as she proceeded to unload a dump truck of gripes. "Since Joe up and left with no money to keep the bills paid, what was I gonna do, let everyone be thrown out on the street? He's on the verge of bankruptcy and they've already signed papers transferring the title to me."

"I had no idea. They never told me what was going on with the house, just that he sends money for food and stuff," I replied.

"Pocket change," she snapped.

Money did seem to slip through their fingers, if they had it, they spent it, and when they didn't, they borrowed.

"He's a lowlife good-for nothing, just skips town, runnin' off all over creation leaving his family, expecting me to pay for everything. I work harder than anyone," she continued. "I'm so darn tired all the time, yet Marge and him think nothing of asking me to bail them out of their money problems," she continued. "Once all the paperwork is done, and the house is in my name I'm kicking him out."

After she finished her rants, I changed the subject, "What about Mom, you gotta get her away from him."

"Don't worry," Betty promised. "I will."

My mind was racing, "I'm getting married in a week, how can she get away by then?"

"Listen Stefanie, her getting away from him is a little more important than your wedding."

"I know, but she's my mom and—"

"I've got customers," she interrupted. "I'll call you later." I started to say something but she had already hung up. Trying to explain how important my wedding was to Betty was probably a waste of time anyway, all she cared about was work. She'd never attended anything for me, no school plays, no graduations. I had overheard her saying to Mom in the past, "I don't care no nothin' about seein' a school play." Between Joe and Betty, the lack of caring about my feelings and achievements was plain as day.

I finished making my wedding plans with Isabel's help and Mom finally called while Joe was mowing the lawn. Her voice was shaky and she spoke quickly. "Stefanie, I'm still here, we haven't been able to leave."

"What do you mean, can't you sneak out when he's in the shower or asleep?" I asked.

She explained that she was still bruised and sore and Joe was holding her captive in her own home.

"He's taken the car keys and whenever we need groceries he makes us go with him to the store."

"Mother, you've got to run away," I pleaded.

"It's not that easy, but Betty's working on it," she explained.

"When? It's been three days, what's taking so long? What about my wedding? Should I postpone?"

"I know, I know, I'm so sorry—no, don't do that, don't put it off." She began to cry. "I'll try to be there… here he comes…"

The phone went dead and I just sat on the floor staring at the receiver in my hand and began sobbing.

It was the day before my wedding and I was devastated. It was becoming more and more apparent that my own mother wouldn't be able to see me get married. The only family that would be there would be my aunt, uncle, grandparents and dad. Rocky and I talked it over and we both decided to go through with our plans. No turning back. I couldn't stay with my relatives forever and this was my only way out.

The next day, the five of us piled into the Cadillac, my aunt, uncle and grandparents, as we made the two hour drive to Santa Barbara. Isabel had reserved a large suite at the same hotel as the wedding, so that they wouldn't have to drive back after the ceremony. She and Grandma tried to cheer me up as they helped me get ready, but with a colossal lump in my throat all I could think about was Mom. At seven o'clock that evening we all gathered in the small chapel downstairs where the brief ceremony was performed by a female pastor who recited the standard dictum.

Just before Rocky and I said our "I do's," the pastor asked who gives this bride away and my dad, responded, "her mother and I." It was at that moment that I accepted that any hope of her showing up at the last minute, was gone. No longer able to keep it together, the floodgates opened as tears gushed down my face like a river, accompanied by a heaving in my chest as I tried to stifle the sobs. I cried throughout the rest of the ceremony, aching for my mother. Everything that was wrong with the occasion filled my head. All I could think of was that this wasn't supposed to happen this way. A wedding is about to take place and then suddenly the mother is so badly beaten that she can't attend her own daughter's wedding! A wedding is supposed to be a happy occasion.

Parents should be there. Any tears that flowed should have been tears of joy not of sorrow.

By the time the simple ceremony was over I was a mess. The whites of my eyes were red, the lids puffy and there were tracks of mascara running down my cheeks like a spider web. Rocky did his best to comfort me, pulling me close and pressing my tucked arm close to his body as he rubbed my hand with the other. Once it ended, we spent time with our families, who had all driven so far to attend. Even his real dad, who he hadn't seen in years attended with his new wife. Everyone on his side seemed to understand my not so subtle display of grief after we explained the situation. My side of the family needed no explanation.

After the twenty-minute ceremony, the hotel waiters served champagne, and then we walked into a small banquet room and ate from a buffet of cold cuts. I enjoyed meeting Rocky's real dad, who could have been his twin, even at 50. His wife, on the other hand was much younger, maybe in her early 30's, and quite beautiful. She had huge warm brown eyes that peeked out from under a wide brim straw hat. There was something nurturing about her and talking to her made me feel better.

The simple affair was lovely and intimate yet for me bittersweet. I was so glad to be free, but of all people not to attend my wedding, my own mother wasn't there, leaving a huge hole in my heart.

We spent the weekend exploring Santa Barbara. They were having a heat wave and the room at the Biltmore Hotel was small and hot with no air conditioning. What few windows there were didn't bring much relief. To top it off, I experienced one of my night terrors while we were there. Rocky was startled awake, never having witnessed anything like that before. "Stefanie, Stefanie, wake up," he whispered shaking my shoulder as he tried to wake me up. It was embarrassing, especially the next day when the front desk clerk called asking if everything was alright? Rocky told him that it must have been the TV.

Hanging out at the beach brought some relief from the miserable heat. We visited the souvenir shops and took a tour boat ride. Sunday afternoon we headed back to my aunt and uncle's house where we were hoping to stay until our apartment was ready in two days. Our original plan was to stay at my house to cover the two-day gap, but that was before Joe showed up.

CHAPTER 29

HOMECOMING

Uncle Antonio was playing catch with his son and another boy in the front yard when we pulled up to the house around five o'clock. A huge smile stretched across his face the minute he saw us. He tossed the ball back to the kids as he moved toward us. As soon as we stepped onto the grass, he wrapped his arms around both our shoulders, steering us toward the house. Isabel appeared at the screen door and smothered us with hugs and squeezes as she beckoned us inside.

Rocky and I followed her into the dining room where she abruptly stopped. Grinning like the cat that swallowed the canary, she turned and said, "Stay here, I have a surprise for you.

We both searched Antonio's face for an explanation but got only a shrug in return.

Seconds later Isabel returned from the kitchen with my mother in tow. My hands flew to my mouth, covering a giant "O"! I threw my arms around her in a big bear hug. "Oh Mother! You're here, I can't believe it!" I squealed. "But how did you get here? When did you get here? I've been so worried." We hugged for a long time, tears of happiness rolling down our faces. She definitely looked better than the last time I saw her. A lot had happened in ten days, as I would soon learn.

The five of us sat around the generous oval dining room table drinking iced tea as Mom began to describe the details to Rocky and me about how she ended up at my aunt and uncle's house.

The remnants of the beating still showed on her face. The bruises had mostly faded to a pale yellow but a couple of prominent scars remained across her eyebrow and her lip.

She started off telling us that Joe was home all the time and wouldn't let her out of his sight. He had threatened to kill her if she tried to leave and she believed him, now that he had gotten hold of a gun. She explained that after she made the call to Betty all she could do was wait for help.

What she didn't expect though was the gunfight at the OK Corral.

"Mother finally showed up a few days after the call with a big black guy that she must have hired as a bodyguard. Joe refused to let her inside," Mom explained. "He hollered at her through the front door, saying things like, 'you and your nigger can turn around and go back to where you came from.'"

Mom said that Betty wasn't intimidated and refused to back down. "Of course Joe jumped down my throat because he knew that I'd called her, but with the distraction, he didn't have time to deal with me," she continued. "Mother yelled right back at him through the door, telling him if he didn't let Sheila and me go, she was going to take matters into her own hands."

Mom relayed that Betty had a key and had told Joe to send them outside or else she was coming in.

"That's when Joe grabbed Sheila and I and shoved us upstairs and then he locked us inside the master bedroom along with himself. The next thing I heard was footsteps on the stairs and then a pop, which pierced a hole in the top of the bedroom door. Mother or her body guard was shooting at us," she said. "Mother yelled, 'That's a warning shot. If you know what's good for you, let them go!'"

Mom paused to take a sip of her iced tea, lit a cigarette and then went on to tell us how she and Sheila crawled into the closet and flattened themselves on the floor fearing that they'd be hit with a bullet.

"From the closet, I could see Joe crouching and sidestepping like a caged animal with nowhere to go until he made his way to the bed, where I saw him retrieve his pistol from underneath the mattress."

She described how the standoff scene unfolded with a combination of verbal threats accompanied by gunfire flying back and forth into the now bullet ridden door. Joe wanted Betty and her 'nigger' to leave and Betty wanted her daughter and granddaughter set free. "After Joe ran out of bullets, he crawled over to the closet and pressed himself against the door until the shots stopped at the sound of sirens."

Mom summed it up. "The shots were meant to scare Joe, but Mother was obviously not thinking clearly. With us in the same room we could have easily been hit."

She concluded that once the cops kicked open the bedroom door and handcuffed Joe, she and Sheila were freed.

"After I spoke to the police and explained the situation—that Joe had beaten me and wouldn't let me leave, and that my mother was only trying to help me—they didn't detain me, so I called Isabel and Antonio and here I am."

Rocky and I sat there stunned. "So what happened to Betty and the black guy?" I asked.

"Nothing to Betty, according to her, except a slap on the wrist for taking matters into her own hands. You know how she manages to fast talk her way out of predicaments, but who knows, there could be more she's not telling me," Mom explained. "I think they booked her helper and then released him after Betty posted bail. I haven't spoken to her much since it happened, just to tell her I needed to get away where Joe couldn't find me. I'm pretty upset the way she went about it, endangering Sheila and me that way."

Uncle Antonio chimed in. "She should have just called the police and then met them there."

Mom nodded, "I know, I know, but she didn't think they'd do anything, like all the other times."

"Where's Joe?" Rocky asked. "Is he still in jail?"

"I'm not sure; it's only been two days," Mom shrugged. "He may have somehow posted bail."

"What are you gonna do now?" I asked. "You can't go home in case he gets out."

"I have to wait for the hearing tomorrow, to make sure he's either in jail for a long time or goes back to Washington. At least I have the car this time."

"You do? Where is it, I didn't see it parked out front?"

"It's in the garage just in case Joe is out and decides to come looking for us," Mom explained.

Isabel and Antonio made room for all of us. They even gave up their bedroom to Rocky and me.

As promised, two days later, our Balboa Peninsula duplex was ready for us to move into—but not alone. Mom had no money and no place to go since Joe had gotten off with only a fine, and she wasn't exactly sure what for? It was a safe bet, however, that he was most likely back in the house. "The judge got confused with all of the he said, she said, and bottom line, he determined that Joe was simply defending his family," Mom explained. "Everything else got thrown out, except the black guy/bodyguard will end up serving some time."

There was no room for Mom and Sheila in our one bedroom, one bathroom unit, however there was space in the upstairs unit. It seems, Emma the landlady, took pity on Mom's situation and gave her the upstairs vacation rental for a week at no charge. Her only condition was to make sure it was clean for the next guests. Apparently someone had canceled at the last minute, which was a lucky break.

The honeymoon was over pretty fast, given the drama that seemed endless. Rocky was a good sport though, and the landlord was more than generous, but still the whole thing was surreal.

Mom and Sheila spent time at the beach and met up with some distant relatives from Oklahoma who had rented a beach house further down the Balboa Peninsula near the wedge. At the end of the week, Mom informed me that they were going to move back home. Evidently she had called Joe from the pay phone at the corner grocery store the night before to see if he was gone yet, and that's when he announced that he was headed back to Seattle as soon as he could get a flight.

"OK, if you're sure he'll be gone," I replied. "And Betty is gonna take over the mortgage so you can stay in the house, right?"

"Yes, she's taking care of it," Mom confirmed. She was well aware that there would be strings attached when it came to Betty. Her help always came with a price tag. In the mean time Betty decided to start making plans for her future retirement by looking for a place of her own nearby. This way she could escape the blight of Los Angeles and be close to her family, but in reality, she also wanted to be driven to work by her daughter and never mind that it was over an hour away.

Rocky and I borrowed a truck and followed Mom home so we could grab the furniture from my room. The house was a mess, but we didn't stick around long enough to assess the damage. We quickly loaded my stuff and left so we could return the truck.

Rocky and I were busy getting settled, he was now working full time for an architect and I had just been hired at the newly built Broadway department store in Fashion Island. It felt good to finally have some peace and to be adapting into a routine. And in about six weeks, as soon as the summer tourist season ended, it would be even better. Living at the beach during the fall and winter was the best time of year as far as I was concerned. I loved having the beach practically to myself.

Two nights later, Betty called in a state of hysteria. "Marjorie Ann is gone!"

"What are you talking about?" I shouted.

"I've been calling the house all day and there hasn't been an answer," she shrieked. "She told me last night that she wasn't feeling well, and that she was going to stay in bed today," Betty continued. "So since I couldn't get in touch with her I went by the house tonight and the front door was wide open and the place was wiped out! The furniture's gone, Marjorie Ann's clothes are gone, and all Sheila's belongings! Can you imagine! The nerve! It looks like a tornado tore through there," said Betty.

I was dumbfounded. "I can't believe it, we were just there two days ago. Did they leave anything?"

"All there was besides the clutter, was a note scribbled on a scrap of paper torn from a grocery bag saying, 'decided to move to Washington, will write when we get settled.' That's it. No call, no discussion! After all I've done for them, and they go and stick me with the house and a huge mess, now I've gotta do something with it. If I hadn't come along and bailed them out, they woulda gone bankrupt, I'm so angry I could chew nails! Ingrates!" She ranted for what seemed like hours. I told her that I would meet her there on Sunday and help her clean out the house.

After we hung up, I thought about what my mother had done and how sneaky she had been. Nothing had changed, no matter how bad it got between her and Joe, she always went back, and now they were gone. I told myself that I had to focus on my own life, now that I was finally free and that at least for me, it won't happen again.

Betty and I sorted through the trail of abandoned belongings for hours. I piled up trash bags filled with discarded clothing, mismatched, cracked dishes, and toys on the side yard for Goodwill to pick up. Black plastic trash bags now took up space alongside my big orange kiln. I would have to get it moved since the house would go on the market soon. So much for my pottery business. Maybe Antonio and Isabel would let me store it in their back yard temporarily?

The only fun part of the cleanup, however, came when I took a hammer to Joe's prized marlin that he'd caught and had mounted on the living room wall. First I chopped off the bill, followed by the fin removal, and then I punctured the remaining body with gashes, all before tossing it onto the pile of rubbish where it belonged. It felt good.

Betty was able to sell the house once the bullet holes were patched, but her anger and resentment toward Mom and Joe held steady.

Mom finally called me and all she said was, "it's better this way, things will be better here, away from California. Everything's OK." Blah, blah, blah.

"What happened? You haven't said a word and why did you suddenly decide to move to Washington of all places?" I asked.

She replied in a matter of fact tone, "Joe came back with a U-Haul and loaded up the house and then we all drove to Washington. It's the only place we can afford to live, he has work here and doesn't in California."

"Mother, he beat you up so badly you couldn't even attend my wedding," I screamed. "What about my family and how they drop everything to come and help you? How are they gonna feel? I thought you were going to hire an attorney and get a divorce and also press charges so that he couldn't hurt you again and another thing... why did you make such a big deal about gathering evidence like the bloody shirt?"

Silence.

"You acted like you were planning on building a case, "I snapped. "And now you're not only back with him but you've left the state! I don't get it?"

Avoiding my questions she said, "I'll write you soon and you can always come for a visit any time you want."

"I don't want to go to Washington. I gotta go, bye."

Calling was too expensive so she wrote letters, and after a month, I responded. I missed her, but I also hated what she'd done. I couldn't understand any of it. Each and every time she got away from him I believed it would be the last time. I couldn't make sense of anything they did, so I stopped trying and tried to move on.

CHAPTER 30

A WHITE CHRISTMAS
FOR ONE

To make it even cuter Rocky and I added our own personal touches to our little Balboa beach house on 34th street. Most of our stuff was a mishmash of his and my bedroom furniture. His double bed and nightstand were all that was needed to fill the tiny bedroom. The living room was cozy with my bright orange studio couch and brass pole lamp. My wicker trunk served as both coffee table and dinner table. We shared Rocky's drafting table as desk and work table, wedged into a corner and slightly obstructing the sliding glass door.

We didn't have to worry about a dinette set, since there was no dining room or breakfast nook anyway. My dad bought us a TV and we received four place settings of dishes along with kitchen gadgets as wedding gifts. My hand made pottery filled with dried flowers popped up in every room.

The place was vintage beach cottage from the front facing patio, dutch door with stained glass, to the knotty pine paneled walls throughout. We didn't mind that the carpet had seen better days and the yellow formica in the kitchen was cracked and coming apart at the seams, or that there was only a wall heater in the hallway to heat the entire house. The space was small and it was no big deal to leave the bedroom door open so we could keep warm. We felt fortunate to have found the little gem in a prime location, just a block from the sand, and at such a reasonable price. It even came with a single car garage, which was golden, given the parking dilemma during the summer and on weekends. The garage even had a nook for my potter's wheel and a small storage area. It was a great place for young people to live and we loved it.

I liked my job at the Broadway even though I got stuck in the millenary department. Selling hats and wigs wasn't exactly exciting. It was, however, located on the first floor near the escalator, right in the middle of the hubbub where people watching and socializing kept me occupied.

With my new job came a new car, well not exactly new, more like a paint peeled, dented, very used VW bug that Rocky and I bought together for a few hundred dollars. But it was new to me, because it was my first car. Rocky usually drove the brand new blue Volkswagen since he had further to go to work. I didn't mind the old red beater, it got me where I needed to be and it was kind of fun driving a stick shift with a clutch, unlike Rita's Rambler that had the gears near the steering wheel.

While things were pretty good on the work front, Rocky seemed different after a couple of months of marriage. He was distant and was starting to act like he didn't want to be married. It was as though he could do what he wanted to push my limits without consequences, now that we were married. It started with him never wanting to do anything as a couple, no restaurants, no movies, no more dates, period. He didn't come home after work either. Instead he chose to play basketball with his old high school friends after work, an activity he had never shown an interest in before. I didn't even know he knew how to play.

One Saturday night, when I had just gotten home from work and Rocky was sprawled on the couch watching TV, I asked him if he wanted to go out to dinner.

"Uh, not tonight, I'm tired from practice and besides we grabbed something afterwards," he casually replied.

As I listened to myself I couldn't help but notice the slight edge to my voice. "Rocky, do you realize that we haven't had dinner together in over a week?"

"Yeah we did, last Sunday, I barbecued those burgers, remember? His eyes never leaving the TV screen.

Losing my patience, "OK, six days, then, I stand corrected."

"Don't forget, you've been working some of those nights."

I took a deep breath, trying to keep my cool. "Can't you skip basketball one night?"

Pause. Irritation in his tone, "I'm on a team now and no I can't. Besides it's fun."

I positioned myself next to the TV so he would be forced to look at me.

"Alright, so when is it over?"

"Year round, and quit nagging me," he barked.

I moved to the couch and sat next to him. "So you'd rather play basketball than be with me," I asserted.

In a flash, he grabbed my wrists and held tightly, something he's never ever done in the two years that we had been together.

"Listen Stefanie, if you don't like it you know what you can do!"

"Ouch, let go of me, you're hurting me."

He released my arms. "I'm outta here." And then he jumped up and grabbed his keys from the clay bowl on the breakfast bar and slammed the door. I sat there staring at the closed door. What was happening to us?

Every day that passed we were becoming more like roommates. He was either working or playing basketball when I was off and when I worked nights, he was asleep by the time I got home. We hardly saw each other.

I started making friends at work. Being a new store, it was filled with young employees. Since my section was near the men's department, I was always talking to the guys who worked there. One of them invited me to go-cart racing after work. I accepted. I thought to myself, why not? If Rocky can go out after work so can I! I followed Kip home to save time, so that we could go straight to the track. I was wearing a dress, so he loaned me his sister's jeans and his fisherman knit sweater. There was six of us, people from work and some of his friends. We had a blast and afterward we all went out for pizza. When we got back to his house he gave me a quick hug as I was about to get in my car. I immediately felt guilty for going and that was when I confessed that I was in an unhappy marriage. That changed things and I was never invited out with the group again. I understood, and realized that I shouldn't have gone in the first place. Even though I wore a wedding band, it just never came up at work that I was married. It was awkward at work after that.

After four months of marriage, Rocky dropped a bombshell that made me feel like I'd been punched in the gut. He nonchalantly made an announcement one evening after he got home from basketball practice. "Oh by the way I'm going skiing in Mammoth during Christmas."

At first I was flabbergasted. I snapped back. "Am I hearing right? Is this some sort of joke? You do know that this is our first Christmas?"

"What's the big deal?" he reasoned.

I couldn't speak. I just stared back at him with my mouth open.

"I love skiing and I haven't been in almost two years," he matter-of-factly stated. "Now I have the chance since the office will be closed for two weeks, so yeah, I'm going."

I was crushed, now sniveling. "And you're telling me you're not going to be here at all?"

He gave me a blank look as if I was speaking in a foreign tongue.

"B–b–b–but, it's Christmas!" I sobbed. "Can't you go for a week and come back sooner?"

He appeared slightly frustrated, raking his hands through his hair. "Go spend it with Isabel and Antonio like you always do and stop making a mountain out of a molehill." He harrumphed away. Muttering under his breath, "Christ almighty."

The more he brushed it off, the more I whined. "It's not the same, I don't want to be left alone while you're off skiing."

Defiant, he got in my face, jabbed me with his index finger on my chest and barked. "Well, I'm going, and I may or may not be back by Christmas. I'm done talking about it."

He strutted off to bed. True to his word the conversation was over.

The scheduled ski trip created a strain between us that kept us from moving forward. It hung over our heads like a mushroom cloud. We were both stuck in a bad place. There was no compromise; we'd both dug in our heels. He wanted what he wanted when he wanted it and I didn't want him to have it at my expense, and neither of us was about to give in. We went through the motions, barely speaking except when necessary.

Everyday I got angrier and angrier until I decided that I wasn't going to be treated like that, and end up like my mother. I made a decision.

CHAPTER 31

REGRESSION

It was nine o'clock on a Tuesday morning in the middle of November when Isabel and Antonio showed up at my house with a U-Haul trailer. The three of us worked non-stop for three hours so that I would be gone in case Rocky came home early. We loaded all of my personal belongings, the few furniture pieces that had been mine before the marriage, consisting of the studio couch, pole lamp, dresser, and of course my potters wheel. I took some of the kitchen stuff, my art supplies and my pack rat things like boxes of Modern Screen and Photoplay movie star magazines that I saved. I left Rocky a letter that I placed on the kitchen counter, telling him that if skiing meant more to him than our marriage, then I was leaving.

Isabel and Antonio had been supportive since the beginning when I first shared with them how unhappy I was. They didn't have to think twice before offering to take me in again, that's just who they were.

They never complained after putting in a full day of moving me out of the beach house, driving an hour to Whittier and then unloading all my stuff into their garage.

Here I was eighteen years old going from life as a married woman in my own place to sharing a room with an eleven year old. My aunt and uncle had three kids; Connie, my new eleven year old roommate, was thrilled to have me move back along with the seven year old boy and a toddler girl. It was a full house where everyone lived in a safe, non-violent environment. Once I got settled, I offered to babysit if my aunt and uncle wanted a night out, which was greatly appreciated and the least I could do.

I took the old red VW bug, since it was paid off, even though I didn't feel like driving. I was falling apart piece by piece and unable to hold it together. My mom had moved physically far away and now my husband moved far away emotionally. I called her once to tell her that I was leaving Rocky and she tried to comfort me by suggesting that I live with them in Sumner Washington. I would have rather lived in a cardboard box under the freeway.

In the end the store let me quit with much notice. Getting dressed and going to work was too much of a chore. I could barely make it through the workday without crying. My co-worker in the hat department became my confidant and shoulder to cry on. She was about fifteen years older and much wiser and experienced in matters of the heart. She had been married and divorced and now lived happily alone on Balboa Island. She was the only one that I would miss.

I was content to stay home with my aunt and her kids all day. Wherever they went, I came along. In an effort to make me feel included, Isabel would say, "C'mon Steffie, let's go to the market, take grandma to the beauty salon, pick up the kids from school." I was on their schedule, that was my new life.

My aunt and grandma were hooked on soap operas, *The Guiding Light, The Edge Of Night* and never to be missed, *As The World Turns.* I found myself watching right alongside them. TV became a big part of my new life. Even with my kiln and potter's wheel now re-located in their back yard, the motivation wasn't there to do my art.

As Christmas approached, I became sadder and sadder. Rocky hadn't even tried to get in touch with me. On Christmas Eve with a big family party planned, I stayed in my shared room brooding. The reality of the holiday hit me along with feelings of abandonment; all I could do was sob.

My dad, who was single again after divorcing Rita, brought along his latest girlfriend for Christmas Eve dinner. Never having laid eyes on her before, here they were standing in my room trying to calm me down.

Dressed in my good sweater and nice wool pants was as close as I got to Christmas, winding up instead in the fetal position on the floor weeping. I just wanted to be left alone, but they kept talking and talking until they finally coaxed me from the room. "C'mon Stefanie, you can't do this to yourself," my dad pleaded.

His date chimed in. "Stefanie, my name is Carol, and I'm a friend of your dad's. I would love to have you sit next to me at dinner."

I just stared at this stranger. She was attractive, with golden blond hair, pale skin and blue eyes and she was dressed in a stylish winter white dress with gold trim.

"You know, I was engaged once and he turned out to be a rotten S.O.B. too, but there are a lotta fish in the sea," she shared. "You are young and things will get better, I promise. They did for me."

Between the two of them not giving up easily, I reluctantly joined the party. With so many family members it wasn't too hard to sit on the sidelines. At least for everyone's benefit I went through the motions of celebrating Christmas. Deep down though, the holiday just made me feel worse.

The days seemed longer and the tears grew more frequent along with the screaming nightmares until the sadness and doom took over my life. I no longer went on errands or participated in family activities, all I did was lie in the bed all day and wail. I heard Isabel on the phone one day saying that she didn't know what to do with me.

She must have been talking to my dad, because the next thing I knew I was taken to a psychologist by Isabel. She shared that she and my dad thought it would be good for me to get some professional help.

This was the first time that I had seen a therapist. It was good to talk to someone other than my aunt and grandma but I still wasn't ready to join the human race. The therapist did a lot of listening, nodding and note taking, on his yellow legal pad. After a half dozen visits over the course of a month, he concluded that my depression was more situational rather than clinical and most likely a result of living in an abusive household, compounded by a doomed marriage.

"The ten plus years of you living in fear, the ten plus years of you holding it all in and harboring anger, had to eventually come out and once it did, you couldn't stop it," he explained. He recommended that I take baby steps toward becoming productive, starting with something as small as picking up a pencil again and drawing pictures.

"Stefanie, the good news is that your personality was formed way before Joe came along, and as a result you were able to determine the difference between right and wrong. In other words, you didn't let him get inside your head and influence your moral values.

"This is not to say, you don't have emotional scars, but because of your foundation of living in a healthy home environment during your early years, I believe that you are resilient enough to move forward and become a productive adult. Whether you know it or not, you have tremendous coping skills."

"I do? Like what?" I asked.

"Your art. The fact that you had an outlet speaks volumes. You could have given up and let the circumstances get the best of you." He went on. "But you're a survivor. Sure, your self confidence needs a boost, but that takes time."

His analysis seemed to make sense as I absorbed his words. He also encouraged me to do something for someone else because that will also make me feel better.

The therapy sessions and the passing of time helped get me over the hump. I took his advice and started taking the kids on long walks and to the park and then I picked up my sketchbook.

It had been about three months since I left Rocky when my dad offered to help get me a job. I was ready. It was time for me to snap out of it. He had a friend who was in management at an insurance office in Orange. I had never worked in an office and I was terrified when I arrived the first time to fill out an application. It was a huge red brick building easily seen from the Santa Ana freeway but nearly impossible to get to. Passing over the Santa Ana freeway several times, I kept missing the street and finally ended up at a gas station looking for help. Now I was not only late but struggled on the test portion of the application. There was too much math and too many trick questions and I simply ran out of time trying to answer all of them.

My understanding was that I was applying for the job of file clerk, but with my poor test score, lack of experience and young age, my assignment was even below a file clerk job. It was the lowest job on the scale with a low salary to match—$1.30 an hour instead of $1.35. Still titled, "file clerk" the job consisted of pushing a basket up and down the aisles of desks dropping off new files and picking up old ones. I couldn't be trusted to file them away, only to pick up and deliver. I wasn't filing anything, just pushing the files around. From seven a.m. until four p.m. five days a week I wheeled the wire-mesh laundry basket loaded with hundreds of stuffed manila folders, until I covered every inch of floor space. It was the most boring job with the unfriendliest co-workers who barely acknowledged my presence. I guess they thought the invisible "file fairy" delivered and picked up a new batch magically? I needed the money so I stuck it out, but not for very long.

It was the middle of February when Uncle Antonio thought it was time to divulge that Rocky had been calling and wanted to see me. Antonio had kept from me the fact that Rocky had tried to see me before Christmas. He wanted to put him through the ringer first. "We thought it would only upset you more if you talked to him and he ended up lying to you again," Antonio explained. "We wanted to make sure his intentions were sincere. We were only trying to protect you, and didn't want to see you hurt."

I nodded and said nothing at first, thinking it would have been nice to know that he at least cared enough to call, instead of believing all this time that he didn't. After the initial shock, I began asking Antonio questions about what had been said between them. He shared that Rocky had apologized and wanted to see me. In the end I couldn't be mad at them, they were doing what they thought was right.

Uncle Antonio agreed to allow Rocky to see me only under certain conditions. He had to come to the house and I couldn't leave with him.

The next night when he came over, Antonio met him at the door and escorted him to the garage so he could talk to him privately first.

When Antonio was satisfied that Rocky was serious about making things right, he came back inside and got me. Rocky was waiting on the front porch with his hands in his pockets and leaning against the railing. As soon as I stepped outside, he moved toward me and threw his arms around me. It felt good. "Stefanie, I'm so sorry, I've been such a jerk. I was going crazy without you."

I pulled away, even though I could have stayed that way forever, but there was too much to talk about. "Rocky, do you have any idea what I've been through?"

"I didn't mean to hurt you, I'm sorry, I don't know what got into me."

We stood outside and talked and when it got too cold we sat in his car. He said that he had called several times and that my uncle refused to let him talk to me or see me. "Antonio was pretty hard on me, he raked me over the coals pretty bad," said Rocky. "I guess I deserved it."

Tears filled his eyes never quite flowing onto his cheeks. "Stefanie, I love you, and I've been miserable without you, please come back. Please give me another chance."

"How do I know you won't do it again?"

"Because I've learned my lesson."

"Do you know what it felt like to have you leave me at Christmas?

"Yeah Antonio told me, and I'll make it up to you. I'll do anything you want. I promise, things will be different."

"The only way that I would consider it is if we live in Whittier and you commute to Huntington Beach for work."

He agreed without hesitation. We talked until we ironed out our problems and at midnight he went back to Balboa.

The next day, he drove back and we went apartment hunting and found a one bedroom about two miles from my aunt and uncle's house. I felt more secure knowing that I had a support system nearby. Not entirely trusting Rocky's word, and just knowing that my family was watching my back and his behavior added a layer of security to the agreement.

Our reconciliation was short lived, we didn't even make it three months before Rocky decided that either I move back to the beach or he was leaving. "Stefanie, I just can't live here anymore," he stated.

He had strong roots to Huntington Beach and although living on the Balboa Peninsula, had been an okay place since it was so close to Huntington, Whittier was too far out of his comfort zone.

"I like the beach too, but I want to be near the only family that I have left," I said. "What if I move back and we split up again? I can't go through the trauma again."

He nodded, acknowledging the fact.

Rocky had lived in Huntington Beach all of his life and was dead set on returning. It was a deal breaker and so he left.

It didn't take much to let the marriage fall apart just like it didn't take much to get it started. The casual proposal, the informal wedding, brief cohabitation. It never really was a marriage, it was just two kids playing house for a few months.

The second go around didn't hurt quite as much. I was stronger now and becoming more and more independent. I had my own place, a job and a better car. This time I ended up with the nicer of the two Volkswagens. Rocky had paid it off and donating it to me probably helped relieve some of his guilt. He pretty much left with the clothes on his back. I would be all right. My family was nearby for the first time since I was a small child back when things were different and everyone relied on each other like a village.

Biding my time at the insurance company was my plan until something better came along. And after three months something did. A new mall was being built in the nearby city of La Habra that included a Bullocks Department store. Getting paid to spend eight hours in an upscale beautiful brand new store sounded much more appealing than withering my life away in that oppressive windowless prison of an office where I currently worked. I wasted no time submitting my application and happily quit the daily grind of the insurance institution once I got the thumbs up that I was hired.

CHAPTER 32

ROCK N' ROLL

When I wasn't working I stayed home alone or visited with my grandparents and aunt and uncle. I had no friends or social life. The insurance company was a dead end as far as making friends. Everyone was older, married and with different interests.

One night I was in my apartment watching TV, when out of the blue my now ex-stepsister Candy called. She had dropped by Isabel and Antonio's house looking for me and they gave her my number. She was asking to come over and five minutes later she was standing at my door.

We hadn't seen each other in over two years, since the summer when I lived with them. My dad and her mom divorced shortly after and that ended our connection. And now here she was.

"I was on my way to the Playgirl Club in uptown Whittier and I wanted to stop by and see what you were up to?"

"Not much, just working a lot. What's the Playgirl Club?"

"It's a bar type club where girls eighteen can get in and guys have to be twenty-one," she explained. "They have dancing to live bands till two a.m.; it's a blast, wanna go with me?"

"No, that's OK."

"Why not, c'mon it'll be fun, I'll do your hair and makeup."

"Maybe some other time."

"C'mon, just go with me for a half hour and if you don't like it, I'll bring you right back."

We went back and forth until she wore me down and the next thing I knew she was giving me a make-over. I have to admit, she worked miracles with my unruly hair. She had it piled onto my head in an updo and it looked really good instead of the usual bangs and headband that kept my shoulder length bob somewhat tamed.

Candy picked through my clothes and found my black bell bottom pants along with a brown turtle neck sweater that met with her approval. Once she was satisfied with the way I looked, she pulled me out the door. I was nervous about walking into a club, something I had never done before.

She let me into the passenger side of a Pontiac Bonneville that belonged to her boyfriend and we drove the few short miles to uptown Whittier, a section of town that I was unfamiliar with.

The club was dark and small and there was a bouncer at the door checking I.D.'s. I was nineteen and she was twenty so we got in OK. Candy was friendly with him and once we got inside I could see that she was a regular since she practically knew everyone.

We sat at a table near the dance floor and a waitress came up and took our order for soft drinks. I started to pay when Candy placed her hand on my purse clasp and said to wait, that we'd run a tab, whatever that meant. She was so worldly about things.

The band was loud, so talking was hard. She got up and danced while I conspicuously sat there and sipped my coke feeling even more out of place. A guy came up and asked me to dance but I shook my head and he moved on. When

Candy came back, she plopped down in the chair across from me, all out of breath and sweating from non-stop Hully Gullying. She lit a cigarette and gulped down her coke.

"Hey, Candy, I hate to be a stick in the mud, but I'm ready to leave."

"OK, I just wanna dance one more dance and then I'll take you home, but before we leave you have to dance at least once."

"It's been a long time, I'm kind of rusty."

"Just watch me and do what I do."

Before I could protest further, two guys came over and sat down. When they ordered us another round of drinks, we could hardly leave.

I did have to admit, the band was really good, doing justice to the current billboard hit songs. The lead singer did an energetic tribute to the original singers of the songs he performed. He and the band sounded just like Gary Puckett and the Union Gap, singing hits, *Woman, Woman* and *Young Girl*. His name was Chris something and he had a loyal following. He slid across the stage—sometimes on his knees—and onto the dance floor gyrating and grooving to the beat. I had never seen a live performance that close up.

He sang his heart out, a true showman and 'soul man'. His rendition of the 1968 Sam and Dave's *Soul Man* and *Hold On I'm Coming*, sounded like the real thing.

One of the guys asked me to dance and after some coaxing, I reluctantly got up and moved around like I knew what I was doing only because Candy was nearby and I could copy her steps. Then before I could sit down, we danced again, I was getting the hang of it. It was midnight by the time we left and when Candy was driving us back, she asked if she could spend the night. It was late and I wasn't going to say no, so I let her stay. I had a double bed, so she slept with me just like old times when we were kids and I would stay over.

Candy left early the next morning so she could return her boyfriend's car and I thought that was the last I'd seen of her for a while. But when I got home from work and found her sitting on my doorstep I thought it was because she had forgotten something. She and her boyfriend had had a fight and she had nowhere else to go so he dropped her off at my place. They had been living together after her mom kicked her out right after she graduated from high school. It was Friday night and she begged me to let her stay just through the weekend, and by Monday she would have a place to go. I agreed.

By the time evening rolled around, she wanted to go back to the Playgirl Club, and she wanted me to drive her there. It being Friday night, I agreed to go with her. "I'll go, but only if you do my hair again. Otherwise, I'll just drop you off."

"OK, so you liked the way I did the updo?" she exclaimed.

"Are you kidding... it looked sooo good. I'm terrible at doing my hair," I said.

"All it takes is practice and a little patience, something you know nothing about," she teased.

We got all dolled up and went back for a second night. I had just danced with another one of Candy's friends when an interesting looking guy came over and sat down at our table. He was different from the others, more serious and intense. He had a strong chin, and a mustache and he wore a sweater cap on his head. He introduced himself as Alex Ward. Candy had seen him before, but didn't know his name.

We didn't dance we just sat and talked as if we were the only ones in the room, completely ignoring the music and everyone around us. I instantly liked him.

It was truly last minute, when he invited me to be his date for a wedding the next day. The only glitch was that he was actually in the wedding, meaning I would have to sit alone during the ceremony, but after that he would be free to spend time with me. Without even thinking about it, I said yes. It was my first date since Rocky and I was both nervous and excited.

During the hour long drive to Westwood we had a chance to get to know each other more. He told me that he was 22 and had just graduated from UCLA and worked nights on the loading docks for a trucking company. He wanted to be a teacher and was living with his parents since moving from the fraternity house near the Los Angeles campus. He came across as an intellectual and liberal thinker who was not afraid to express his opinions. I noticed that he had especially strong views about racial equality influenced in part by the fact that his best friend was black.

The wedding reception ended up being the first of many dates. Alex and I fell for each other in a big way. I liked that he was so different from any of the guys that I had known before. He was so serious, smart and philosophical, yet he still had a sense of humor and never ran out of witty remarks. We went to the Playgirl club occasionally, and did the usual stuff like movies and spending holidays together. He wasn't crazy about Candy, though. Sometimes he acted kind of jealous when she was around. Candy had nearly become a permanent house-guest. I felt sorry for her; she didn't have a job and had no place else to live, plus I had a hard time saying no.

After she had been there a month, we began to bicker, and I really wanted her to move out. She got angry when I suggested that she start looking for another place to live.

When I came home from work the next night and tried to use my key to unlock the door, the chain was attached.

"Candy, Candy, can you hear me?" I shouted through the crack in the door. "The chain is hooked, come to the door and unhook it, I'm locked out."

She yelled back from the bedroom, "Tough shit."

"What's the matter with you? Let me in, this is *my* apartment!"

"Yeah, well not anymore, that'll teach you to kick me out."

I decided to climb through the living room window, but when I tried to open it, it wouldn't budge; she'd put a stick in the track. I couldn't believe it. I paid the rent, bought the food, and was basically supporting her on $1.30 an hour and she has the nerve to lock me out of my own house! Chain on the door, sticks in the windows. I sat outside on the walkway leaning against the building waiting for her to cool down or go out, whichever came first.

After an hour, I heard the chain slide and clank against the door. She exited the apartment without a word, pretending like I wasn't there as she stepped around me. Once she got to the end of the walkway, she stopped. "And don't get any ideas about trying to lock me out she said over her shoulder. "Leave the chain off, or I'll kick the door in."

That was the last straw.

The apartment manager got wind of the incident and gave me an ultimatum, kick her out and stay without her or else you both leave.

Two weeks later, we both left, separately. I don't know where she moved, but I decided to move back to Huntington Beach temporarily. Betty arranged for a moving van to move me to the garage apartment behind her new condo in Huntington Beach. She was only there on weekends since she was still working at the cleaners. I didn't have the deposits needed to get a place of my own; this was the only way to maintain some sort of privacy and a place of my own.

CHAPTER 33

WORKING GIRL

With the Fashion Square shopping center nearly completed, I saw no reason to stick around the insurance company. Bullocks informed me that they would be calling within the next ten days to come in for store set up. There was no way I was going to miss that by being tied down with another job, so I gave my one-week notice and happily quit.

With a few days off, I played a lot. Aside from high school shenanigans, I hadn't done much in the way of kicking up my heels. Now that Alex had gotten me a fake ID, I could drink in bars, which made it much more exciting. I went to the Playgirl club almost every night, sometimes alone if he was working, and I usually stayed until the two a.m. closing. Even Candy had once commented in passing, "I've created a monster."

Seeing Candy there was awkward, we pretty much ignored each other, until she decided that she wanted to make up. We did.

She was with a new guy who was in a band, and now lived with him. Candy shared that she and her mom were getting along better, except her mom wasn't crazy about the musician she was shacking up with.

One night as I was leaving the club, she was sitting outside smoking a cigarette while waiting for her ride from the new guy. She asked me to sit with her. That's when she broke the news that she was pregnant. "I was going to have an abortion, but my mom said, 'what if you can't ever have another one?' I've been thinking about her words a lot, which is why I decided to keep it."

"Aren't you scared?" I asked. I didn't know what else to say.

"Yeah, of course, but when I told Gil he said that he would help me out."

"You mean the guy you were living with right after high school?"

She nodded, "Uh, huh, he wants to get married, but I can't stand him."

"Oh, um, well, you know… I'm glad he's going to be there for you."

"I know, and my mom will too, if I move back in with her," she said. "But if not, who knows, maybe she'll come around after she sees her grandchild?"

"So are you going to move back with her?" I asked.

"Nah, we'd just kill each other after a week."

"Well, I hope it works out with the musician, so you don't have to move back with your mom, and I hope she gets over it."

"I haven't told him yet, so ya never know."

We said our good-byes and I drove home, but couldn't get her situation out of my mind.

My week long vacation was cut short when Bullocks called the next morning and asked me to report to work that afternoon. I didn't care; I was thrilled and couldn't wait to start. Opening a new store was exciting. Most of the employees were new trainees just like me. We all wore jeans and tee shirts and worked in the basement marking room, where we received, checked in and priced new shipments for two weeks until there was enough inventory to stock every department in the store.

It was super easy to make friends, unlike the insurance company, and most of the employees were young adults just starting out. Ron Maris and I became buddies right away. He was a college student and worked part time during school breaks. His mom was a store executive, therefore, his job security was ensured.

Once the store opened, I became a floater for the first few months, which was a great way to figure out which departments I liked. Most new employees who hadn't been transferred from other stores moved around just like me.

The perfume bar in "Cosmetics" was fun, especially during the holidays. It was always busy and I earned a commission on top of my normal wages. What I didn't like, however, is when I had to sell products from the other cosmetic lines. Every time I approached one of the Revlon or Estee Lauder cases to look for an item, the assigned salesperson was ready to scratch my eyes out. They were territorial and greedy. They resented a newbie coming into their domain snooping around for a lipstick or a moisturizer to sell to one of "their" customers. Once Christmas was over, I couldn't wait to leave.

Probably the worst department was the maternity and ladies half-sizes—neither fat or pregnant—I knew nothing about either of them. That fact was proven when an undercover store shopper wrote me up because I didn't know anything about selling her a nursing bra; a low blow.

It was when I landed in the junior sportswear department that I knew where I wanted to be. I loved being surrounded by all of the latest hip styles and working with a bunch of young women my age. It felt like a sorority.

I worked forty hours a week and whatever schedule they gave me—days, nights, and Saturdays—with a different day off each week.

No more burning the candles at both ends; it was time to cut back on the Playgirl Club nightlife. If I was off or had the one p.m. late shift the next day, I'd pop in on a weeknight. Saturday nights were reserved for Alex, unless we went there together.

The long drive back and forth to work between Huntington Beach and La Habra was getting old, so I decided to move after three months—much to Betty's disappointment. She tried unsuccessfully to talk me out of it, which ultimately became the cause of our estrangement.

It was Alex who helped make it possible both financially and physically for me to move back to the same apartment complex in Whittier. He chipped in to help me with the deposit and he borrowed a truck to move my stuff.

Alex was glad to have me close by again but after a month I was feeling suffocated by him. We had been together for a year when things started to deteriorate between us. The fact that he was becoming so possessive began to take the wind out of our relationship. He had to know where I was and what I was doing whenever I wasn't with him. Even though I had strong feelings for him, in the end I thought it was for the best to break it off. He didn't.

As for Candy, she continued to be a regular at the club. Neither the pregnancy or giving birth slowed her down. She was tall and hardly showed even at eight months and about a week after her daughter was born, she was back on the dance floor. Now, no longer feeling like she was a threat, I made the mistake of telling her that I moved back.

What I didn't expect though, was to become a babysitter. Candy got wind of the breakup and thought since I was home alone, why not drop the kid off on the way to the club. She had given birth in Hollywood, where she was still living with the musician and now she was ready to party.

Pushing past me as soon as I opened the door, Candy set the basket containing the baby on the sofa and began her pitch. "C'mon Stef, please can you babysit," she pleaded. "She's sound asleep, you won't even know she's here."

"Candy, I have to get up early for work, and I don't know anything about babies, what if she wakes up?" I reasoned.

Candy refusing to back down, "She's not gonna wake up, what's the big deal? You'll be asleep."

"But what if she does wake up?" I repeated. "Why can't your mom babysit?"

"She's out of town and don't worry, the baby never wakes up."

She pointed to the pile of gear that was now sitting on the floor, "There's a bottle in her bag. All you gotta do is heat it up and give it to her," she explained. "C'mon, I've been cooped up, I really need a night out, and Chris is performing tonight."

The baby seemed harmless, sound asleep in her portable bed, so I gave in. "Fine, but you better be back by midnight."

"Thank you, thank you, thank you, you're a doll," she cooed.

Candy was now primping in front of the bathroom mirror, making some last minute touch-ups of more black mascara and hair spray before she went out. "Stop going all agro about it," she reiterated. "You'll never know she's here."

She was mostly right, but after a half dozen times of accommodating Candy and the sleeping baby, the spell finally broke and the kid started wailing and wouldn't stop. The bottle didn't work, nor the diaper change and back patting made no difference. Knowing it would be a lost cause to phone the club, with a 50-50 chance of them answering their phone and 100 per cent guarantee that they for sure wouldn't stop pouring drinks to go find a customer, I got dressed. I put the screaming baby on the seat next to me in the car and drove uptown to the Playgirl Club. Once parked, I scooped her up and when I got to the door, I asked the bouncer to get Candy.

When Candy arrived at the door she was fit to be tied. "What the fuck are you doing here?" she screamed.

I handed her the baby. "Don't ever drop her off again," I said. "I can't do this."

Patting the baby on her back and rocking her sideways, she demanded information. "What happened, did you try to give her the bottle?"

Unloading my car, illegally parked in the red right in front of the building, I began piling all the baby paraphernalia on the sidewalk. "Of course I did and she won't take it," I snapped. "She just cries, and cries, and I don't know what to do."

"Did you try rocking her, you have a rocker, ya know."

"I tried everything; rocked her, walked her, talked to her, sang…"

"You're incompetent, that's all!" she shrieked. "She's never done this before, she's a good baby."

The baby continued to wail, now getting the attention of the bouncer and two men that entered the bar.

Candy walked toward my car, screaming at me over the baby's cries. "You can't even take care of a two month old baby." Turning her attention to the baby, she took another swipe, "Aunt Steffie is an idiot, huh Doreen."

"All the more reason, not have me babysit, Candy," I asserted. I got back in the car and drove away without looking back.

CHAPTER 34

THE MANAGER

I missed being close to Alex and was sad that things hadn't worked out between us. Being friends seemed like a good alternative but I was wrong. After we broke up, he continued to visit me with the pretext of wanting to talk about 'us'. It was just too familiar, too comfortable to slip back into the way things were. I knew that if the friendship continued, we would end up back together.

It was hard, but I knew that I would have to force myself to disentangle those feelings in order to stay strong. One night when he stopped by my apartment, he greeted me with the usual hug. This time, though I held my ground. "I'm sorry, it has to be this way, but I don't think we should see each other anymore… even as friends."

He instantly removed his hands from my shoulders and raised them in a 'hold up' position. Now he was in a snit. "Fine, if that's the way you want it, I'm gone!" He opened the door and closed it a little too loudly.

The growing interest in my job at Bullocks took my mind off Alex. It also helped that he had gotten the message and hadn't been back.

My department had been a training ground for managers who wanted to get promoted to a buying job. I had been there almost two years and worked under five different managers, now I was ready to move up. I was an assistant by now and wanted to become a department manager rather than be transferred to a buying position somewhere else. An executive training course within the company was required for anyone to be considered for a management position.

The school was part of the corporation and run by each individual store. It also included frequent field trips to the headquarters in the downtown Los Angeles store.

There were just ten of us out of 20 or so applications chosen to attend the classes, which occurred one day a week during our normal work schedule. We sat at desks in the designated room that mimicked a classroom setting in the executive office section of the basement. It was just like school; we had study manuals, lectures, homework and tests all about the Bullocks standards and business of retail. The technical section contained a lot of math about profit and loss and gross merchandise margin, which caused me to seek out a study buddy. Bob was not only a math whiz but he had a knack for explaining the concepts so that I could grasp the principles.

In twelve weeks, all ten of us graduated and became official managers. No more punching a time clock for an hourly wage. As salaried employees the company could work us longer than 40 hours a week without paying overtime. To compensate for the longer hours we received hefty discount perks. My salary went up and now I was running one of the largest volume departments in the store, Collegian Sportswear. It was a dream come true to be a manager by 21 years old.

The hours were long and the pay was still low by most standards—after all, it was retail—but I loved every minute of it. The girls I worked with became my best friends. Darla and Judy were married so our social time was pretty much going to lunch or dinner during our shift breaks. Donna, Marie and Rhonda were the ones that I spent time with outside of work.

I didn't have much money leftover to spend on entertainment, so if we went to a bar, we shared a pitcher of beer. At the Playgirl club, however, we never paid for drinks, a good reason to go there. Men were always approaching us to dance and buy us drinks; some were regulars that I had become acquainted with since I started going there. The place was becoming a popular entertainment spot rather than just a dive bar. The owners were booking headliners such as Ike and Tina Turner. To see them up close in such a small venue was a thrill. The place was jammed and yes, Candy was there too. She had her friends and I had mine, but we were cordial to each other.

The Playgirl club was a good place to meet up with friends and catch one of the shows, but other than that it had lost its appeal for me. It sure wasn't a good place to find a mate. Most of the guys that hung out there got stupid when they drank and were mainly interested in one night stands. I reversed course and decided my job was much more interesting than wasting my time in bars. My social life would take a backseat, which was fine because I loved my job and couldn't wait to get there every morning.

Meanwhile, my mother had been nagging me to come for a visit. She was always sending me care packages filled with a bunch of weird stuff that she had made or grown in their garden; jams made from fruits I'd never heard of, home-made wine, banana bread. Inside the box was always a letter offering to pay for my flight, but I was too uncomfortable to go alone. I had never been away from my mother this long and although I wanted to see her. I just wasn't sure I was ready to recapture the heartache that went with the memories.

The thought of facing Joe again sent chills down my spine. I hadn't seen him in over three years, not since he'd ruined my wedding when he beat the shit out of Mom.

The letters were becoming more frequent. Mom had an agenda. She wrote them, but I could tell the effort was collaborative dangling concert tickets, ski lessons and excursions, as way to entice me to come. I couldn't be bought by anything they had to offer.

One Sunday after dinner at Grandma's house, I discussed the dilemma with my aunt and grandma. Isabel and Grandma had strong opinions about taking anything from Joe. They were equally concerned for my safety. "Stefanie, letting them pay for your flight so you can go for a visit is one thing, but taking Joe up on extravagances will only give him something to hold over you and brag about," Isabel reasoned.

"I know, you're right," I said.

"He's not doing it out of the goodness of his heart, he's just showing off."

I nodded in agreement. "I don't want to ever be obligated to them again. They'll just throw it up in my face later."

"I know how much you want to see your mom. Can you maybe take one of your friends and just go for a couple of days?" Isabel asked.

The wheels were turning in my head. I smiled widely at my aunt and grandma. "I know! How about I take Grandma and Grandpa, Joe likes them and they would be a perfect buffer." They loved the idea.

Grandma and Grandpa were excited to be taking a trip on an airplane. Their first ever. They usually took road trips back and forth to Arizona or San Diego, so this was a big deal. "Are you nervous to fly," I asked Grandma in the car on the way to the airport.

She chuckled. "Oh no, I'm more excited to be going to the Northwest, where all you see is green for miles. And I'm so glad to get away from staring at those four walls all day."

We both laughed. I was actually the one who was a little nervous only having flown once before with my dad on a short flight to San Diego.

Mom picked us up at the airport in the now battered Buick Riviera. The car wasn't that old, maybe less than seven years, but looked more like seventy by the look of the rusted chrome trim and cracked leather upholstery, not to mention the stained and cigarette burned headliner fabric and carpeting. I could see how the outside elements had gotten to the exterior, but the inside deterioration was pure neglect.

Mom also looked a lot different. She had gotten kind of heavy and her hair was another story. The color was yellowish-orange and the style was the windblown look or more like an eggbeater had gotten to it. She wore a loose fitting shirt with rolled up sleeves and faded dungarees.

In spite of the first impression jolt, I was happy to see her. She was ecstatic and couldn't stop smiling. Her Benson and Hedges sat on the console and as soon as we got in the car, she lit up and then she offered me one. I must have mentioned during a phone call, that I now smoked along with all of my friends. Anyway, I declined, it felt weird for her to see me smoking.

It took about forty-five minutes to get to the small town of Sumner and another ten minutes to their ramshackle house that sat at the end of a gravel driveway. I didn't see any other houses nearby, although there could have been some behind all the overgrown vegetation that surrounded the property—it was impossible to know.

The outside of the dwelling was flecked with peeling yellowish paint and once we got out of the car the whiff was unmistakable and got us before we saw them. It was evident they had acquired a slew of barnyard animals, a couple of cows, a few goats and too many chickens to count. But it was the six or more cats that threw me for a loop, an animal that Joe had clearly disdained in the past. Now here they were?

There were numerous fruit and vegetable orchards, with ripened peaches and tomatoes that had fallen from the vines and trees and were now scattered all over the dirt yard amongst the animal droppings. Mom pointed out the berry vines where their homemade wine had come from. They had become farmers of sorts, living off the land. Mom got into canning her own fruits and vegetables, baking fruit pies, making jams, preserves and pickles. Now I could identify the source of the care packages.

The inside was just as dilapidated as the outside, except the dim lighting and Mom's artwork helped conceal the flaws. The house had a stench of cigarette smoke and cat litter combined with traces of mustiness. It felt claustrophobic; small separate rooms, few windows, precarious, timeworn stairs that seemed like an e-ticket ride to the second story.

My grandparents slept in Mom and Joe's room, and they slept on the couch and recliner downstairs. I had to share a bed with Sheila, who now at fourteen was pretty big for her age. All that cold and rainy weather probably stimulated her appetite. She had a bad case of acne and was self-conscious and somewhat shy unlike her father. She was happy to have her older half-sister back and sharing her room, even if for a few days. "I wish you could stay here forever," she professed.

"I know you do, but I have a job, and I like living in California," I explained.

"Well, you can get a job here, there is a nifty store called, Nordstrom."

"Yes, I heard. Can't wait to see it tomorrow, but it still rains too much here," I emphasized. "I wouldn't like that. I'd rather have it be sunny." Of course, I wasn't about to tell her the real reason was that I wouldn't be caught dead ever living under the same roof as her father!

That night when Joe came home from work, he was his usual gregarious self, acting like the past had never happened. After hugging all of us, he focused on my grandparents, which had been my plan all along. He was on his best behavior. The less interaction he had with me the better.

The next day Mom took us sightseeing in Seattle. We visited the Pioneer Square, the Space Needle, Seattle Center and the famous Seattle based department stores. The shopping was the best, everything bunched together within walking distance. The boutiques were cute but the Bon Marche and Nordstrom were the highlight of my trip. Both built in the early 1900's, the time-honored, elegant architectural masterpieces were massive, covering an entire city block with eight or more floors. It felt like I stepped back in time. What a treat!

The next day was less than thrilling, having to spend the entire day with Joe playing tour guide. He took us to a horse-breeding farm. He was now involved in horse breeding and local horse racing with some of his pals. It was pretty boring walking around looking at a bunch of horses except when we all got an eyeful seeing two gigantic horses mating. Grandma was so embarrassed she covered her eyes and turned away giggling like a schoolgirl.

By the end of the three days I was ready to leave. There were no incidents to speak of, other than picking up on some of Joe's put-down remarks to Mom. A reminder of the past, I could feel myself cringe and my jaw tighten the minute he opened his mouth to criticize, like when he scolded Mom about the cats crawling across the kitchen counter while we were eating breakfast. It was gross for sure, but his belittling tone peppered with profanity made it distressing.

"God damn, Marjorie Ann, will ya get them fuckin' cats outta here!" Mom instantly picked them up and put them outside, like an obedient child. I'm sure it wasn't the first time the cats made themselves at home in the kitchen, but typical Joe, putting on airs acting all irritated like it was a new thing.

Overall, the trip had ended up being reasonably pleasant. Mom seemed content and when I asked her about the hitting, she said Joe was a changed man and no longer hit her. Did I believe her? Not completely.

It was hard to say goodbye to my mother. I loved her and missed her, but the conditions in which she lived were stifling and now I had a choice. Never would I allow myself to be under his thumb again. I would rather live in my car.

CHAPTER 35

THE CAR

The Collegian junior sportswear department was always busy, considering it was one of the top grossing departments in the store.

For that reason my job kept me on my toes, every day was different and filled with new challenges, which I liked. The more responsibility the better.

The floor space alone was a challenge. The department was enormous. It was wallpapered with black and white polka dot walls and red carpeting that covered the greater part of the second floor where the bank of elevators opened onto an array of contemporary junior fashions.

The wide range of clothing included all of the latest in pants, shorts, skirts, tops, sweaters, and jewelry expertly displayed to attract female customers.

Merchandising the floor was my thing. Re-arranging the clothes that filled the rods and racks by order of color provided me an opportunity to exercise my artistic creativity. And once the arranging was done I enjoyed pulling it altogether by creating displays with coordinated top to bottom fully accessorized outfits. Accelerated by the shear volume, it was an ongoing process, keeping the department fresh and replacing sold goods. I would no longer put the finishing touches on a display when a customer would come along and rip it apart. But that was the point after all!

The Bullock's philosophy was sell, sell, sell and managers weren't exempt. Spending time on the selling floor wasn't measured in hours but in dollars. So as long as I showed some sort of sales activity on the weekly reports they left me alone. I wasn't a natural born salesman. I much preferred spending time behind the scenes merchandising and doing paperwork. Selling was a skill that I had to psych myself up for. It was an effort each and every time I approached a customer. Taking the initiative to walk up to strangers and talk to them was uncomfortable for me. Each time I approached someone I could feel my mouth go dry, my face grow warm and my armpits begin to drip. Knowing the merchandise helped lower the anxiety. Even though the very nature of the job, with the constant public exposure opportunity was a plus, it remained a struggle. I simply had no self-confidence.

Part of the increased responsibility that came along with the manager job was supervising a staff of six or more employees. The administrative role changes the dynamic from peer to boss, another thing I found hard to get used to.

The employee evaluations were a killer, sitting across from someone and critiquing their performance was awkward enough, but when the employee was much older and I had to point out mistakes.

"Bonnie, I'm sorry but your raise will only be 10 cents this time because your sales aren't high enough." Fortunately those types of uncomfortable scenarios only occurred twice a year and the camaraderie more than made up for it.

The very best part of my job was the clothes, though. I did love wearing the hip clothes and being a part of the junior apparel fashion movement. So much so that every bit of my paycheck after rent and gas went into buying clothes. I couldn't help it, it was addicting. My justification: How can I sell the clothes if I'm not wearing them? I needed to look good as the manager, didn't I? As for food, I was especially frugal, existing on peanut butter and jelly or tuna sandwiches. Thanks to Mom, I saved money by spreading her homemade preserves on my peanut butter. Eating dinner at Grandma's or Isabel's house broke the monotony of my otherwise predictable diet.

One night while I was enjoying one of those weekly home cooked meals at my grandparents' house the conversation turned to cars. They thought the bug was unsafe and I was getting a little tired of manually shifting gears, along with the mounting repairs that came with owning an older car. Plus, I wanted to buy my first car instead of driving the hand me down that Rocky transferred to me. The scrimping and saving on food and entertainment had paid off, so I knew that I could do it for a car. The clothes buying addiction was another story.

Now that I had a trade-in to cover most of my down payment, all I'd have to worry about was a car payment. I could surely sock away enough money each month to handle that.

My grandpa suggested that we take a drive over the hill to the city of Covina and see what the Chevrolet dealership— where he used to work—had to offer. Grandpa had been an auto body painter for Hartman Chevrolet for over 20 years, as well as a loyal customer. He was proud of his 1964 Biscayne and the dealership's stellar customer service that they gave him along with the good deal. He hadn't worked there in five years, but wanted to give them the business just the same and hopefully request a discount for his granddaughter. It was worth checking out.

We planned our trip for the following week on one of our dinner nights. It was my day off, so we ate earlier, closer to 4:30, leaving plenty of daylight so grandpa wouldn't have to drive home in the dark. It was summer and didn't get dark until after eight so we had plenty of time. As I was helping Grandma with the dishes, I heard Grandpa call a guy named Timmy to confirm that he would be there to show his granddaughter some cars.

We all piled into Grandpa's Biscayne and off we went. On the way over, I learned that Timmy was actually the owner's son. Grandpa was vague about providing details about who was who and what kind of deal to expect. I guess I would have to keep my eyes and ears open.

Grandpa found Grandma and me admiring the new Camaros on the showroom floor just before he ushered us down the hall to one of the offices. I followed my grandparents into the cramped space where I stopped dead in my tracks at the sight of a cute guy sitting behind the desk. I'm not sure what I expected, maybe the stereotype greasy used car salesman with a shiny suit and a comb-over? But certainly not wavy blond hair, sparkling blue eyes and dimples. This was Timmy? Wow! You could almost see the sparks flying both ways! His face lit up about the same time that he sprang to his feet, practically diving over his desk to shake my hand. I was dressed casually in white Jamaica length shorts and an untucked fitted sleeveless blue and white printed top. He was wearing a short sleeve white dress shirt with a navy and red diagonal stripe necktie and gray gabardine suit pants.

The four of us squeezed into the tiny office and got down to the business at hand. Now sitting directly across from him on one of the two metal chairs facing his desk, his eyes never left me as I answered the typical car questions he ticked off.

I kept thinking, why hadn't my grandparents told me about him before? He was single, no wedding ring, good looking, had a job, and within my decade, yet no matchmaking on behalf of my grandparents! Any indication of a fix up was clearly not in their radar.

Grandpa, who was pressed against the back wall continued to call him Timmy, as if he were still a child, but I noticed that "Timmy" introduced himself as Tim.

The initial pleasantries now out of the way, 'Tim' didn't waste any time going into his car salesmen routine. "What kind of car are you looking to buy?" Notice, he said 'buy' not 'see'.

"Do you have a car to trade-in?" And then the zinger, "So, tell me, Stefanie, how much of a monthly payment can you afford?"

Without a beat, I proclaimed, "I want a Camaro, yes, I have a 1965 VW bug, and I can afford exactly $80.00 a month." I noticed a twitch coming from the corner of his mouth as soon as I relayed my monthly car payment budget. In fact he looked like he could barely keep a straight face. I didn't understand what was so funny at the time. But Uncle Antonio later explained, after I told him about the car the next day.

"You see, car salesmen love it when a payment buyer shows up. They don't have to negotiate the sticker figure and can keep the price high and the payment low, but what they don't tell you is that the finance term, with interest, will go on for a very long time."

Eventually we all went for a test drive in a lime green Camaro and after that Tim checked out my VW. He suggested that I would get more money if I tried to sell my car myself, rather than trade it in. I said that I would be back once I sold my car.

He was leaving for Hawaii in a few days and said for me to leave my number and if a customer came into the used car department of the dealership looking for a VW, he would send them my way. I gave him my work number because I no longer had a home phone. Disconnecting my phone had been part of my money saving plan. The funny thing about it was, when they did cut off service, it was incomplete, leaving me with the ability to dial out, but no one could call in. I never reported it, because I liked having the security of knowing that I had a way to call for help in an emergency.

On the way home Grandma was the first to speak, "Eddie, did you see the way that young man looked at Steffie? I thought his eyes were going to pop out of his head when she came into the room."

"Uh, no. I never noticed."

She gave a gentle whack on the back of his head. "That's because you're a rattlebrain, man."

I was laughing, but I had to agree with Grandma, Tim did do a double take when he saw me. I don't know what he expected when Grandpa said he was bringing his granddaughter? Just like me, he may have had a preconceived notion? I have to admit, I was somewhat interested too, but Tim seemed like a bit of an operator and much too slick for me. He was older and seemed more worldly, which I found intimidating. I'm sure his little black book was filled with plenty of phone numbers. I put him out of my mind.

CHAPTER 36

THE STEAK

About a month later when I picked up the phone at work Tim was on the on the other end. "Hi Stefanie, this is Tim Hartman from Hartman Chevrolet. I have a buyer for your car," he announced. "You still have it, right?"

I was completely caught off guard. "Oh hi, um, wow, that's great. Yeah, I actually haven't done anything about it since I was at your dealership," I explained.

He got right to the point. "A father and son came into the dealership looking for a used car for the son, but there was nothing that fit his budget, so I thought of your Volkswagen bug."

"I've never tried to sell a car before and I don't know how much to ask?"

Tim came to the rescue. "That's OK, let me handle it," he declared. "Here, I'll look it up in the blue book, hold on a second."

"Uh OK," I said. I pulled the pencil from behind my ear and started doodling while I waited for him to return. What was going on? This guy sure seems anxious to sell me a car, even coming up with a buyer for my old one.

He was back on the line in a minute and then he suggested that I ask $900.00 for my car. "Listen, Stefanie, I've already accounted for the scratches and dents, so I wouldn't go too much lower if they try to hammer you on the price."

"Are you going to tell them the price before they look at it?"

"Yeah, yeah, of course, but they may still try to talk you down, so don't go lower than $875.00, OK?"

"OK, I'll try."

"I'll send them right over, and if they buy it you owe me a steak dinner," Tim said with a chuckle.

Giggling, I said, "Oh, OK, tell them to meet me in the Bullocks parking lot in an hour. And thank you."

The dad and son showed up and bought the bug on the spot, for $900.00, but that meant that they also drove it away. I called Tim when I got back to my office. "Well I guess I owe you a steak dinner."

"What time do you get off work, and I'll give you a ride home," he responded.

It was all so sudden. I drove myself to work with every intention of driving myself home and now my car was gone and I really did have to buy a new one. After I stopped to catch my breath, I replayed the sequence of events in my head. As I mindlessly attached price tags with the tagging gun to some blouses, I concluded that the strategy was pretty clever: sell my old car so you can sell me a new one and oh yeah, get a date out of it!

When I walked out at 6p.m., Tim was parked in front of the employee entrance driving a brand new shiny black Malibu. Trying to contain the heart palpitations, I put on a perky smile and gave a casual wave as I slid into the passenger seat. He was grinning from ear to ear. "Are you hungry?"

I fidgeted with my skirt, smoothing imaginary wrinkles with the palms of my hands as I got comfortable in the passenger seat. "Sure, I guess."

"I thought we could grab dinner, but first I want to go home and change my clothes."

"OK, sounds good. Where is home?" I inquired.

"Belmont Shore," he answered nonchalantly.

"Like in Long Beach? Isn't that kind of a far drive to work?"

"Not for me, I like to drive and I'd rather live by the beach than Covina, know what I mean?"

"Yeah, I grew up at the beach."

"You did? What the hell are you doing living in Whittier then?"

"My grandparents and my aunt and uncle are here," I explained, leaving out the Rocky part. "I also lived with my aunt and uncle before I got my own place, right after my mother moved to another state. I decided to stay and wanted to be near my family and since they all live in Whittier, here I am. Besides I like living near my work. I'm not crazy about long distance commuting."

"Which beach are you from?"

"Huntington Beach."

"Bitchin', so you must have gone to high school with all of the famous surfers?"

"I sure did, did you ever surf?"

"A little bit in high school, but now I like to water ski. I have a boat and we ski in the marina near my house and also at the river, whenever I can get away during a weekend."

"Oh wow you have a boat? I water-skied at Lake Elsinore once and also in the Newport Beach back bay."

"Lake Elsinore is a mud hole," he proclaimed. Hmm, I guess he's an authority."

"I didn't notice. It was pretty fun, though," I replied.

"The best water skiing is at the river, just like glass and the water's warm and clean."

"Sounds like you're a good skier."

He shrugged, "Yeah, well, I've been at it a while." No

modesty there. I'm surprised he wasn't blowing on his fingertips before brushing them across his chest.

We were talking so much, the forty-five minute drive seemed more like ten minutes.

The two-story contemporary house in Belmont Shore that he shared with two other guys, was a block from the beach. It was a typical bachelor pad, the black leather sofa, the matching veneer end tables and glass topped coffee table stacked with Playboy magazines.

No one was home when we got there and I waited in the living room while Tim quickly changed into a tee shirt and navy and white striped bell bottoms. Instead of going out for a steak dinner, he wanted to barbecue, which was fine with me. We got back in the car and drove to a neighborhood market a few blocks away where they had a butcher shop. Tim selected two large Porterhouse steaks along with some potatoes and a head of lettuce, and when I reached for my wallet and offered to pay, he wouldn't hear of it. "I thought I was the one who owed the steak dinner"? I asked.

He chuckled. "That was just my way of getting you to go out with me."

I turned red and looked down shifting my weight from foot to foot as we stood in the checkout line.

We made the dinner together in the small kitchen and since steak was not in my budget, I devoured every morsel along with the baked potato and salad. My hearty appetite didn't go unnoticed by Tim who commented a couple of times that I must have been hungry.

We drank scotch and water and talked for hours. There was nothing romantic about the evening since all we did was talk from opposite ends of the sofa.

We shared bits and pieces about ourselves. Not true. I'm

the one who shared the bits and pieces and he's the one who shared larger portions about himself. I was right, he was older by six years, divulging that he was 27. Before we knew it, it was one o'clock in the morning. Tim yawned. "Listen Stefanie, it's pretty late, and I've had too much to drink and I don't think I'm in any condition to drive."

"I know, I didn't realize it had gotten so late."

"Would you mind staying over? You can have my room and I'll take the sofa, perfectly respectable."

What could I say, it was late and we had been drinking a lot of alcohol.

Clearing my throat, I replied, "I just need to be at work by ten tomorrow."

"That's fine, I have to go in too."

He gave me an extra toothbrush and one of his tee shirts to sleep in and then he sort of tucked me in with a quick 'good-night' peck on the lips.

CHAPTER 37

HUGGER ORANGE

The next morning Tim drove me home as promised and waited while I got ready so he could drop me off by ten. It felt weird not having a car, but I kinda liked being chauffeured around by a cute guy.

This time the offer to again pick me up after work included a movie, "Catch 22." I accepted and when he took me home and said good night, he gave me a real kiss.

The next day was Sunday and my day off. Tim arrived at my apartment around two in the afternoon to take me to the dealership so that I could buy my new car. Once we settled into his office, he switched into salesmen mode and was all business. As he was writing up the transaction, he rattled off so many figures my head was swimming. On top of the sales price were tax, registration and then the financing terms—I had no idea what all those fees meant, let alone what I was paying for the car. All I knew was that my payment would be $80.00 a month, probably forever. The car that I wanted would have to be traded from another dealership. Although they had an orange one similar to the one that I wanted, it was loaded with a performance package of optional equipment, including air-conditioning, which were extras that I didn't need and were beyond my budget. Tim was kind enough to loan me his Malibu until Monday when my car would be delivered. He said, not to worry about him finding a way home, he'd just grab one of demos off the lot.

Tim had the "Hugger Orange" Rally Sport Camaro detailed and filled with gas by the time I arrived at 6:30 Monday night. I was about to take possession of my first new car that I bought with my own hard earned money. It was sleek and sporty and best of all it had an automatic transmission—no more shifting—black vinyl bucket seats and a simulated wood console. It was beautiful. And that new car smell was like no other. I was so excited I couldn't wait to show it off to my friends at work. Tim was almost as happy as I was, beaming ear to ear when he opened the door for me and handed me the keys.

He called the next day to see how I liked my car and then asked me out. "Hi Stefanie, how's the orange bomb so far?"

Giggling at his intro I said, "It's perfect, I love it. Oh my gosh it has so much more power compared to the VW, I barely tap the gas and it takes off."

"That's because it's a Chevy and it doesn't hurt that it has a V-8 engine," Tim responded. "What are you doing Saturday night?"

"Um, nothing, why?"

"You want to go to Disneyland," he asked. "I haven't been in ages?"

"OK, sure. I haven't either, not since my high school graduation all-night party three years ago."

"Well, it's been a little longer for me both graduating and going to the magic kingdom," he said with a chuckle.

Once we had walked from one imaginary land to another, gone on a few rides like the Matterhorn bobsleds and Pirates of the Caribbean, we both decided that we had pretty much outgrown the happiest place on earth.

Tim called me everyday now, and we saw each other at least twice a week. We went bowling, miniature golfing, attended the play "Hair," took in a lot of movies, sometimes his choice, sometimes mine. I liked that. Same with eating out, it was a toss up between going to casual places like El Cholo and Bob's Big Boy, and swanky ones like Reuben's and Dal Rae. When we stayed in and watched TV, we ordered pizza.

My relationship with Tim felt solid and free of drama. He was spending several nights a week at my place and whenever we both had a weekend off we towed his boat out to the Colorado River to go water skiing. We would meet up with some of his friends in Parker Arizona or Lake Havasu, where we all booked a block of rooms at a local motel.

Most of his ski friends were married couples that he had grown up with, except for one guy, who was indeed married but to someone other than the girlfriend he brought to the river. B.J. was an occasional fixture at the river because of his friendship with Tim through the car business. The guy was a wheeler dealer, claiming to have a big used car wholesale business and bragging about all the money he made. Everyone knew the scoop about him two-timing his wife, but seemed to go along with it. I thought he was an arrogant creep from the minute I met him.

Everyone else was at least five or more years older than I was, some even had kids. They were nice enough and OK to be around in small doses. Other than the mutual affection for skiing, we didn't have much in common. It was more of a group date, with beer drinking and joke telling, rather than one on one conversations. The cheater and his mistress were both twice as old as I was and I could have done without either of them. She was tall and statuesque and he was short and portly. She was Caucasian; he was Asian. She had long blond hair and wore elegant jewelry and stylish sportswear that showed off her figure. He, on the other hand, was going bald, out of shape, owned a big boat and had a gutter mouth. He had no filter when it came to communicating, tits, pussy, cock, were his go to vocabulary choices. He was simply a dirty old man, nasty and vulgar. He laughed the loudest at himself, the men snickered and the women were embarrassed. Fortunately he and his concubine weren't one of the regulars.

Towing Tim's fifteen foot speed boat behind the car for the five hour drive on Friday nights, provided us some quality get-acquainted time. He brought the Coors beer and I brought chocolate-chip cookies that I made from scratch. An unlikely combination, but the cookies and beer actually tasted great together. As for the made from scratch cookies, I can thank my neighbor Claire, who happened to be a gourmet cook and accomplished baker, for turning her chocolate chip cookie specialty into mine. She was always dropping off her baked treats for me to sample, and one day I mentioned that I wished that I could make something for Tim that tasted that good. She suggested that I start with the chocolate chip cookie recipe and that she would help me. Claire and I spent hours over the next couple of weeks, baking batch after batch until I got it right. She was meticulous about measuring and mixing and emphatic about using only the highest quality ingredients.

"I insist on using only real butter, like Challenge—never margarine—and not straight out of the fridge; it must be softened at room temperature in order to blend properly.

"What's the difference?" I asked.

"Trust me it's major; real butter tastes better and enhances the flavor, and not only that, margarine has hydrogen added so it's like eating plastic. That's the secret to why my cookies are so good, I use the real thing."

The cookies were consistent in their shape, not too thick, not too thin, and with just the right amount of crispness on the outside and chewiness on the inside. Each one was a masterpiece. No wonder Tim was dazzled, going on and on that they were the best chocolate chip cookies he'd ever tasted.

I willingly accepted the compliments even on those early occasions when I'd passed off Claire's as mine until I got the hang of it.

No one had ever taught me how to cook before. What I learned about cooking growing up, I picked up from the one and only cook book that was in the house: Watkins. My mother didn't own measuring cups or measuring spoons because she never measured anything. When she wasn't using her fingers to add a little of this and a pinch of that, she would grab a coffee cup or silverware spoon as a measuring device. Cakes were made from a box mix, cookies were from a slice and bake pre-made roll of dough.

It was true Tim was impressed with my cookie baking ability, but Claire said that I needed to learn how to make more than one thing if I was serious about learning to cook now that I had someone who appreciated it. She suggested that I invite Tim over for a home cooked meal. I was game, as long as it was going to be a simple dish and as long as she would be there guiding me. But her idea of a home cooked meal was stuffed pork chops. Heck I didn't even know how to make an unstuffed pork chop? She said not to worry she would help me from start to finish. I shopped for the list of ingredients she provided, including four expensive thick chops with pockets in them.

I was all set for our Saturday afternoon cooking lesson when of all things, I ended up having to work until 6p.m. due to a power outage that occurred at work, forcing a time consuming manual switchover. Since Tim was coming over at 6:30, Claire ended up making the dinner and popping it into the oven. So much for my cooking lesson.

I had just removed the chops and rice dish from my oven when Tim arrived and announced a change of plans. "Hey, Stefanie, I have a little problem, I need to go back to my house and deliver a car to one of my neighbors. So maybe it would be easier if we just went out to dinner."

I couldn't believe it! After all the time, money and trouble spent orchestrating this? And poor Claire, she would have a conniption fit!

Hands on my hips and now tapping my foot. "What! Are you kidding me? Dinner is already made."

"Oh jeez, I'm sorry."

"It's just that, it's not something that should be saved."

Tim stood there massaging his chin thinking about what to do.

"I have an idea... how about we pack up the dinner and transport it to my house? It'll be OK in the car for 45 minutes, won't it?"

Trying not to panic I nodded. "Uh, sure, I guess."

We pulled out the breadboard and wrapped dishtowels around it and then placed it in the trunk of the car. Once we arranged the baking dish of hot food on top we added a roll of towels to form a wall of protection so it wouldn't slide. It made the trip just fine and I took the bow and praise that Tim heaped upon me for my cooking skills as if I had slaved over a hot stove all day.

CHAPTER 38

GETTING TO KNOW YOU

Those five hour car rides to and from the river lasted a couple of months until the season ended in November when the water turned cold. Since we were each other's captive audiences for all those hours, we got to know each other on a somewhat deeper level pretty quickly. Tim revealed what it was like growing up in a big Catholic family with three older sisters and a younger brother.

"The nuns were strict and unreasonable, but I gave them a run for their money," he chuckled. "Man, I was always getting slapped with that ruler for something."

"You mean the teachers, uh, nuns actually hit you?" I asked.

"Better believe it, those sisters are a mean bunch. You don't wanna mess with them."

"I never knew that, so what did you do to get slapped?"

Tim tapped a tune on the steering wheel as a warm-up to confessing his transgressions. "Well, where do I start… teasing girls, talking in class, skipping mass, sassing the nuns, ditching school, playing with matches… shall I go on?"

"Sounds like you were a handful with all those shenanigans," I said smiling.

"Yeah, I guess and when I was about nine, I burned down the garage."

"Oh my gosh, that's terrible. Were you a pyromaniac?"

Tim now busting with laughter. "What can I say? I was bored and matches were fun to play with."

"Scary."

"Yep, and here's the one I'm most proud of: When I was about eight I would sneak inside one of the cars on the dealership lot and take it for a joy ride around the dirt lot behind the service department until someone caught me."

I swiveled in my seat to face him. "C'mon, no way, you're making this up, how could you even reach the pedals, let alone see over the dashboard?"

"I couldn't see over the dashboard at all, so it looked like a runaway vehicle cruising around the several blocks of dirt on the back field of the property."

We both laughed hysterically picturing the scene in our heads.

When I asked if the rest of the kids were as adventurous, he professed to being the black sheep. "My sisters were little angels, followed the rules and attended mass. They were also big fat tattletales," he explained.

"They were always getting me into trouble, like when I was a teenager and I'd sneak out at night after my parents went to bed."

"I would have been locked up forever if I had tried something like that plus I would have been too scared anyway."

"Yeah, well my parents were older, in their 40's, when I was born and were clueless about raising a boy after all those girls. Besides, I think they were worn out by the time I came along."

"How about your little brother, was he as busy as you?"

"Not so much, he was a little tamer when he was younger, and once he became a teenager, nobody cared."

"Is that because all the kids moved out by then?"

"Yeah, pretty much, and my parents were ready for their rockers."

I just shook my head.

When the time came for me to talk about my upbringing, I knew it was going to sound more like "Dr. Terror's House Of Horrors" than his "Adventures Of Ozzie and Harriet."

Sure enough, the next words out of Tim's mouth were, "What was your childhood like?"

I wasn't sure how much detail I wanted to share, so I sort of eased into it beginning with the good stuff that the early years brought, living as an only child with my mom and grandparents.

"I would have loved being an only child and gotten all that attention," said Tim.

"That I did; everything was great until I turned seven years old." I said softly.

"Why what happened then?"

"Well to put into car-speak, my mother traded me in for a new model, a man, actually—who happened to be the devil. That's what happened."

"Oh man, that's a drag, a real jerk, huh?"

"You can say that again," was my retort and then I flashed on the mashed potato episode.

He waited for me to continue.

I took a deep breath and then said, "My mom's husband, Joe has a bad temper and basically takes it out on women and children."

"Like how do you mean, did he get physical or something?"

"Yes, for instance I got spanked for not eating my mashed potatoes right after they got married."

"Shit, that's kind of drastic isn't it? What'd your mom do when he hit you?"

"She asked him to stop, but not much else."

"Did he ever hit her too?"

"He didn't just hit her, he beat the shit out of her several times, and yes, she stayed with him."

"Jesus Christ."

Hearing my stories must have sounded like I was raised in a loony bin. There was nothing normal about it. I also divulged about my brief marriage at eighteen. The intensity of the domestic violence was a lot to digest within the matter of a few hours and could have sent him running. It didn't.

He was spellbound, mostly listening at first as if I was describing a movie. The more I opened up, the more disturbing the details and the more astonished he became. The two black eyes were what really stunned him.

"Stefanie, that is the most disgusting thing I've ever heard, how can a grown man beat up a little girl? Especially one that isn't even his, and worse, how could your mom allow it to happen? Jesus, no wonder you felt like she traded you in, because she did in a way. Shit, what a coward."

"Yeah, my grandpa said the same thing about Joe, since Mom and I got the brunt of his anger."

"A real gutless lunatic afraid to pick on someone his own size."

"Well, come to think of it, there were others. I did see him pop the teenage kid next door—who used to babysit for us—because I guess he made a remark about Mom."

"No kidding, and how big was the kid?"

"Tall and super skinny, about half Joe's weight, I suppose, probably why he went flying backwards over the shrubs between the houses?"

"What a messed up S.O.B. I don't blame you for running off and getting married right outta high school," Tim said.

Tim reached over and laid his hand on my knee, giving it a squeeze in a comforting way. "Things are better now."

I gave him a smile and said, "I know."

There was no way he could ever understand what it was like growing up under that reign of terror in a house full of evil and violence. From his portrayal of his home life it contained a good deal of controlled chaos and some degree of ugliness probably lurked behind the scenes, but nothing as conspicuous as what I described.

Now, after two months of being together, I was about to meet Tim's family. The topic of holiday customs had come up in conversations and since I wasn't bound to strict family obligations of my own, he invited me to spend Thanksgiving with him and his family. I accepted the invitation with both enthusiasm and trepidation. Tim was used to them, but I wasn't and he did his best to prepare me on the drive over.

The dinner was being held at his sister Patty's house. She lived in Pasadena not far from his parents. His first characterization was to the point, "Patty is a bitch."

Pause.

I whipped my head in his direction. "What an awful thing to say about your sister."

"Oh she'll be nice to you, don't worry about that," he mollified. "She's bossy, and sticks her nose in the family business, trying to run the dealership from her kitchen. My brother-in-law, Bud, her husband, refers to her as a bitch all the time."

"I can hardly wait, so who else do I need to watch out for?"

Chuckling, Tim continued. "You'll love my other sister, Mona, and her husband Verrill, he's a short little Greek with a big personality, super funny guy."

"OK, getting better, go on, how about your parents, anything else I need to know?" I inquired.

"My dad is the best, nicest man you'll ever wanna meet, and my mom makes the best stuffing in the world. My mother isn't the best cook, but she knows how to make two things really well, stuffing and banana nut bread. She is sweet, and all that but overly religious," he divulged. "She attends mass everyday—"

"What do you mean everyday?" I interrupted. "I thought church was only on Sunday?"

"Not for devout Catholics like her, six o'clock mass every morning," he explained. "She even has her own priest who visits the house and never misses a free meal."

"You're telling me she has a priest who makes house calls?"

Snickering. "Yeah, Father O'Hara, every Christmas… puts on the feed bag."

"Well, my dad and his family are all Catholics. My dad took it upon himself and went behind my mother's back to baptize me Catholic, when I was a baby, but I wasn't raised that way," I clarified. "My mom baptized me as a Methodist, and I always attended protestant churches, some of which were non-denominational."

"So, you're a double Christian, then!"

Shrugging.

"If it comes up just tell my mom you're Catholic."

CHAPTER 39

HOME FOR THE HOLIDAYS

With seven kids under the age of eight running amok and ten adults talking over each other, I was barely noticed. His mom, however, didn't waste any time inquiring if I was Catholic.

We had barely sat down on the sofa in the family room— where most of the adults were chatting when Tim's mother came over and shook my hand before she sat down beside me. Mrs. Hartman was a pixyish woman, small boned with dainty features. She wore her salt and pepper gray hair in a bun that was nesting in a backcombed bouffant. Her jewel necked, midi length floral printed dress that bore shoulder pads was belted at the waist and flattered her petite figure.

Her demeanor was sweet, and her voice squeaky. Clearing her throat she started, "…uh where are you from, dear?"

"Well, I grew up in Huntington Beach and now I live in Whittier."

"Uh huh, and do you work?"

"Yes, I'm a department manager at Bullocks Fashion Square in La Habra, have you been there?"

She hadn't and after the pleasantries were established, she dropped the bomb.

"That's nice, and are you Catholic?"

Before I could respond, Tim, said, "Yeah she is Mom, did you make your famous stuffing?"

"Oh yes, Timmy, I made it at home but Patty made the turkey, so it won't have the flavor of the juices, but it'll be fine just the same. I'll go see if Patty needs some help; we're about to eat."

Minutes later, doors could be heard opening and closing along with the pitter patter of little feet running through the house as everyone gathered around the dining room table and the kids' table.

He was right about the dressing, it was truly the best that I had ever had. But then again, my mom emptied a box of Mrs. Cubbison's seasoned breadcrumbs combined with some un-sieved turkey drippings and that was her version of turkey stuffing.

All things considered, I guess you could say I survived our first family get-together unscathed. Everyone was friendly, including his so-called, "bitch" of a sister, from whom I saw nothing of the sort.

Next on the list was Christmas. This time Tim accompanied me to my aunt and uncle's house on Christmas Eve, where he received a hero's welcome, especially from Grandma and Grandpa. They were thrilled. After all, they'd started the whole thing. If it hadn't been for them, I most likely wouldn't have met Tim. By the wide grin on his face, I could tell my grandpa was in heaven seeing the two of us together.

No pressure and no third degree at my family celebration. It was a relaxed and casual traditional holiday with lots of food and beverages and a load of gifts that cascaded across the living room floor far beyond where the tree sat. Everyone was given a gift to open at midnight. Tim was caught off guard and especially touched when my aunt handed him an unexpected gift. It was a bottle of "Brut" cologne, the official cologne of legions pitched by Joe Namath.

My family served tamales on plastic plates that had a pattern of stenciled red and green ornaments circling Santa. The dinner was buffet style and you sat wherever you wanted. Tim made a complete pig of himself scarfing down at least a half dozen of the homemade tamales. "This is the first time I've had homemade tamales, the only ones I've had before are in a restaurant, and I've never had beans this good," he raved. He couldn't stop himself from taking seconds and thirds, to my grandmother's delight.

Christmas Day was reserved for the Hartman family, only this time the holiday would be spent at the parent's house. They still lived in the Pasadena house that Tim had grown up in. It was an original 1930's two-story Spanish style stucco home with a tile roof. It sat far back from the street with a sweeping lawn. A cement driveway ran the entire length of the property leading to a single car garage in the back.

In addition to the same group from Thanksgiving, the parents, the siblings and a slew of nieces and nephews, there was now, an aunt and uncle and a set of in-laws and of course, the priest.

It was pandemonium when we arrived, with the kids running in and out of the house playing hide-and-go-seek, while the grown-ups were seated in the formal living room sipping stiff cocktails. Before we joined the adults, Tim took me on a brief tour of the back yard where the hiding kids had taken cover behind the enormous shade trees. I was admiring the perfectly manicured yard that stretched umpteen feet from the concrete patio all the way to the planter that rimmed the back fence. But then as I looked closer, I noticed some figures strategically positioned amongst the plants inside the flowerbed. Oh my gosh, I was standing in a holy sanctuary. Those figures were religious statues placed throughout the planter that bordered the property.

Tim had left me standing there with my mouth agape while he intercepted a flying ball and then tossed it back to one of the boys. When he returned, he took my hand and led me back into the house. I kept my opinions to myself.

Now back in the living room, Verrill, the Greek, was engaged in an animated discussion about college football, maybe UCLA and USC, anyway it was something I knew nothing about and something Tim didn't keep up with either.

As we sat and listened, I took in the surroundings and then leaned over and whispered to Tim. "Do your parents spend much time in here?"

"Rarely, this room never gets used except during Christmas and special occasions," he explained. "There's a family room in back that was added on, and that's where they watch TV and spend most of their time."

"I was wondering about that, everything looks so fragile," I commented.

"Another reason no one goes in here," snickered Tim.

The room opened through arched doorways and was traditionally furnished with maroon colored heavy velvet tie back drapes that framed the matching arched windows with wrought iron bars on them. The circa 1930 curio cabinets were full of pink Depression glass and porcelain figurines. Tim and I sat together on a vintage settee that was upholstered in a rose colored silk brocade. It wasn't very comfortable, in fact I think I maybe felt a spring poking me. The mahogany wood coffee table and end tables with carved legs had probably been elegant in their day, but were now in need of some refinishing to restore the rich grain of the wood. There was a cute little random needlepoint footstool with Queen Anne style legs that must have been a family heirloom. The rose bordered wool area rug covered most of the hardwood flooring, adding a touch of warmth to an otherwise somber room. It was an interesting old house that appeared to be frozen in time.

By five o'clock everyone was crammed close together, some straddling the legs in order to fit all thirteen of us around the formal dining room table that normally sat ten. With the candles, fine china, crystal, silver and linen napkins this holiday meal was far from casual.

On a silver platter in the center of the table sat an enormous Honey-Baked Ham. It was surrounded by an array of side dishes in china serving bowls that concealed most of the Irish lace table cloth. I did, however, eventually get to make myself useful by carrying in a bowl of marshmallow topped candied yams.

Seated next to Tim at the dinner table, I soon realized he wasn't kidding about his mother being a religious fanatic. Aside from the priest showing up for dinner and the hallowed garden, the dining room walls were papered with holiness. It was hard not to notice the variety of crucifixes (ivory, gold, wooden, large, small) and religious paintings that covered every square inch of the walls. Unlike the backyard that had fresh air and plants, this felt stifling.

The dinner was festive with the boisterous Greek brother-in-law overpowering the conversation with more sports. Tim made every effort to include me in the conversation, but since I had little to say about sports or politics I mostly listened, nodding and laughing whenever appropriate. To begin with, I was already shy in front of groups of people that I didn't know. I felt a lot of pressure walking into a big Catholic family gathering and being the only non-Catholic in the room. I didn't know the words to their grace that was spoken before we ate, nor did I participate in the crossing ritual or understand the holy references, making it obvious that I wasn't a practicing Catholic. Of course that was one of the first things his mother zeroed in on. As I was carrying Tim's and my empty plates into the kitchen, his mother inquired again about my religion. "Oh,… uh, Stef, I thought that you said you were Catholic? I noticed that you didn't say grace or cross yourself."

"Well, actually I was baptized Catholic, but my mother raised me protestant."

"Oh, dear, that's a shame," she said with a sigh.

"My parents divorced when I was a baby, and my dad baptized me Catholic, but I didn't live with him."

"Well, at least you were baptized a Catholic, that means you will always be one in the eyes of the church."

"Uh huh." I gave her a polite smile and busied myself rinsing the dishes as more family members entered the room toting empty plates and bowls.

After dinner cordials, consisting of *creme de menthe* and sherry, were served in the living room during the gift exchange. Tim and I had already opened the gifts we'd given each other the night before. He bought me a faux fur trimmed genuine leather coat that I had had on hold at work, no surprise, but something I wanted. My gift to him was a rather bold clothing statement that was currently in style. I gave him a combination mixed pattern ensemble of a multicolored striped dress shirt with a coordinating striped tie of the same colors. His wardrobe needed some excitement and a shot of color and mixed patterns was a good start. He said that he liked it and would wear it. I believed him.

I sat next to Tim and watched as he opened a half dozen gifts from his parents and siblings, consisting mostly of ties and socks along with a Christmas sweater. He was nearly finished when his mother approached me with a small foil wrapped flat box with a red stick on bow. "Here Stef, this is for you, so you don't feel left out."

With her standing there and waiting, I opened it. Inside was a wooden crucifix. Concealing my uneasiness with a stiff smile, I graciously accepted. "Oh, thank you Mrs. Hartman, um, this is very thoughtful of you."

"You're welcome and it's got a little adhesive sticker on the back, so you can hang it on the wall without a nail," she explained.

Tim rolled his eyes. "Thanks, Mom. I'm sure she'll figure it out."

On the way home, I informed Tim about the conversation in the kitchen between his mother and I. He explained that in his mother's world, once a Catholic, always a Catholic, so the fact that I wasn't practicing, fell on deaf ears. Yikes!

CHAPTER 40

KEEPING THE FAITH

Some time in January my neighbor and good friend, Claire invited me to be her roommate. She was moving to a newly built apartment complex about twelve miles to the east in Placentia, a city in north Orange County.

I liked what I saw after touring the complex. I thought it would be fun to be roommates and also easier on my pocketbook, so I said yes.

Since Claire and I barely saw each other we didn't have a chance to get in each other's hair. She was an elementary school teacher with a set schedule that had her out the door by seven and off on weekends. I on the other hand, working in retail, went to work later including some nights and Saturdays. It was a good fit, plus she was always leaving her gourmet leftovers in the fridge for me.

Tim and I went out more than we stayed in now. Even though I was paying half the rent, it was still someone else's furniture we were sitting on.

We had been dating about six months with talk of our future together coming up a lot in recent weeks. The proposal wasn't planned and there was no ring. It just kind of happened one night when we were saying goodnight at my door. Tim's face became serious as he place his hands on my shoulders. "Stefanie, it's a drag having to leave. I think it's time we get married.

My head titled slightly as I asked for clarification.

"Are you teasing me or do you mean it?"

"I love you Stefanie, and yes I mean it."

"I love you too, and yes, I will marry you."

I threw my arms around his neck and we kissed a long lingering kiss.

"Start making plans, I want a place of our own, enough of this bullshit going back and forth."

"I know. I don't like it either, so how big of a wedding ceremony are you thinking?"

"I don't care, whatever you want."

"Gosh, I don't know, I mean of course I'd like a real wedding with a wedding dress, but I don't think I should expect my dad to pay for it," I reasoned. "Even though the first one was more like a civil ceremony, he did foot the bill, and my mom is in no position to pay for it."

"Don't worry about the money, Stefanie, I'll take care of it."

"Are you sure? I feel bad, the bride's family is supposed to pay for the wedding."

Tim raised my head upward with his index finger under my chin so we were face to face. "There is no supposed to, OK? It's a done deal."

I nodded.

"One more thing before I leave, how about a ring? What kind do you want?"

"Oh gosh, I don't know, I haven't thought about it. I know, how about we go ring shopping at Bullocks so we can use my discount?"

"Okay, just tell me when and don't worry, it will all work out, OK? Good-night, I love you."

"I love you too, I'm so happy," I shouted as I blew him a kiss.

The next day, we paid a visit to the fine jewelry department at Bullocks, a place that I had only admired from afar over the past two years. "Tim, I'm overwhelmed," I said quietly as I tucked my arm through his. "There's so many. How will I ever be able to choose from such a huge selection of sparking diamonds?"

Tim looking serious with a slight frown, turned to face me. "Listen, Stefanie, I want you to be happy and get the ring that you want, don't settle for one that's just OK because the price is less, OK?"

He spared no expense, and in the end, I chose a flawless diamond that was encircled by smaller diamonds. Once it was on my finger, I couldn't take my eyes off of it. I had never seen anything so sparkly in my life. Tim and I settled on a June wedding that we would pay for ourselves. Not exactly 50/50, but just the same I contributed whenever I could. No one would be giving me away either, not my real dad and especially not Joe. The thought crossed my mind a few times about approaching my real dad to walk me down the aisle but, since I barely saw him and we weren't that close, it didn't feel authentic to me.

As for my mother and Joe paying for anything to do with my wedding, that was a joke. I saw the way they lived, barely having two nickels to rub together. Even if they had a windfall and offered, it would have opened the door for Joe to think that he was a part of the wedding. No, Tim and I would manage on our own. It was better this way.

We would not be explaining to his family that it was my second marriage, either. On our way over to announce our engagement to his family, Tim said that his mother wouldn't understand because as a devout Catholic she didn't condone divorce.

"Isn't that dishonest?" I asked.

Shrugging. "Nah, it's just not worth it to upset her and then listen to her preaching," he reasoned.

"I know but won't she wonder where I got the last name Murdoch?

"She's in another world half the time, but if she asks, we'll just tell her it was your dad's?"

"Tim, she's going to meet my dad at the wedding!"

He had an answer for everything. "There will be too many people around and she won't remember, trust me, she's scatterbrained."

"OK, if you say so, but I don't like lying. Sooner or later it'll come back to bite us."

Pulling up to the curb, Tim leaned over and gave me a smooch on the cheek. "You worry too much."

***

Mrs. Hartman, I still called her that since she hadn't corrected me, even after the engagement, decided that it would be nice to invite my grandparents over for dinner in honor of our engagement. Grandpa wore his good suit and Grandma got a new perm for the occasion. My grandfather and Tim's dad really seemed to enjoy seeing each other again. Grandma was pleased to be invited to their house since it was a first, and they had only met a couple of times at the company picnics during the time Grandpa worked at the dealership.

But when Mrs. Hartman brought the food to the table, I did a double take! All I could do is stare in amazement. The woman actually had the nerve to open a can of Hormel beef tamales and dump them into a baking dish with some grated yellow cheese on top and call it dinner. My grandma looked a little stunned herself. I stole a glance and noticed her bite her bottom lip to keep from laughing especially after she caught sight of Tim and I exchanging looks.

His mother was clueless. I'll never know if she did it on purpose as a prejudicial insult or if she honestly thought it was appropriate to serve imitation Mexican food from a can to someone who was of that nationality. It's not like she wasn't aware, Tim had done nothing but rave about my grandma's homemade tamales to his mother and everyone else on Christmas Day. Yet there they were, not even a close forgery.

Grandma was too polite to say anything in front of Tim on the ride home so after we dropped them off we discussed it. He brushed off his mother's behavior as status quo. "Stefanie, I guess I'm used to her strange ways, and her horrible cooking."

"Well, I'm not. What's the matter with her?" I asked. "What was she thinking, you don't open a can of chow mien and serve it to an Oriental, or Chef Boy R Dee ravioli to an Italian." What was I getting myself into? First I find out this woman was a religious fanatic, then I discover she's prejudiced. I kept telling myself, "I'm marrying him, not his family."

Tim clarified that the religious obsession with his mother and her thrusting her beliefs onto her children was a turnoff for him. He admitted he hadn't been inside a church since he was drafted into the army at age eighteen. The strict edicts and rules of the Catholic religion that had been the foundation of his family no longer confined him, much to the chagrin of his mother. His dad, on the other hand, had been a convert and didn't carry the same religious compulsion.

All that was fine with me, except Tim insisted on getting married in the Catholic Church. Why? Because it would kill his mother if he didn't and he didn't want the conflict.

"But Tim, I've been married before and I'm not a practicing

Catholic?" I protested.

"That's OK, your marriage doesn't count. You were never married in the eyes of the church, they don't recognize non-Catholic weddings."

"Are you sure?"

"Yes, but we can check with the priest, if you want?"

"Well, I guess we need to find a Catholic church now?"

"That won't be hard, there's one on every corner," he proclaimed.

"I still think we should tell your parents about my previous marriage."

"Trust me, we can't."

Finding a church was pretty easy, just as Tim had said, there happened to be one right around the corner from my apartment. The priest was young and laid back and wore sandals. After Tim and I met him he mostly put my mind at ease, with the exception that we had to attend marriage classes before the wedding.

It was a Saturday, following our third out of four classes, when we attended a barbecue at Tim's parent's house. We were both tired, and I didn't feel well after just having a wisdom tooth pulled. True to form, when his mother inquired about the classes. Tim's comment about how useless the classes were, set her off. She preceded to defend the classes.

"Timmy, Catholic teaching on marriage is a really beautiful thing and helps young couples like you and Stef get off to a good start."

"I'm sure it is, but these classes are so boring, I fell asleep."

She took offense and lit into him. "What a disrespectful thing to do, you have no regard for your religion!"

"Oh, jeez mom, give it a rest, half the people in the class were nodding off."

Fortunately he didn't include me in the count, otherwise his mother would have scolded me too and maybe worse, held a grudge. As it turns out I did nod off a few times.

The subject was getting blown out of proportion by the minute. The woman was a staunch Catholic who took every criticism personally.

Tim was able to calm her down, and she finally let it go.

CHAPTER 41

HERE COMES THE BRIDE

My mother was thrilled when I told her the news. Much to my delight, she was planning on showing up for this one. It was unlikely that Joe would attend, but if he did, I wasn't going to let it spoil my day. It was an exciting time and all I could think about was planning my wedding.

Every night after working eight hours, I had appointments. Three months isn't that much time to organize a wedding ceremony and reception. I lost so much weight, from all the running around, that my dress had to be altered twice.

I did consult a wedding planner to help coordinate the event, but I still ran myself ragged picking and choosing every detail; invitations, flowers, gift registry and on and on. Since there were so many of us at work getting married at the same time, we all traded names of florists, photographers, and performers. All of our wedding dresses of course, came from the Bullocks bridal department.

The best part of planning the wedding was selecting the music portion for the ceremony.

Kathie, back in the Lingerie department had a fantastic soloist at her wedding the month before. The singer had the most beautiful voice I had ever heard. When she sang 'Ave Maria,' it took my breath away. I had to have her even though my playlist would be much more modern and less traditional than she was probably used to singing.

With conflicting schedules and time constraints, the singer and I arranged an audition that would take place over the phone. I knew that I wanted her, but I wanted to make sure she could deliver the same performance singing contemporary music.

She assured me that she had sung one of the songs at another wedding and that she would be able to obtain the lyrics for the other one in plenty of time to learn them before the wedding.

Just before Ellen began, she asked if it was OK if her sister accompanied her on the guitar, explaining that it would sound better than acapella.

The telephone audition brought me to tears. "Oh my gosh, you sound as good as Karen Carpenter," I gushed. "I'm all choked up, I have chills, you did an absolutely beautiful job. I'm so excited to have you sing at my wedding."

She thanked me and asked if I also wanted her sister for the ceremony.

"Yes, yes, yes," I giggled.

If she had that effect over the phone, I could only imagine what it was gonna to be like in person. I now had a vocalist with the voice of an angel who would set our ceremony apart from all the others. I hoped everyone would be so enthralled with the ceremony overflowing with beautiful music performed by my singing angel that they wouldn't notice the scrimpy food selection at the reception.

A week before the wedding, Mom and Sheila flew down. Joe couldn't come because of work. I was relieved.

Tim and I picked them up at LAX airport and brought them back to our newly rented apartment where, as of the day before, I was now living alone. Tim would stay in Belmont Shore until the wedding. We liked the apartment complex where I was living with Claire so much that we rented a first floor apartment in the next building.

While I was at work, Tim became the chauffeur for Mom and Sheila, driving them to Huntington Beach so that they could see old friends from the neighborhood. He even took time off work a few times to accommodate my family and never complained once.

On the Sunday before the wedding, Tim's parents invited all of us over for dinner. They wanted to meet my mother, which I thought was a kind and thoughtful gesture. The whole family was there, including the sister from Philadelphia, whom I had never met. I have to admit, I was somewhat tense about meeting her after the negative stuff Patty had told me she had said about Tim and the wedding.

It had been during one of the family get-togethers, that Patty had shared Diane's comment about Tim getting married. "When Diane heard about Timmy finally tying the knot, first thing out of her mouth was, 'I'll believe it when I see it!', so that's why she's coming. Just thought you should know."

When I had asked Patty why she'd said that, she rolled her eyes. "Oh everybody knows he was such a player, screwed anything in a skirt."

Just what I needed to hear.

"Well, that doesn't make me feel very good," I replied. "In fact he's been completely faithful the whole time we've been together."

"Well, lets hope he's changed," she said. "Diane is such a bitch, loves to stir the pot, which is why no one likes her."

Hard to know what to believe. I knew Tim had been with a lot of women, but that was the past. I'm the one he was marrying.

My anxiety was diminished once I finally met Diane. She was pleasant enough, in a cool sort of way, but she seemed more interested in catching up with her sisters than talking to my mom and me. Fine with me, at least I didn't have to worry about any curve balls. Her husband on the other hand, couldn't have been friendlier.

When it came time to have dinner, all of the adults were seated in the dining room and the children were relegated to the kid's table in the kitchen as usual.

My mom was having a nice chat about horses with Diane's husband, when Tim's mom began inquiring about the wedding details. Assuming that we were having a mass, she wanted to know if she should contact Father O'Hara so he could participate. When Tim responded, "We're not having a mass." She lost it.

"What do you mean Timmy? You can't have a wedding without a mass," she demanded.

Tim's reply consisted of two words. "Too long."

His mother's voice became shrill. "You have no respect for your religion," she wailed. "You've always turned your back on the church!"

Silence fell over the room. My mother and I looked up from our plates and just stared at each other in disbelief at the embarrassing turn the evening had taken.

"Mom, I'm not making all of our friends sit through a mass," Tim said, matter-of-factly.

Tears were now streaming down her cheeks. "You've always shunned your religion, Timmy!"

His dad remained focused on his steak while his mom threw her napkin onto her plate and abruptly left the table. Diane scooted her chair back and said, "I'll go after her and try to calm her down." Everyone else resumed eating as if the scene hadn't occurred.

Finally, his oldest sister broke the silence. "Don't worry she'll get over it."

The conversations tentatively started up again, only in a more subdued form. His mom eventually returned and joined everyone for dessert and coffee that the girls had taken upon themselves to serve during her absence. No apologies.

My mom wasn't there for the first episode—about the boring classes—but I was, and his mom didn't care who was around when it came to defending her church. Religion was everything and her life revolved around it.

The subject never came up with Mrs. Hartman, but during one of the meetings with the priest, I declined to sign a document agreeing to raise my children Catholic. Tim didn't care, and the priest who would marry us didn't push it since it was an option. I can't begin to fathom what his mother would have done had she known. She probably assumed since we had attended classes and would be married within the church, that anything to do with children was also part of the program.

CHAPTER 42

FAMILY FEUDS

Weddings seem to bring out the best and worst in people. Tim's mom wasn't the only disgruntled family member. Betty was still carrying a grudge against my mom for deserting her and sticking her with all her debts and against me for flying the coop.

My fallout with her had begun when I moved from the back unit in her Huntington Beach condo sooner than she expected. Back then Betty had been hounding me to come and live with her and I thought it would be a good idea. It wasn't. First of all there was no kitchen, so I had to schlep downstairs to her place every morning in order to make a cup of coffee or anything else food related. She also ran me ragged, picking up groceries, gassing up the car, returning purchases at department stores on top of driving myself one hour each way to work in La Habra. She hated to drive, so I even ended up driving her to work in Los Angeles a handful of times when her regular driver was on a bender.

Betty was no longer the same person I'd known when I was a child living with her and Charlie. During the brief time that I stayed in the condo, I began to notice things about her that I had either overheard as a child or were a distant memory. Her mood swings, her glassy-eyed stare, her getting up before the sun came up, going to bed late, never eating and her obsession with evangelical pastors and their TV shows.

When she wasn't around, I started snooping. At first glance I noticed that her bathroom seemed a bit untidy, which was unusual for her. There were cigarette burns around the sink, and clothes strewn on the floor and hanging behind the door. I opened the top drawer and found a dozen or so red and green capsules lying loose in a plastic drawer divider. No evidence of prescription bottles. From whatever knowledge I had picked up about drugs, I was pretty sure the red ones were for sleep and the green ones were for staying awake. I decided to sample one of each to confirm.

Sure enough, the red one made me drowsy and the green one made me wired and took my appetite away. The pill popping would justify her mood swings, her lack of appetite and why she was able to work such long hours. It would explain why she would crash and fall face first into her plate of food at the dinner table and have to go to bed by seven p.m. I was pretty young but I do remember that part.

She was my grandmother and I loved her but I really began to dislike her. She was unreasonable and difficult to get along with. I finally realized that she was also controlling and manipulative. Whenever she doled out money to Mom or to me, she always had an agenda.

She'd become furious when I'd told her I was moving out. "After all I've done for you, now you're running out on me," she protested. "I gave you a free place to live and spent all that money letting you decorate it the way you wanted and now you think that you can just turn your back and leave?"

I did my best to reason with her. "I'm sorry, Betty but it's too far for me to drive to work. I can't do it anymore."

"Well, look at me!" Placing both hands on her hips for

emphasis, "I drive further than you, and work longer hours so that we can have a nice place to live!"

Yeah and you pop pills in order do it.

"Can't you rent it out?" My voice a little too upbeat.

"Why, and have some stranger living there?"

It was a losing battle; Betty wanted it her way and wouldn't take no for an answer. There was no two ways about it.

Fortunately I was able to move back to the same apartment complex, this time to a different unit. The move took place one morning after Betty had gone to work. And sure enough, the next morning, she called me at work and began raking me over the coals. "First your mom leaves without telling me and now you!"

For every defense, she had an offense. I finally had to hang up on her.

Now Mom had come back for my wedding and we were about ready to step into the lion's den.

Although there had been a small breakthrough, with Mom sending cards and letters, she hadn't seen Betty in four years. For me it had been three and unlike Mom, I gave up trying to get along with her. She never tried to make amends or apologize for the mean and hurtful things that she had said to me.

Tim and I drove Mom and Sheila to the Huntington Beach condo where Betty was living, to make some sort of peace with her. I was hoping that since we had Tim with us, as a buffer, she might warm up a little. At least she let us in the door and she was cordial. Cool, but cordial. She knew about the wedding from Mom's letters and after the initial pleasantries, I extended a verbal invitation, which only made her indignant. Now she was offended because she didn't get an official one in the mail.

"Betty, I'm sorry, but I didn't think you would want to come," I said.

"Well, you could have at least asked, by sending me an invitation."

"I'm asking you now."

"It's not the same."

Mom added, "Steffie didn't mean anything by it. She's not trying to exclude you, Mom, she just didn't think that you'd want to come."

Poor Tim kept shuffling his feet looking the other way and getting more and more uncomfortable by the minute.

I tried to change the subject by asking if I could show Tim around. Betty turned her attention to Mom and waved us off with a flick of her wrist. As Tim and I climbed the stairs, I overheard Betty's familiar whining about how hard she works.

"I'm so darn tired," was her favorite phrase. "You know, there's no one to help me. I gotta do everything myself." Those words drew a smirk reminding me of how much comedy material I had gotten from it as a child. Making fun of Betty's, 'I'm so darn tired', used to make everyone laugh whenever I went into my impersonation routine. My Aunt Isabel and Grandma had egged me on whenever they would ask about Betty during my visits. They even got into the act after awhile.

Tim asked what was so funny, and I told him I would tell him later. On our upstairs tour, I noticed the little white portable TV I had forgotten, sitting on a dresser in the guest bedroom. "Oh wow, so that's where my TV was," I exclaimed. "I thought I lost it somehow."

Tim, said, "Do you still want it?"

"Sure, let's disconnect it."

He undid the rabbit ears, wrapped the cord around the

holder in the back and then picked it up. As we were coming back down, Betty threw a fit when she saw Tim carrying the TV. "Hold on there!" She said, putting her hand up like a stop sign. "You can march that right back up the stairs and put it back where you found it."

Tim came to a halt, and then in a continuous motion swiveled on his heels and preceded back up the stairs to return it. He wasn't about to get into it with a crotchety old woman over a cheap TV set. I was more upset than he was. "Betty, that's mine, my dad gave me that for Christmas."

"It's mine now," she asserted. "Say, uh, Stefanie, you know… all the money I spent on you living here for free, it's the least you can do."

Before I could respond, Tim, who had returned from the TV caper, grabbed my arm and steered me toward the door, saying, "c'mon lets go outside for a smoke."

"But, it's mine," I contested as I glared at Betty over my shoulder.

"I know, Stefanie, but it ain't worth it, I'll buy you a new one just like it. Shit, I'll buy you a bigger, better one than that old thing. Forget it, OK?"

Tim was right. Arguing over a TV was petty. She was nuts though. I guess that's what being a drug addict does to you.

With her hostile attitude toward me, I didn't see her coming around any time soon or in time to attend my wedding, nor did I expect her to send a gift or any acknowledgment. She did, however, make nice with Mom. Betty also did her best to monopolize my mother's time while she was in town for the wedding. According to Mom, she acted jealous and seemed resentful about the upcoming nuptials, almost like a competition.

I didn't let Betty get under my skin; she'd made herself so disagreeable I didn't want to be near her. She would have embarrassed me had she showed up for my wedding anyway. Her appearance had gotten so bizarre. She now wore a bouffant platinum wig that was so fluffy it could have passed for a gob of cotton candy. Her make-up was thick and greasy and her eyes were heavily lined with bright blue eyeliner. She was always saying that the wig made her look younger and more like her daughter, who had always had blond hair. Once upon a time, Betty had applied Henna to create an auburn tint to her natural dark brown hair. Her short stylish bob was now long stringy locks of steel that were concealed under her glamorous wig.

She was also on her fourth husband. Charlie had been her third and the one before that had been my mother's father. I'm not sure who the first one was. Number four's name was George and he was a piece of work. I had no idea where she dug him up. I only met him a couple of times just before I moved from her condo. He was hardly ever around, always traveling back to Louisiana where he was from and where he would stay for months. He even looked like maybe he had some mixed race with his darker skin color. His face had some serious creases, must have been from all that hard drinking and heavy smoking. He too, was an alcoholic. He seemed illiterate; we could barely understand him with his Cajun drawl.

It was a weird union. I guess he helped out around the cleaners whenever he was in town and also provided companionship. George was a nervous kind of guy, always jiggling keys in his pocket and pacing, maybe he drank a lot of coffee or maybe he was a pill popper too?

Betty also jumped on the religious train with vehemence, watching televangelists, and sending donations to Oral Roberts. Mom also divulged that Betty had been corresponding with inmates, which sadly didn't surprise me.

CHAPTER 43

WE'VE ONLY JUST BEGUN

With Mom arriving a week before the wedding, she was able to attend my wedding shower and help me with whatever I needed to be done in our new apartment—where she would stay with me until she went home after the wedding.

Just when I thought everything was done, I realized that my mother had nothing nice to wear to the wedding. I decided it was time for a complete head to toe make-over. With my employee discount, I bought her a lovely cocktail length dress of silk shantung in kind of a shimmery platinum color. The sheath style was flattering and camouflaged the bulges that she had acquired from the weight gain.

Her hair was yet another challenge and a bit frightening. She was in desperate need of decent haircut—it looked like it had been chopped with pruning shears. As for the color, a mere touch-up wouldn't begin to cover the major outgrowth of dark brown intertwined with shades of a brassy yellow.

She had let herself go in just about every way. Her clothes were a disaster, too. They were well worn, dingy and pretty far out of style. I noticed she had this stale smell, which could have been a blend of the lingering cigarette smoke mixed with body odor and grungy clothes. Everything about her was unkempt. Probably moving to the woodsy rural community of Sumner sped up the process. Mom blamed her weight gain on all that fresh farm food and the cold winters that kept her inside where she was forced to bake breads and pies—which of course they all ate to keep warm.

Any remains of the disheveled appearance was erased by the time the wedding day arrived. She was transformed into a "mother of the bride" to be proud of.

Sheila was a challenge as well. She was at the awkward age of fourteen and to top it off she was nearly as wide as she was tall. Finding her an age appropriate dress in an adult size was not easy. She wore a woman's size fourteen but she needed a youthful teen style. In the end, we were successful, finding her a powder blue age-appropriate dress in the women's budget department.

The wedding was on a Friday evening in June. All of Tim's family was there, approximately 30 of them, along with about a dozen from my side, the rest were friends. All in all we had around 75 people in attendance.

Tim and I stood at the back of the church waiting to walk down the aisle together as we listened to the words that I believed would come true. Words about love, being strangers at first and then taking a lifetime to know each other well. The young woman with the crystalline voice had performed the song *For All We Know* perfectly, almost as well as Karen Carpenter.

Once the bridal march played, we made our way, arm in arm, to the alter where the priest took over. When it was our turn to recite the standard vows, Tim was so nervous he said, "I Stefanie instead of I Timothy." Everyone laughed, and then he quickly corrected himself. The highlight of the shortened version of the Catholic ceremony for me as well as the audience was the moment when Tim and I kneeled before the priest just after we kissed. Everyone sat captivated once again by our lovely vocalist and accompanying guitar as she sang, *We've Only Just Begun.*

Everyone loved the music and said so. "Oh Stefanie, the music was spectacular." "What great choices." "Where did you find such a good singer?" "I've never heard anyone sing like that before and the Carpenters too!" Just as I had hoped, the wedding was more about the ceremony than the reception. That's all everyone could talk about and Tim was even blown away by how well the popular music had turned an otherwise routine ceremony into an enchanting event.

Our reception was fairly short, The guests seemed happy, they mingled, drank some champagne, nibbled hors de oeuvres, ate their slice of cake and then were on their way. It was dinner time and most people didn't want to stick around where there wasn't much food.

Tim and I took off and headed to the Century Plaza Hotel where we had a room service dinner and spent the night.

The next day we drove to Lake Tahoe where we water-skied and swam for a week. Not the most romantic setting with a group of Tim's friends turning up for most of the week.

It was still fun but I couldn't wait to get home and start my life as a married woman. I was anxious to set up housekeeping and return to work as a Mrs. like so many of my co-workers.

I was so happy. We had a nice place to live that was filled with new things along with his furniture and mine, and we had plenty of food in the refrigerator. For the first time I didn't have to skimp at the grocery store. To be able to go to the butcher and pick out prime cuts of meat was a luxury.

Living on peanut butter and tuna sandwiches for so long, I had forgotten what it was like to fill up a shopping cart. Tim had been good about contributing to the cause when we were dating, especially after he caught a glimpse of the inside of my bare cupboards and fridge, which horrified him.

"Stefanie, what the hell kind of way is that to exist?" he exclaimed. "Man oh man, that's the sorriest looking refrigerator I've ever seen. One can of tuna, a jar of peanut butter and some kinda home-made wine!" It made for a good story and plenty of laughs about how he saved me from hunger, after we were married.

Out of habit, I was still a frugal shopper and didn't buy anything that we didn't need. This was a new experience for me, which I was grateful for and didn't take for granted. I knew what it was like to count pennies and to barely eek by each week. Growing up we had a sufficient amount of food except when Joe's paycheck came up short. There were lean times, but Betty would step in and make sure that we were fed.

CHAPTER 44

THE HOUSE

Mom and Sheila stayed in our apartment the night of the wedding and they went back to Sumner the next day.

When we came back all of our presents had been waiting. It was great fun opening them and putting away the stoneware and china place settings, the beautiful crystal wine glasses and grandma's silverware that she had carefully wrapped in saran. We really were starting a new life together. We loved our new apartment that was barely six – months old and conveniently located close to both our places of work.

We had lived there about six weeks, when one night I got home from work, opened the door and noticed a blanket laying on the floor in the entry way. "That's weird, what's Tim doing dragging a blanket out here," I asked myself. I called out for Tim. No answer. I walked further into the living room and then I saw it... the TV was missing, and also the stereo. The room had been ransacked, lamps askew, drawers and doors open. It didn't take me long to figure out what happened. I bolted out the door and ran directly into the manager's office where I borrowed their phone to call Tim, while the manager contacted the police. Too scared to go back, I waited outside until they arrived and then reported what had occurred. It was scary and felt like such a violation of privacy. It never felt the same living there after that.

A few weeks later we started looking for a place to move and that's when we stumbled upon a new tract house a few miles away in Brea. Just for the fun of it we pulled into the community. The models were stunning, each one with a different color palette of matching appliances, window coverings, plush carpeting and bold wallpapers. When we toured the actual home sites, we found that the homes themselves all had big yards and two car garages.

We borrowed most of the down payment from Tim's dad and took the leap and bought our first house! I had to pinch myself to make sure I wasn't dreaming. It was the smallest model, 1700 square feet with three bedrooms, but to us it was a castle. With a brand new home, there were so many decisions to be made about floor covering, paint and appliances. We went with the harvest gold range, refrigerator and dishwasher for our new kitchen, tile for the kitchen and bathroom floors and neutral brownish shag carpet for all the other rooms. We moved in a little over a month later. Every weekend, instead of going water skiing or anywhere for that matter, we chose to work on our new home.

Once the inside was done, we tackled the outside. We seeded grass, planted flowers, and had paving stones installed to finish off the yard. Everything was new, and best of all, ours. We continued fixing up the house to our liking from the window coverings to the fencing. Everything needed to be done.

The only sad part about the move was when Tim informed me that I would have to give up my beautiful 'Hugger Orange' Camaro. It suddenly dawned on him—that as the owner's son and assistant new car sales manager—his new wife should also be driving a demo. He dropped the bomb one night as we were finishing dinner. "Hey Stefanie, we need to sell your car."

I was dumbfounded. "What are you talking about?"

"I'm not making car payments," he reasoned.

"I don't understand?"

"You're family now, so you should be driving a demo, like my sisters."

"But, I love my car, I want to keep it," I pleaded. "I'll make the payments out of my check."

"That's not the point. Don't worry, I'll get you another one just like it."

"I don't know, this is my first car that I bought all by myself. It has sentimental value."

"C'mon, Stefanie, it's just a car… a piece of metal."

"Not to me," I argued.

Tim reached across the table and lifted my chin with his finger. "I promise I'll get you another one just like it, only this time it'll be loaded."

Maybe I was over-reacting; after all it was just a car.

"Alright, as long as it's Hugger Orange," I conceded.

The next night when he came home from work, he was driving a bright yellow Camaro. 'Daytona' yellow, he called it.

Standing on the front step with my hands on my hips, I shot daggers as I blurted, "What's that?"

"Your new car, loaded, real leather, air conditioning, and a year newer", Tim said grinning ear to ear.

"And yellow!!!!!" I declared.

"No one in the area had an orange one, and this just came in," Tim reasoned. "Come on let's take it for a spin. Wait till you get a burst of cold air on your face. It's six o'clock and still hotter n' shit, trust me you'll appreciate the air conditioning in this heat."

"I hate yellow," I muttered as I slid into the driver's seat.

"Don't worry, you'll only have it a few months until the new ones come out for next year and then you'll get another demo.

"Wait! Are you saying, I'll be getting a new car every year?"

"That's exactly what I'm saying, and whatever model you want. Feel better now?"

"Uh, sure, I mean… I had no idea, but I'm still deeply attached to my original Camaro."

"You'll get over it. And now do you see why I said not to get hung up on a car? You're not gonna have em long enough."

"Yeah, I guess."

As happy as I was, with the exception of the car, I continued to suffer from screaming nightmares, something Tim simply couldn't begin to comprehend. It jolted him the first time it happened and then he would shake me awake until it stopped.

Once when I was talking to my mom on the phone, I asked her when my bad dreams began. She said that she couldn't remember, guessing that maybe some time after we moved to the house in Hawthorne.

The recurring nightmares that now continued into adulthood must have been my way of keeping the past alive. It felt like I was torturing myself with demons of the past. No matter how deep I tried to bury it, the dreams were a reminder of traumatic occurrences that took place after my mother brought Joe into our lives. The theme was consistent, the threat of being brutality assaulted replayed itself in living color. There was always a faceless man about to strangle, shoot, or stab me. They averaged about once month—sometimes more, sometimes less—and I couldn't figure out what triggered them.

Things were so much better now. Surely the dreams would go away. I felt safe for the first time since I was seven years old. Because I had lived in so much fear all the time, I desperately wanted someone to protect me. No one had, until now. It would take time and work to build inner strength, and to overcome the inability to say what was on my mind, or stand up for myself. The environment had been toxic and emotionally unhealthy. Becoming independent and self sufficient on the outside was one thing, but on the inside I was cowering and afraid of confrontations and scolding. Every time I had any kind of negative encounter, there was that urinary muscles reflex that made me feel like I was going to pee. If someone was angry or reprimanded me it happened—the urge to pee. I fell apart inside if I got yelled at or scolded. Overly sensitive and thin-skinned, the physical reaction couldn't be overcome. It was a reflex. No matter what I told myself or how many deep breaths I took, it happened each and every time there was a raised voice.

CHAPTER 45

THEY'RE BACK

We had been married just over two years when I became pregnant. I wasn't the only one at work who was expecting, however. Bullocks' entire second floor of new brides were all in the family way! From wedding bells, to the stork. It was the talk of the store. Everyone wondered if there was something in the water?

Coincidentally Mom, Joe and Sheila decided to move back about the same time. Apparently the construction work had dried up and flowed back down to Southern California. Mom added in her letter since Sheila had just graduated high school, there was no reason to stay in Washington. I had mixed feelings about them coming back. On the one hand, I wanted my mother in my life and for her to be a part of her grandchild's life but, and it was a big but, that meant if she was in our lives, so was Joe.

With both of them having been out of sight, and particularly him out of mind for the past five years, it had been a lot easier to stash away my feelings of resentment. Now that they were returning so were the ill feelings.

Would I be able to empty the garbage of the past? Stop playing those old movies of adversity in my head? Dislodge the ill feelings and replace them with all of the good things in my life? Or would I simply sweep it all under the rug?

Mom and Joe rented an apartment in the San Fernando Valley, which we never visited. They were the ones who always made the trip to see us in Brea.

Mr. Charming and Tim hit it off from the beginning. Why wouldn't they? Joe poured it on thick, like he always did in front of people. Joe would throw his arms around our shoulders, and say, "Hey Steffie, how'd you reel in such a good lookin' guy?" Then he'd burst out laughing. Tim didn't quite know what to make of his unrestrained in-your-face personality at first but, after a while, it became a familiar tune that he accepted.

Joe couldn't do enough for us. If he offered once, he offered a hundred times to help us around the house with building projects. "I'm pretty handy with a hammer," he would declare. "Y'all just give me a holler and I'll strap on my tool belt and be on yer doorstep in a flash."

Tim took it all in stride. He didn't know any different—only what I had shared about my childhood anguish—because he had never seen the other side. Whenever we were around them, Tim became the buffer so I didn't have to interact with Joe separately. It was an unspoken understanding and Tim just wanted to keep the peace.

Joe insisted on giving us a wedding gift in the way of building our patio overhang one Saturday when he and Mom came over. He acted like he didn't want any money. But he sure didn't require much in the way of arm twisting when he snapped up the wad of bills that Tim pulled out of his wallet. I started to say something to Tim later, but he waved it off like it was no big deal. "Hey, babe, we got a new patio overhang, for not very much money, so I'm happy."

It was around my seventh month of pregnancy that Tim and I got the bug to move to Newport Beach. The move made sense; we both loved the beach and had always wanted to move back. We found a two year old house in a tidy neighborhood filled with kids, known as Harbor View Homes. We sold our house right away and moved six weeks before our baby was born.

Tim said he liked driving and didn't mind the longer commute to work. I quit my job, which I'd planned to do once the baby was born. I wanted to be a stay at home mom. My plan was to move my kiln from my aunt and uncle's house so that I could get back into my art and to go to college and get my degree.

My entire family was so excited about my pregnancy. Even Betty was starting to come around by making inquiries to my mother about the coming birth. Mom came over a few times wanting to help with baby stuff. She came with me to Manhattan Beach to pick up a wicker bassinet that I had seen in a magazine and she helped make curtains for the baby's room. With Joe always working and Sheila, at seventeen, doing her own thing it was good having Mom around by herself. She was even looking for places to move nearby so that she could be closer to her first grandchild.

The more time I spent with my mother, the more I noticed different things about her. She seemed overly impressed with material things and accomplishments. She gushed over our furniture, clothes, cars, Tim's job, my previous job... anything to do with status. "I just tell everyone that you were the youngest buyer in Bullocks," she would say.

Rolling my eyes, I would correct her. "Uh, no, Mom. I was a manager, who got to select some jewelry now and then, but the buyers were all downtown."

Defending her belief, she pressed, "But you were the youngest to be promoted to such a high position."

What was with her making such a big deal? "Mother, there were lots of us the same age who were managers."

Maybe this behavior had always been there, and I had been too young to notice? But it really started to bother me.

Also, she was continually looking for a hand-out. There were a few times when she would ask to borrow a few bucks until Joe got paid. Whenever we would go out to lunch, she would dig through her purse when the check arrived, feigning shock whenever she came up short. Bottom line, she never paid. Ever. She would drop hints about clothes and shoes too. "Whenever you decide you don't want it anymore, give it to me."

Mom, Joe and Sheila did end up moving closer to us, into a rental in Laguna Beach. It was a dilapidated back unit of a duplex that was dark, dingy and cramped. It hadn't seen a paintbrush in decades and could have been a shade of green once? The carpet was threadbare and stained. The kitchen and bathroom tile countertops were chipped and cracked. The shower was full of mold. Their well-used furniture blended well, along with the live tarantula in the recycled fish aquarium. The only source of heat was a wood burning fireplace and a wall heater in the hallway. Mom would turn the gas flame on full blast inside the fireplace whenever she didn't have any wood—which was often—in order to keep the place warm.

The Mr. Coffee machine was always on and the burnt odor hit you as soon as you walked in the door, along with the stench of cigarette smoke mixed with cat litter. You'd have to practically burn your clothes when you got home.

As much as Mom loved her coffee and cigarettes, it was her naps that were her favorite activity. Between the naps, coffee and cigarette breaks, I couldn't say what else she did all day. The TV seemed to always be on with Merv, Mike and Dinah talk shows. She claimed to do Joe's bookkeeping and she liked sewing and mending things. I noticed the row of liquor bottles lined up on the kitchen counter, and I wondered if Joe was the only one who indulged? I caught a whiff of something strong on her breath a few times when I stopped by during the day. I was in denial at first, saying to myself that it must have been strong mouthwash. But after it happened more than once I decided she must have been spiking her coffee.

Mom was still a bad housekeeper. I wondered if Sheila had to take over the bed making back-up position?

Sometimes it was hard having Mom and Joe living so close. Sure everything was fine on the surface, because no one ever talked about anything of substance and certainly not the past. Everything they did seemed to bother me, though. I tolerated Joe because of Mother, but she could be irritating, too, the way she played the helpless victim game. She was only 45 years old for God's sake, but she acted more like she was 75, she couldn't open a jar of mayonnaise let alone carry the Sunday paper to the trash. "My pleurisy, my arthritis, my sternum."

It was hard to know what was real and what was exaggerated. No doubt her health had deteriorated, but I think she milked her ailments for sympathy.

Mom and Joe were beginning to live up to something Betty had once called them—'white trash'—the pigsty house, their slovenly appearance, the manner in which they conducted themselves. Even Sheila was bedraggled. In a few months she would start junior college, but in the meantime, she mostly cruised around in a beater car that Joe had bought her.

In spite of her woes, my mother was thrilled about becoming a grandmother. And, of course, Joe got in on the act, bragging to everyone about his new grandchild. Ugh!

CHAPTER 46

AND BABY MAKES THREE

I gave birth to our daughter, Charli, two days after Thanksgiving, which I confess was the happiest day of my life. Tim was in the delivery room since we had taken the Lamaze classes and now we had a healthy baby girl. The first thing I did when they handed her to me was count the fingers and toes—two, three, ten times at least. I suppose all new mothers do that. Afterward, I stroked her little fat cheek with my index finger as she slept in my arms. I never wanted to let her go, all I could do was stare at this little miracle.

A few days later we brought our little bundle home. Sometime during the middle of the night, Tim and I were jolted awake by a strange and unfamiliar sound. "What's that?" asked Tim.

It took me a few minutes to answer. "It's the baby." Neither of us admitted it, but I think we both forgot that we had one in the other room after we fell asleep.

In 1974 the hospitals didn't have rooming in, which meant the mothers weren't awakened by crying babies. The nurses usually gave supplemental bottles at night so the mother could get plenty of rest and not be woken up for two a.m. feedings. Once everyone got home, however, reality sunk in pretty quickly.

I padded down the hall to see what the ruckus was all about, Tim right behind me.

Tim held Charli's little hands and did his best to shush her as I changed her diapers. Once she was dry and still wailing, I began to nurse the hungry baby until she fell back asleep. It was good to have been pampered in the hospital, but it would have been nice to be prepared for what was in store once I got home.

The middle of the night feedings weren't so bad after all. In fact, I began to look forward to the stillness of the night when it was just the two of us bonding. I settled into the Windsor rocking chair that sat in the corner of Charli's pastel green and white striped room and carried on lengthy conversations that would be just between us.

"Charli Elizabeth, you wanna know how you got the name Charli? You're named after your great grandpa, Charlie. It's also a boy's name… anyway, I'm sorry to say you never had the honor of meeting him. Besides being my grandfather, he was my best friend, and the most important person in my life—maybe even more than my mom, especially after her priorities changed. Anyway, that's how you got your name. It has significance. So wear it well."

A child remembers those adults in their life who made a difference. Charlie was that adult in my life. Just being together was all that mattered. Sure, the adventures were fun, but so was sitting next to one another on the sofa, talking, not talking, it didn't matter. There was never a doubt in my mind that he wanted to spend time with me or that he loved me.

The middle of the night feedings were a time for contemplation as well as conversation. It became a safe outlet for my thoughts and feelings, even if my only audience was an infant.

"Charli, I don't know what kind of mother I will be, but I do know this: I will love you unconditionally forever and I will protect you. Always. And should anything ever happen between your dad and I, I promise I will never allow anyone to come between us. I will be there for you no matter what and I will never abandon you or allow anyone to harm you. Ever."

EPILOGUE

A friend once said that bedtime was his dessert. For me going to sleep at night was more like eating my least favorite dish. It's ironic that my friend associated food with sleep and my nightmares are a result of living in a fearful situation, which first began because of food. The screaming dreams never occur on a schedule, I never know when they will come. The anticipation produces anxiety whenever I lay my head on the pillow at night. Even though I will myself to think of something pleasant, the nightmares are always the same; someone, usually a man is after me.